UNSANCTIONED
CRIMSON POINT PROTECTORS

KAYLEA CROSS

UNSANCTIONED

Copyright © 2022 Kaylea Cross

Cover Art: Sweet 'N Spicy Designs
Developmental edits: Rhonda Merwarth
Line Edits: Joan Nichols
Digital Formatting: LK Campbell

This book is a work of fiction. The names, characters, places, and incidents are products of the writer's imagination or have been used fictitiously and are not to be construed as real. Any resemblance to persons, living or dead, actual events, locales or organizations is entirely coincidental.

All rights reserved. With the exception of quotes used in reviews, this book may not be reproduced or used in whole or in part by any means existing without written permission from the author.

ISBN: 9798849762050

AUTHOR'S NOTE

Fasten your seatbelts! Get ready for a wild ride through danger and mayhem and heartbreak—as well as a surprise appearance from a badass heroine from a previous series I hope you'll be excited about.

Kaylea

PROLOGUE

One year ago

Standing in the shadows in a corner at the back of the large ballroom, Callum scanned the assembled guests seated at their tables beneath the glittering crystal chandeliers in the upscale hotel lobby. Rick Vanderzalm, the man he'd been sent here to Amman to guard was sitting near the front with a wealthy Jordanian businessman and his wife, along with three of their associates.

So far, the gala had been uneventful. And in his line of work, uneventful was exactly what he wanted.

Some of the most influential people in Jordan were here tonight—and at least one who may or may not be unwittingly spending his last few hours as a free man. Security was tight but discreet, positioned throughout the room out of sight from the guests. Two of Callum's own men were dressed in the same uniforms as the wait staff, able to move around the room without drawing any notice, their weapons concealed beneath their tailored jackets.

"Table eleven," one of them murmured, his voice transmitting through Callum's earpiece. "Saleh's on the move."

Callum's gaze swept over the other tables to land on the man in question, now circulating between the tables at the front of the room where the richest guests were sitting. Callum had directed his team to watch the suspected arms dealer closely tonight.

The latest intel received prior to the gala hinted that a Jordanian security force planned to move on Saleh soon. Maybe even tonight. That wasn't Callum's concern. He and his team were here to make sure Vanderzalm remained secure and escorted back safely to his hotel.

He stayed at his post, surveying the room with an expert eye, and getting sporadic updates from his team as the evening progressed. After dinner, the speeches started. Mostly in Arabic, with English translation provided in subtitles on the huge screen acting as a backdrop behind the podium at the front of the room.

Saleh stayed seated, looking completely relaxed and smiling as presenters took the stage to begin the awards portion of the program. Callum tuned it out, focused on the main players in the room instead. Vanderzalm had both powerful friends and enemies in the region.

Someone at the podium spoke in heavily accented English.

"We are proud to present this next award to an outstanding volunteer within our organization. This year's recipient has gone above and beyond in providing emergency care for children orphaned by the ongoing war in Syria and was unanimously selected by both her coworkers and members of SOS Children's Villages International Regional Office, Middle East." The presenter paused, aiming a smile off into the audience. "Ladies and gentlemen, it is my honor to present this award to Nadia Bishop."

Callum glanced toward the stage in time to catch a glimpse of swirling blue paisley fabric sweep up the steps. A young woman walked across the stage, her flowing dress standing out amongst the much more formal attire in the room. Fair-skinned, her long brown hair tumbling freely down her back.

At the podium she accepted the award, shook the presenter's hand, then stepped up to the microphone to address the audience. Her gaze swept across the packed room, and Callum felt an almost physical jolt when it stopped on him, seeming to pick him out in the shadows. A ripple of awareness slid through him, then she glanced away and began her acceptance speech.

His attention was now as much on her as Vanderzalm. She was poised, her smile warm and to him seemed far more genuine than most of the other people gathered in this room.

"I'm honored to help the children put into my care," she said in an accent that was pure American, "to give them love, comfort and hope during the darkest time of their young lives. I love doing what I do—and yet my greatest wish is that one day our work won't be necessary."

A murmur of agreement rippled through the crowd.

She raised her award slightly, gave a nod. "Shukran." With another bright smile she stepped back from the podium, her gaze once again seeming to connect with his for an instant.

Callum watched her leave the stage and stride into the sea of tables, the fabric of her flowy dress standing out in the crowd. He couldn't believe he hadn't noticed her before.

The awards ceremony finished twenty minutes later, and a final speech by the host concluded the gala. Guests immediately rose and began mingling in amongst the tables to talk and finish their champagne. Callum divided his attention between Vanderzalm and Saleh, now working opposite sides of the room.

After another flute of champagne and a round of shaking

hands with several dignitaries, Vanderzalm finally reached up to adjust both sides of his bow tie. The signal Callum had been watching for.

"We're leaving. Bring the vehicle around front. I'll escort him out and meet you at the curb in five," Callum murmured, his voice low.

"Copy that," one of his guys answered. "Heading out back now."

Callum moved through the throng of people wandering toward the open double doors at the back of the room, scanning for any sign of a threat as he strode toward Vanderzalm. The businessman from Utah didn't so much as glance at him as Callum passed by and took up a position behind him, ready to go for his weapon at the slightest hint of trouble. He didn't really think anything would happen, but after so many years of living by his instincts in combat zones in the shittiest parts of the world, he was always ready for anything.

"Your six is clear," one of his guys reported as Callum stepped outside onto the sidewalk as the rest of the crowd spilled through the exit doors onto the street. Limos and luxury vehicles lined the curb to pick up their wealthy passengers.

"ETA on the vehicle," Callum said, watching around him. Saleh was off to the right and slightly behind them, lingering near the entrance where he was talking to some men. His security team was posted close by, watching the crowd as intently as Callum.

"Turning the corner in about five seconds."

Right on cue, the big black Escalade came into view and stopped along the curb. Callum stepped forward to signal Vanderzalm, staying at his back as he and another team member escorted him to the vehicle.

Callum opened the back door. Vanderzalm got in, Callum's guy right behind him.

Shutting the door, Callum stepped back and scanned the sidewalk and street before giving the order. "You're clear."

"Roger. See you back at the hotel." The Escalade pulled away from the curb and sped away up the street.

Callum relaxed a little but didn't completely drop his guard. He couldn't when he was in a crowd. Saleh was still over by the entrance holding court with two men in tuxes.

A tingle of awareness made him turn slightly just as a mix of patchouli and vanilla drifted toward him. Nadia Bishop was standing several feet away, watching him.

She smiled, a teasing gleam in her eyes. "Hi. Do you speak English?"

If Vanderzalm had still been here, Callum would have ignored the comment—ignored her. But he was officially off the clock now and that cute line, combined with her impish smile made him crack a grin. Being a ginger made him stand out here. "I do."

Her smile widened and she offered her hand. "I'm Nadia."

He shook it, taking a good long look at her as his hand engulfed her small, slender one. She was about five-five or so, medium build. Poised and confident. Her dress was loose but skimmed her body enough to hint at the curves beneath. "Callum."

"Nice to meet you." She cast a quick glance around and focused on him again. "So, what brings you to the gala?"

"Work," was all he said, then nodded at the crystal award in her left hand. "Congratulations."

She glanced down at it, her pretty face twisting in a grimace of embarrassment. "Oh, thanks. I don't know why they chose me when there are so many others who deserve this award more. I hate being dragged up on stage."

No one would have guessed that from the way she'd handled herself up there. "Worked in Jordan long?"

This time the smile she flashed him was a bit strained. "Long enough. I've mostly been working in the refugee camps."

He nodded, becoming more curious about her by the minute. Her out-of-place dress and carefree style of her hair at this upscale event told him this wasn't her usual scene. He liked that. It told him she was comfortable with herself, and after only a few moments in her presence he could already tell that the warmth she radiated was genuine. "Do you have a ride to wherever you're going?"

"I'm not sure, actually. I—" They both looked sharply to the right when a racing vehicle suddenly pulled up next to the parked cars. Doors flew open, then a wall of uniformed men rushed at Saleh.

Shit.

Callum grabbed Nadia and whirled her around, taking her down on the sidewalk and covering her with his body as shouts and screams broke out around them. She was rigid beneath him, jerked when several shots rang out in quick succession. He stayed on top of her, kept one hand on the back of her head and reached for the Glock 22 in his holster while he assessed the threat.

It was already over, the whole thing taking only seconds.

Jordanian security personnel had already swarmed Saleh and taken down all his bodyguards. Two were bleeding on the marble tiles outside the entrance, their weapons efficiently stripped away. The crowd stood or crouched in corners or behind the row of parked vehicles, staring in shock at the scene, too afraid to move. Callum assessed the scene, ready to react if things got ugly.

Cops came rushing from all directions. More vehicles roared up, lights and sirens on. Callum waited until the Jordanians had dragged Saleh into a waiting SUV with tinted windows and sped off before easing his weight from Nadia. "Are you all right?" he asked, scanning her quickly.

"Yes," she answered, eyes wide. "What happened?"

"Jordanians just took a suspected arms dealer into custody," he said, helping her to her feet and holding her arms until she steadied. The Jordanian security forces were pros. He and Nadia hadn't been in any real danger, except maybe for a stray bullet from one of Saleh's men if they'd managed to get a shot off—which he doubted.

Nadia stared up at him for a moment, face pale. She started to turn her head to look behind her. He caught her cheek in one hand, stopping her and bringing her gaze back to his. He didn't want her seeing the blood, even though there was a good chance she'd been exposed to violence and bloodshed in her work. "It's okay now. All over."

She put a hand to her chest, right over the tempting valley of her cleavage where it was exposed by the tight bodice and let out an unsteady breath. "I was *not* expecting anything like that tonight," she murmured, then eyed him. "Are you security?"

"Yes."

She seemed to relax a bit, held his gaze, his hand still cupping her cheek. Her skin was smooth and so damn soft. He had to fight the urge to stroke his thumb across it, the need to soothe and reassure her pulsing through him. "And you don't want me to see whatever's going on behind me," she said.

The Jordanians were hauling the wounded men away, leaving bloodstains on the slick marble floor. "No."

"Okay," she said with a tiny nod. "Definitely not turning around."

"Good." She was pale but seemed to be recovering quickly enough, trusting his word. Trusting him, and it lit up his protective instincts even more.

"Thank you, by the way. For covering me like that." Her

eyes were like melted dark chocolate under the overhead lights as she smiled ruefully. "Never had a guy jump me that fast before."

He let out a startled laugh and reluctantly lowered his hand, his palm tingling from the contact. Everything about her was unexpected. "Can I give you a ride back to wherever you're staying?" She still seemed a little shaky. He wanted to make sure she got back safely. And he also wasn't ready to say goodbye to her yet.

She quirked an eyebrow at him, the look in her eyes turning speculative. "Okay. But since you've already been on top of me, I think you should probably take me for a drink now."

He smiled, the attraction between them sending a spike of arousal through him, and unable to shake the feeling that he'd been destined to meet her tonight. Drinks together sounded like the best thing that had happened to him in forever. "Deal."

ONE

Crimson Point, Oregon

"So, how did it go in Jordan?"

Stretched out on the comfortable leather sofa in front of his best friend and former captain's fireplace, Callum picked up the ice-cold beer Boyd had just given him and took a sip, happy to be able to relax after a long two weeks at work. "It went." The job had gone fine. Few hassles, actually one of the smoothest he'd been on.

Except everything about being there reminded him of Nadia. Of that incredible weekend in Qatar last year that had changed his world, and that she was just over the border in Syria. So close, yet so far away.

Story of their entire relationship.

Boyd nodded and let it go. Though he'd left the military behind and was now pushing fifty, he'd kept himself in top shape and looked exactly like he had on their last mission together overseas, though there were a few more streaks of silver in his hair. "You hungry?"

"I could eat." He'd grabbed something at Whale's Tale in town at lunch hours ago and hadn't eaten since.

"Come on, I'll make you a sandwich."

Boyd made the best sandwiches.

Callum got up and followed him through the open concept room to the kitchen. "How's Ember? You guys set a date yet?"

"We're thinking maybe September. Something simple, either here or at the beach." Boyd started pulling ingredients from the fridge and putting them on the counter. "You want bacon?"

"Is this a trick question?"

That hard mouth twitched once. "No, but I guess it was a pointless one. Of course you want bacon." He turned on the oven, took a slab of bacon from the fridge, got out a baking sheet and started peeling off strips onto it. Thick cut with pepper, the good stuff.

Callum glanced past him to the loaves of fresh bread sitting on the counter by the sink. "Guessing you didn't sleep much last night, huh?" Boyd often made bread from scratch when he couldn't sleep. Said it was meditative. Callum wasn't sure about that, but he knew it was damn delicious.

Boyd popped the tray in the oven under the broiler before answering. "It's Ember. She's been having nightmares lately. About the murders."

He made a sympathetic sound. She had seen her brother and several other people shot on the dunes last winter and buried in the sand while they were still alive. She had barely escaped with her own life that night, forced to crawl over her brother's body on the way out. No one would ever forget a trauma like that. "Sorry to hear that."

"She'll get past it. She's strong, and the quiet up here's good for her."

Callum liked it too. Boyd had built his place high up in the hills outside of Crimson Point as a sort of sanctuary from the rest of the world. Away from the town, his nearest neighbor a half-mile or more away, the entire property surrounded by a band of thick forest.

It suited Boyd. After serving his country honorably and bravely as a Delta operator for so many years and then being shit on by his own government to cover its ass, Boyd deserved all the peace he could get. "Where's she tonight?"

"Over at Poppy and Noah's place. They're having a girls' night." He started slicing a plump, ripe tomato from his garden on the wooden cutting board he'd probably made out in his workshop.

"It's great that she's made such a good group of friends here," Callum said, getting up and crossing to the butcher block to pull out a long, serrated knife. "Pass me that loaf."

Boyd pushed it over and Callum began cutting thick slices of it, inhaling the scent. "Sourdough?"

"Yeah. It's my new thing."

"I like it." His phone rang. He answered the video call even though he didn't recognize the number, in case it was work related. But when the caller appeared on screen a moment later, his heart seized and his mind went blank.

Nadia stared back at him, her pretty face breaking into a smile.

"Hey, stranger," she said in a bright voice.

Callum unfroze himself and immediately strode for the front door, aware of Boyd's gaze following him. "Hi," he answered, keeping his tone neutral as he stepped outside onto the verandah and into the warm July evening air.

She'd messaged him a few days ago saying she might be getting a new assignment. They had only communicated by text and email since she'd called from London back in April. When he'd offered to fly over to meet her for the weekend and been turned down flat. After that, he hadn't been interested in repeatedly ripping the bandage off by hearing her voice.

"This a bad time?"

"No." He hid his reaction, locked down his emotions so she wouldn't be able to see them. She was outside too, the sky behind her turning purple with the dusk. Which was impossible, because she was ten hours ahead in Syria, so it should have been early morning there. "Where are you?"

"Where are *you*?" she countered, an impish gleam in her eyes. Big brown eyes that he could still easily get lost in if he wasn't careful.

"Boyd's place. I thought you were in Syria."

"I was. Now I'm on the West Coast."

Despite his resolve to stay cool and detached, his pulse accelerated. This was the closest they'd been in forever. It was rare enough they were on the same continent together, let alone in the same time zone. But why this video call now? "Oh. You in between assignments?"

"Yes." She turned her phone around and held it up so that it showed the background behind her. "What do you think of my view?"

Tall evergreens stood silhouetted against the few clouds in the sky. Cedars and firs. She panned over a bit, showing a yard. A neatly mowed lawn with a bordering row of shrubs that looked really familiar, then the gray cedar shingles on the side of the house.

His jaw nearly dropped. Holy shit. "You're at my place?"

She came back into the screen, a big grin splitting her face. "I am. But you're not." She shook her head, her expression turning sardonic. "We really do have the worst timing."

Yeah, among other things. But dammit, he wanted to see her. Maybe he could finally get a straight answer out of her about whether she wanted a relationship or not. She obviously still cared about him, or she wouldn't have shown up tonight. "Hang tight, I'm on my way." He shoved the door open and strode back inside. Boyd looked over at him, holding the tray of bacon in one oven-mitted hand.

"Your roommate told me you were out and asked me in," Nadia said, "but I told him I'd wait outside. You were right—he's sarcastic. I like him."

Groz was sarcastic all right. It was one of the reasons Callum liked the PJ so much. "I'll be there in fifteen minutes." The drive took twenty minutes minimum without traffic, but he'd blow every light and stop sign on the way home if it meant getting a few extra minutes with her.

"Okay. I'll be here."

He slid his phone back into his pocket and met Boyd's stare. "Sorry, but I gotta go." He needed answers.

In typical Boyd fashion, he merely nodded, but his buddy never missed anything. He must have seen Nadia on the screen and figured out exactly what was going on. That awareness was part of what had made Boyd such a good operator and an even better commander.

"Here," Boyd said, measuring him with that piercing green stare. "Toasted turkey, bacon and tomato to go. Extra mayo and pepper."

"Thanks, man. I owe you." He took it, clapped him on the back with his free hand. "Talk to you later."

He jumped in his truck and roared down the hill, his mind whirling as he turned onto the coastal highway. In the distance to the left, the sky was turning purple over the darker, indigo ocean in the distance.

The ride home was a blur. North along the highway. West down the hill toward town. North on Front Street along the waterfront, and up the hill on the north side of town to his neighborhood.

With every mile his heart beat a little faster, even as a hard knot pulled tighter and tighter in his gut. He didn't know what to think of her showing up here like this. She'd made it pretty clear before that she wasn't really into him, first with the brushoff and then the sporadic attempts at communication that followed.

Next to Groz's candy-apple red Mustang an unfamiliar car was parked along the fence out front, he assumed Nadia's rental. He went through the wooden gate and along the side of the house, still unsure what he was going to say.

Then Nadia stepped around the corner and the breath whooshed out of him.

He stopped, his whole chest squeezing tight as he fought the impulse to rush over and haul her into his arms, the need to touch her, hold her almost overwhelming his self-control.

They were in relationship limbo. He needed to keep that firmly in mind, and the rest of him firmly in check until he knew what was happening here.

Her smile faltered a bit at his reaction as she tucked a lock of long, chocolate brown hair behind her ear. She wore a flowing, ankle-length dress in swirling pinks and corals, making her creamy skin glow. He'd thought he'd been prepared to see her, but seeing her in the flesh now… She was so goddamn beautiful she took his breath away.

"Hi," she murmured, expression uncertain.

"Hi." He hated the awkwardness between them. The disappointed, almost hurt look on her face. What did she expect him to do, pretend nothing had changed and pick up right where they'd left things in Qatar?

No. He was done chasing after her and settling for the bits of her time she was willing to give him.

Except he'd literally just dropped everything and rushed straight home to see her.

Hell. Her showing up here out of the blue was fucking with his head. "What are you doing in Oregon?" he asked, shoving his hands into his pockets.

"Had emergency meetings in LA and decided last minute to fly up to Portland on my way home to surprise you. Was that…bad?"

He wasn't sure. Right now, he was more confused about them than ever. She wasn't the manipulative type. Whatever had motivated her to show up tonight had to be important. "Come on inside," he said, motioning to the side door as he strode toward it.

He let her in, got a whiff of her patchouli-vanilla scent as she stepped past him into the house. The familiar smell triggered an instant memory of them together, naked in that Qatar hotel room bed. He slammed the door shut on it in his mind. "Are you hungry? I can order us something, or—"

"No, I ate on the way here. And I can't stay long anyway. My flight from Portland leaves in a few hours." She paused inside the entry, shooting him an uncertain look.

So she'd flown to Portland and then driven all the way out here just to see him for a couple hours, hoping for…what? What the hell did she want from him?

He didn't know what the hell to say to her, but he definitely wasn't giving into a moment of weakness and taking her to his bed, then watching her waltz out of his life again. No matter how badly he still wanted her. "Okay. Go sit on the couch and I'll bring you some tea."

"That would be great, thanks."

He busied himself in the kitchen, half an eye on her as she wandered around his living room. Glad to have some space from her while he collected his thoughts. It was scary how much she affected him. How intense his feelings for her still were.

"How long have you lived here?" she asked, checking out the photos on the mantel. Some of him and his family. Others of him in uniform with men he'd served with. Some of them he'd helped bury.

"Few months." Having her in his home was something he'd fantasized about way too often over the past year. Though in his fantasies it had happened under completely different circumstances. He'd always imagined them the way they'd been in Qatar. That she would fall in love with him and want to build a future together.

He couldn't believe he'd ever been that naive.

He carried the mugs of tea into the adjoining room and handed her one. "Thanks," she murmured, giving him a measuring look.

He took the couch opposite her, unable to bear being any closer, and kept things light as he tried to get a read on her. "So what were the emergency meetings about?"

She curled up into the corner of her couch, tucking her pink-painted toes beneath the folds of her dress. Looking every inch the free-spirited flower child she was. "My new assignment."

Her tentative expression told him he wasn't going to like it. At all. "They're not sending you back to Syria?"

"No. Afghanistan."

His fingers tightened around the handle of his mug, every muscle in his body going rigid. "What?" His voice was low. Strained.

Afghanistan was about to implode. With the US and other western countries withdrawing their troops, the security situation was already unstable as the Taliban and other militant groups got ready to take the country back. It would only get worse from here on out.

Her big brown eyes held his. "I know. But they desperately

need volunteers to support the locals working at our orphanage there, and I have a lot of experience. The number of kids needing support there is skyrocketing. Villages are already being overrun up in the mountains, with more children becoming orphaned every day and being brought to Kabul."

He didn't respond, tamping down his reaction. He'd done a lot of tours in Afghanistan over the years. Could still smell the mountain dust in his nostrils when he closed his eyes. He didn't want Nadia within a hundred miles of its borders. Thinking of someone as gentle and untrained as her living in Kabul while all this shit went down… Christ.

"We're going to have proper security on site this time," she said, as if that made it all okay. "Former Afghan military, apparently."

Who would abandon their posts the instant their homes and families were threatened by encroaching militants. And he couldn't blame them. "Why do you have to be the one to go?"

She lifted a shoulder, her chin coming up in that defensive gesture he knew so well. They'd had this argument about her safety so many times in the past, but her going to Kabul now was the most dangerous thing she'd ever done. "They asked for me specifically because of my experience and because I speak decent Dari after working in Pakistan early last year." She shrugged, her expression holding a defensive edge. "If I don't go over there to help them, who will?"

He was so fucking torn. On the one hand, her determination to help children in need and her hardwired desire to make the world a better place were two of the things he loved most about her. On the other, her stubbornness and insistence upon always choosing to see the good in humankind made him want to shake her.

It was a major effort to clamp his mouth shut and not tell her how he felt. Because nothing he said would change her mind, and he didn't want to fight with her. Things were already strained enough between them. "How long do they want you there?"

"As long as possible, until the official withdrawal date."

"Do they have a plan to get you out if things go to shit?" Because there was a good chance they would.

"They're working on that now."

Working on it? Jesus. That should have been the first thing they did after deciding to ask this of her. They were sending her into another fucking war zone.

Somehow, he tamped down his frustration and concern and managed to contain it. "When do you leave?"

"I fly out of DC on Monday morning."

Three days from now. Putting her on the ground in Kabul Wednesday morning local time, in the middle of scorching summer temps while infrastructure and security broke down all around her. "And before that?"

"I'm going to spend the weekend at my dad's. Anaya's coming too. I'm excited, because I haven't seen them in months."

The sister she was closest to. He'd only met her once before on a video call. He'd liked her, felt she was a good and level-headed person. "What do they think about all this?"

She glanced down, smoothed a fold in her dress. "I haven't told them yet."

They were going to hate it as much as him, but they wouldn't be able to change her mind either. "How is your dad?" he asked to change the subject. Her father had suffered a mild heart attack a few months ago, while she'd been overseas. She adored him but wasn't close to her mother.

Her face brightened, the love and pride in her expression piercing him. She'd looked at him that same way in Qatar. As if he'd hung the damn moon.

He'd give damn near anything to have her look at him like that now. Didn't know what he'd done to make her stop.

"He's doing great. Back to his old tricks and looking forward to hunting season this fall. How are your parents?"

"All good. My mom's already planning for Thanksgiving and asking for my availability." She was big on holidays and family tradition. If she had to delay a family celebration by a few weeks either way to ensure everyone could be there together, that's what she'd do.

Nadia nodded, more relaxed now, everything about her radiating the natural warmth and kindness that had captivated him from day one. It was no wonder why she was magic with children. "And how do you like your new job?"

"It's great. My boss is a good guy, easy to work with and for." Ryder Locke was a former Marine and gave Callum all the latitude he wanted while organizing and carrying out a job. Ryder trusted him, never micromanaged him in any way. Callum appreciated that.

"Do you work on the security details much personally, or are you mostly in a managerial role now?"

It was a telling statement about their situation to know they'd drifted so far apart that she didn't know all of this already. It left a hollow feeling in the middle of his chest. "Mostly behind the scenes, but I still work the odd detail personally. I just got back from one in Jordan a few days ago."

Something flickered in her eyes. "Amman?"

"For a few days."

"I have fond memories of that place. Remember my terrible first line to you the night we met?"

"I thought it was a great line."

She grinned. "I'm glad." Then her smile faded, and she leaned across the narrow coffee table to stretch out a hand and set it on his knee.

That simple, innocent touch sent a shockwave through him, set his pulse racing.

The way she was looking at him, with such open caring and sincerity… He wanted to drag her onto his lap, bury his hands in her hair and kiss her until neither of them could breathe. Erase this awful, brittle distance between them and go back to the way things had once been.

"I know you're upset about me going to Kabul," she said softly. "But I wanted to see you before I left because you've been so distant lately."

Yeah, and why do you think that is?

She continued before he could say anything. "And I don't want you to worry about me while I'm over there. I'll be careful, won't take any undue risks."

He stared at her, unsure whether to snort or laugh. Of course he was going to fucking worry. She always tried to put a positive spin on things, downplayed the danger her work placed her in and put way too much faith in humanity, but she had to know how risky this upcoming assignment was. "You know I will anyway."

He drained the last few sips of his tea and stood before she could say anything else, aching at the loss of her touch and the confusion on her face. She had no clue how hard this was for him, the constant struggle not to touch her, wanting a clear and decisive answer about where they stood. What each of them wanted going forward.

Because if she didn't want to move forward together, then he needed to distance himself from her. "Want more tea?"

"No, I'm… No thanks."

He wasn't thirsty and wasn't a huge tea drinker, but he needed an excuse to get out of the room for a few minutes to regroup before he either caved or started asking her some really hard questions he was pretty sure he didn't want the answers to.

And now he was glad he hadn't asked her about the status of their relationship.

While he was pouring water from the kettle into his mug, a hard lump sitting in the pit of his stomach, he glanced over when footsteps came up the stairs down the hall.

Groz appeared at the top of the stairs in jeans and a black button-down, dark hair wet from a shower. He stopped when he saw them, then flashed Nadia a smile. "Hi again," he said to her before entering the kitchen. "Just on my way out," he added to Callum as he opened the fridge to peruse the contents. "Mia's coming for the weekend to look at a few places together. I'm meeting her for dinner at Travis and Kerrigan's."

Callum nodded and dunked the teabag in the mug a few times, going back and forth in his mind about what to say to Nadia. "Tell her I said hi."

"Will do." Groz emerged from the fridge with a white bakery box from the Whale's Tale and raised his eyebrows at him. "So that's her, huh?" he whispered, dark eyes gleaming with interest as he pulled out a cupcake and started devouring it. Groz was either eating or talking most of the time.

Callum nodded as he disposed of the teabag. Yeah, that was her. The woman who'd turned his world upside down, stolen his heart but didn't seem to want it.

"Outstanding." Groz chuckled and slapped him on the back once on his way to the living room where he opened the box and held it out to Nadia. "This is from our favorite spot in town. Best bakery you'll find on the Oregon Coast. You have to try one of these."

Nadia grinned up at him. "Oh, well, if I *have* to." She selected one, gave Groz a little smile and scooped some of the frosting into her mouth with a finger. "Yum. Thanks."

"My pleasure."

It was a good goddamn thing Groz was happily taken now,

because before Mia he had been an insatiable flirt, and there was no way Callum could have withstood watching his roomie working his charms on Nadia. But given that Groz knew how he felt about her, he didn't think Groz would have done that.

"I'll leave the rest of these here for you guys, just in case," Groz said, placing the box on the coffee table in front of her. He shot Callum a sly wink. "See you guys. Don't wait up, honey."

"I won't, sweetheart," he answered, deadpan. Normally he loved bantering with Groz. Tonight, his heart wasn't in it. Probably because it was still in the hands of the woman sitting in the other room.

The door shut behind Groz, and the sudden silence that filled the house pressed in on him like a physical weight.

"I like him," Nadia proclaimed, taking another bite of her cupcake.

"Yeah, me too." He walked back to the opposite couch, ready to explode with all the things he wanted to say. Everything he wanted to ask but refused to because he would be an idiot to bare himself to her now.

Nadia popped the last bit into her mouth and neatly put the paper wrapper in the box as she chewed. She glanced at her watch and sighed. "Well. I guess I should get going too."

Don't go.

He bit the words back, knowing they would be useless. And worse, make him vulnerable. "Sure," he said instead, and followed her to the door.

He walked her to the gate. She stopped in front of it, looking hesitant. "I'm sorry if I overstepped by just showing up like this. I thought… Well, it doesn't matter what I thought, but I didn't mean to make you uncomfortable…"

His normally long fuse and the self-control he prided himself on suddenly snapped. "Why did you come? Really."

She blinked, watching him warily. "Because I wanted to see you."

"Why?" Why, dammit? Why now, after she'd blown him off months ago? When she ran from him every time things got serious between them?

"Because I've missed you," she whispered, a sheen of tears making her eyes glisten.

Fuck. Her tears were like a knife to the gut. He'd never seen her cry, and knowing he was the cause tore him up inside. *I've missed you too.* Every goddamn day.

He bit the words back, refusing to let them out. He wasn't a toy she could pick up off the shelf to play with when she felt like it.

"Callum," she said, looking down at the grass between them. "I know I've hurt you in the past, and for that I'm truly sorry. I didn't come here to hurt you more. Truly. I just… I really miss you, and I can't stand feeling like I'm losing you."

"*Losing* me?" he managed, unable to keep the bitterness out of his voice.

Those big brown eyes lifted to him again and she shifted her feet, clearly uncomfortable. "I care about you. A lot. But I don't know how to give you what you want."

Staring at her as he absorbed her words, he wavered. She'd never been this vulnerable or direct with him about this before. She was also going to Kabul in a few days. The threat of something happening to her was way too real. Hurt as he was, he couldn't let her go with this coldness between them.

Against his better judgment he reached out and drew her to him, banding his arms around her and holding her tight. The feel of her soft curves pressed against him, her scent swirling around him, almost broke what remained of his control. Especially when she wound her arms around his neck and burrowed in close, her cheek resting against his heart.

She angled her head up. Their gazes locked, and he knew he'd made a critical mistake.

A tidal wave of desire and possessiveness roared through him. He didn't stand a chance as her eyes dropped to his mouth. She lifted her face…

The instant their lips met he was lost, every argument about keeping his distance suddenly gone. He gripped handfuls of her hair and kissed her back. Managed to rein in the driving hunger for a few moments, until her tongue flicked his.

He took over, alternately soothing and tormenting. Giving and taking. Claiming her in the only way he could in this moment. Knowing he was going to have to let her go yet again in the next few minutes.

He broke the kiss, his whole body strung taut as he stared down at her. Her pupils were dilated, her breathing unsteady. Hair mussed from where his hands were burrowed into it, pink, kiss-swollen lips parted slightly.

It took an act of will not to scoop her up right then and carry her into the house. Lay her on his bed and strip that dress off her. He wouldn't stop until he was buried as deep inside her as he could get, until she was digging her nails in his back and crying out his name as she came apart for him.

His hand was slightly unsteady, his heart thudding as he eased a hand from her hair and stroked the side of her face. "You be careful over there," he rasped out, a hollow ache forming beneath his ribs.

Nothing was resolved between them. They were standing feet apart, yet a yawning divide stood between them, and she was afraid to risk taking the leap to meet him on the other side. Maybe because she didn't trust him to catch her. And if she didn't trust him on that level by now, then it was pretty clear she never would.

She nodded, tried to smile, but for the first time he saw

doubt in her eyes. Maybe even a little fear. "I will. I'll call you when I can, okay?"

He nodded, hoping it was true.

Her smile dimmed. Turned wistful, the naked longing there killing him. What was she so damn scared of? "I wish I could have stayed longer. Our timing sucks, doesn't it?"

He'd been thinking the same damn thing. "Yeah."

Watching her drive away to face the unknown in one of the most hostile places on the planet, he swore he felt his heart crack in two.

TWO

"*Kabul?*"

Nadia studied the two faces that were the dearest to her in the world. One dark brown, one light-skinned but flushed with sunburn, both currently wearing identical expressions of disbelief and anger. "Yes. I fly out Monday."

"Why?" her dad demanded, his face flushing a shade darker.

She took a deep breath and explained the same things she had to Callum last night. Had it really only been sixteen hours since she'd seen him? It felt like an eternity.

Her dad got up and started pacing the kitchen floor, dragging a hand through his hair. "Dammit, Nadia."

"Dad," Anaya said quietly, ever the peacemaker.

He whirled to face them. "What? She's about to go risk her life in that hell hole for people who don't give two shits about her, and I'm not allowed to be upset?"

"You're allowed. But it's not going to help the situation—or change her mind." She gave him a pointed look.

Nadia reached out and squeezed her adopted sister's shoulder. "Thank you," she whispered.

Anaya shot her a glare. "Hey, I'm mad at you too. Don't think I'm not."

"Okay." Nadia withdrew her hand and sat back, chastised.

"It's because I love you. That's why I'm upset. I'm worried about you." She glanced at their father. "We both are."

"I know. You were both terrified when I told you I was going to Aleppo, but I made it through that assignment okay, didn't I?"

Their father muttered something under his breath and left the room, heading for the stairs. Nadia sighed but Anaya touched her arm. "Just let him be. He'll get over it in a bit and come back down when he's ready."

"Yeah. Let's go sit outside," Nadia suggested, wanting to shake everything off and enjoy family time. "I need some fresh air before my jet lag catches up with me." The long meetings, whirlwind flights and that pit stop in Crimson Point had depleted her energy reserves. She needed to fill them back up before she left Monday.

They went outside to sit on the back verandah that ran the width of the house. The West Virginia afternoon was already hot and muggy, a heavy bank of dark clouds forming over the western hills promising rain.

"Looks like we're going to get a thunderstorm later," Nadia said as they rocked the rocking chairs set along the railing overlooking the neatly tended yard. Already gusts of moisture-laden breeze made the wind chimes dance, filling the air with their delicate music. "I've missed it," she mused. "Lying on the top bunk in our room all snug under the covers while a summer storm blew up outside. Remember that?"

"Yeah."

"I used to hate thunderstorms."

Anaya gave her a doubtful look. "You did?"

"Before I came here, when I was really young. They used to

terrify me." Back then she'd been afraid of so many things. Now, the things that still scared her she buried deep.

"Me too," Anaya said. "I only remember the last hurricane that hit when I was still in Haiti, though I know there were others before that."

"It's funny how that happens, isn't it? How you can start a new life somewhere else when you're young and forget so much of what came before."

Anaya nodded, gazing out at the hills, seeming lost in thought. One of the things Nadia loved best about her sister—other than her loyalty and kindness—was her appreciation of quiet. Of the peace neither of them had found as young children. Her sister had been through a lot in her life, most recently including having her heart and dreams smashed into a thousand pieces by a man who had never deserved her in the first place. Nadia thanked God that Anaya had finally seen the truth and found the strength to walk away before it was too late.

"It's so different here now," Nadia murmured. "So quiet." There were no toys or bikes or scooters strewn all over the backyard. The huge play gym that had stood in the center of the lawn had been replaced by neat rows of raised beds their dad grew vegetables in.

"I know. It still feels weird, doesn't it?"

"Yes." Her childhood seemed like another lifetime ago.

Back then her parents had still been married and the house had been full of all the noise, drama and chaos that came with raising a family of six kids, four of whom were adopted from different regions of the globe and couldn't speak English when they first arrived.

Nadia was number five. The Bishops had come to Romania to adopt her when she was six. Anaya was the baby of the family, adopted from Haiti when she was just starting elementary school.

Her sister glanced over at her, expression somber. She'd become too somber over the past eighteen months, more withdrawn, even from her sometimes. "How long do you think they'll keep you over there?"

"Could be a few weeks, could be a few months. Just depends on what happens."

Anaya nodded. "Hope it's short. Just saying." She shook her head. "When are you going to realize you don't have to prove yourself to the world anymore?"

The words weren't meant to be harsh, that wasn't Anaya's way. But they hit hard anyway. She'd felt the need to prove herself ever since she could remember, and likely always would.

An abrupt change of subject was in order. "I, uh, made a stop to see someone on the way here from LA."

Anaya frowned. "Who?"

"Callum."

Her sister gasped and smacked Nadia's arm. "No way, the hot Viking warrior?"

That was actually a pretty apt description of him. An incredibly *sexy* hot Viking warrior, especially when he had a beard.

Anaya twisted her rocking chair around to face Nadia head on, her expression avid. "Spill. Every detail."

"He wasn't all that happy to see me at first."

Her face fell, a frown creeping in. "Really?"

"No." She'd thought he would be surprised in a good way to see her, but his reaction had been downright chilly when she'd stepped around the side of the house. "Things are strained between us. He's still upset that I said it wasn't a good time when he offered to come meet me in London in April." She regretted it now, that stupid knee-jerk reaction to retreat when things began to look serious.

"That was three months ago. Haven't you guys talked since then? Smoothed things out?"

"Well, sort of, but things haven't been the same since. He's distant now." That bothered her. She truly hadn't meant to hurt him.

"*Nadia.*"

She winced at her sister's exasperated tone. "What?"

"You know what. He offered to fly all the way to London just to see you—probably only for a day or two at that, knowing your schedule—and you blew him off."

"I'd already made plans and booked things—"

"Don't bother with the lame excuses. If you'd wanted to see him badly enough, you would have canceled whatever plans you had. Instantly. And you've had plenty of time to set things right since." She shook her head in concern, tight black ringlets swinging around her heart-shaped face. "What's up with you? You have deep feelings for this guy, I know you do."

Deeper than anyone who'd come before him, that was for sure.

"I've never seen you as happy as when you got back from Qatar, and you still always talk about him."

"I know." She slumped in her chair, knowing she deserved the well-meaning lecture. There was something wrong with her. And she felt even worse because she knew Anaya would secretly give anything to find a man like Callum. "He's amazing."

"Then what's the problem?"

"He's…intense." Much more into a long-term, committed and exclusive relationship than she had expected.

Anaya's deep brown eyes widened. "Like, in bed? Because, whew, girl, if that's what you meant, please continue." She fanned herself, all eagerness again.

Nadia cracked a grin. "Well, since you asked, yes. He can

be." Okay, most times he was. And in the best possible way, capable of reducing her to a puddle of need with a single touch or look. "But I meant in terms of his expectations about being in a relationship with him."

Anaya looked confused. "Meaning?"

"You know me, my life is crazy. I never know where I'm going next, or how long I'll be there. For him it's all or nothing. I'm not exactly stable relationship material, and he wants more than I can give him."

One perfect black eyebrow arched in challenge. "You said he was military. No, 'badass military' I believe was the exact phrase, so he would understand your lifestyle better than anyone else you've been with. Try again."

"Yeah, except he's traditional at his core. Comes from a picture-perfect nuclear family, parents are stable and still married, actually love each other…" She sighed, trying to put her misgivings into words. She hadn't intended to bring this up, didn't want to inadvertently hurt Anaya by saying it, but there was no avoiding it if she wanted to be honest. "That's what he wants too. Someone to settle down with, raise a family and grow old with."

"He's told you that?"

"I just know." She'd dated enough guys to know that Callum was different from all the others. He wanted what his parents had. "He's the marriage-and-babies type."

Anaya's expression tightened ever so slightly. As if she had hidden a flinch. "And you're more the babies type than anyone else I know, plus you're seriously into him, so I fail to see the problem here."

She shrugged, feeling defensive, and hating that she'd caused the little flare of pain she'd just seen in her sister's dark eyes. "I'm not ready yet. I don't think I'm cut out for that traditional lifestyle, so I don't want to lead him on when it can't go anywhere long term." She wanted to settle down eventually. Probably. Waking up to and going through life with Callum at her side was pretty tempting in a lot of ways.

Anaya eyed her in the way only a sister could, her expression saying Nadia was full of shit. "We both know it's more than that. And that it's time you let all that BS go. Past time, if I'm being honest." She shifted in her seat. "Does he know about your past?"

"Yes. Mostly," she hedged when Anaya kept staring.

"And does he know whatever you guys have is the longest and most serious relationship you've ever had with a guy?"

Ugh. It sounded so pathetic out loud. "No."

Her sister made a frustrated sound. "You don't think he deserves to know that?"

"No, it would make me sound pathe—"

The screened door to the verandah opened and their dad stepped out holding a trio of mason jars in his big hands. "Thought we could all use some cooling off," he said in a gruff voice that told her she wasn't quite off the hook yet.

"Ooh, blackberry sours?" Nadia said, accepting a jar filled with gorgeous purple liquid. Her father's signature summer cocktail was made from fresh blackberries picked around the property that he turned into puree and simple syrup, then mixed with lime juice, brandy, and poured over ice. Yum.

He grunted and sat down in the chair on Nadia's other side, the wood creaking as it took his weight. "So? What were y'all just talking about before I came out?"

"Girl stuff," Anaya said, her eyes dancing with amusement.

Nadia took a sip of the cocktail and moaned, closing her eyes as the tart-sweet flavors burst on her tongue, the brandy giving a kick of mellow heat down her throat as she swallowed. "This takes me back." When she glanced at her dad, he was smiling to himself. A good indication that he was pretty much over his mad. "Thanks, Dad."

"Welcome," he said in that same gruff tone. He wasn't fooling anyone. He had a marshmallow center and everyone who knew him was aware of it.

Except his ex-wife, who'd done everything in her power to take advantage of it during their turbulent, dysfunctional marriage. Nadia still had deep, conflicted feelings about her adoptive mother, along with a lot of gratitude and some great memories too.

"So? What were you saying before?" he pressed.

"Well, I was just getting around to telling Anaya about the kiss Callum and I had last night—"

Anaya smacked her shoulder, mouth open in a scandalized gasp. "You said he wasn't happy to see you!"

"I said he wasn't at *first*. By the end he was." She'd been thinking about that kiss constantly since, wishing they'd had more time together, at least enough to finish what they'd started. She'd fallen so fast and hard for him, but what she'd said to him was true.

The stars never seemed to align for them. When he pressed for more, she got spooked and pulled away. Now she was edging toward trying to meet him part way, ready to consider trying a real, committed relationship with him, and he was the one being distant.

It made her wonder if the universe was trying to send her a message. That maybe they weren't meant to be.

"And? How was it?"

Their dad groaned and shifted in his chair. "Why'd I have to have so many daughters?" he muttered to himself.

"Oh, hush," Anaya told him, leaning across Nadia to smack his shoulder too. "Go on, Nadia. How was it? Scale of one-to-ten."

"Oh, I dunno... Twelve." Unforgettable, just like the man responsible.

Anaya crowed and stomped her feet on the wide plank floor while their dad made a strangled sound. They all laughed, and just like that, all the tension from before vanished.

Yet as they sat talking and laughing together, her upcoming assignment sat heavy at the back of her mind. She would never say it, but the truth was, she was nervous this time around.

She couldn't forget that look on Callum's face when she'd told him. That haunted expression in his eyes that she wished she could wipe away. Fear for her, brought on by all the things he'd seen and done over there during his elite military career.

But her organization had asked her to go specifically, and she couldn't say no. Didn't want to. She'd worked all over the world, starting in the US, then moving into Europe and beyond, slowly taking on work in more dangerous settings around the world.

The prolonged war had left too many Afghan children without homes or anyone to look after them, and the violence would continue long after the US pulled its personnel out. It broke her heart, and if she could do something to make even a few lives better during her time there, then it would be worth the personal risk she was taking.

"Rain's coming," her father said during a lull in the conversation, squinting at the clouds boiling over the distant peaks of the hills surrounding their little valley. "Be here within two hours."

Taking in that ominous line of black clouds in the distance, Nadia set her empty jar on the arm of the rocking chair and let out a slow breath. The storm that was going to break here later was nothing compared to what was coming to Afghanistan.

Thankfully, she would be out of there before the worst of it hit.

THREE

Aref looked up from his tea when someone banged on the door, his body tensing. "Who is it?" he called in Dari.

"Gaffar."

He turned to his wife, who was holding their infant daughter. "Go," he whispered. Eyes wide, she hurried off and disappeared in their bedroom at the back of the house.

Aref went to the door, one hand on the butt of his pistol at the back of his waistband. He stood to the side of the doorframe, then quickly leaned over to check the peephole. It was Gaffar, and he appeared to be alone, dressed in dusty jeans and a T-shirt, his beard untrimmed.

He unlocked the door and opened it. "Come in," he urged, and his friend rushed inside. Aref shut and locked the door, turning to face him. "What is it?"

Gaffar gulped, the strain on his face making Aref's insides curdle. "They're coming," he rasped out.

No. They couldn't be. Not this soon. They'd already fled Kabul and come here to escape the people hunting him. "Are you sure?"

"Yes, I swear it. My cousin just alerted me twenty minutes

ago. Taliban are in the eastern part of the city asking about you. It's only a matter of time before someone tells them where you are."

Aref clenched his jaw and gripped his friend's upper arm. "I owe you a great debt."

"Think nothing of it. But please, you must leave now."

He nodded. "I know. And you should leave for a few days as well, so you have an alibi if anyone tries to question you." If the Taliban found out that Gaffar had helped him and his family escape, they would make an example of him.

"I'll wait for you at the bottom of the village."

Gaffar hurriedly left and Aref strode to the bedroom where his wife was huddled on the edge of their bed, cradling their daughter. Her long hair was pulled back in a thick braid, her brown eyes filled with love and concern.

"We have to go. Now," he said in as calm a tone as he could manage in the moment. They had planned and prepared for this, even expected it to happen, though not this soon.

While she rushed to collect their bags, he swept through the small, three-room house they'd been staying in—collecting ammunition, food and the little money they'd managed to save up for this day. Getting rid of anything that would tie them to this place.

Within minutes all was ready. Aref opened the back door and checked the yard, going around the side of the house to ensure no one was waiting for them in the street.

He waved his wife forward, kept one hand on her lower back and the other on the butt of his pistol as he hurried them down the dusty road. It was empty except for a few children playing with a soccer ball, but as he led his wife through the town, he could feel eyes on them peering from behind curtained windows.

An eerie sensation blended with the quiet, and he knew

Gaffar had come not a minute too soon. They needed to get away from here as fast as possible. American and other foreign forces were withdrawing steadily every day. Only a few pockets of resistance remained in Kabul, and soon those would be gone as well. As soon as the Americans pulled out, the Taliban would sweep back across the country to reclaim the territory they had lost over the past twenty years.

And they would show no mercy to those who had aided the enemy.

Gaffar eased the ancient Toyota out onto the road at the bottom of the village. Aref helped his wife into the back seat as she tried to settle their fussing daughter, then jumped in the front next to Gaffar.

The drive out of the village was tense, and the sole road that led in and out of town was the perfect place for a checkpoint— or an ambush.

But they passed through the chokepoint without incident, and Aref breathed a little easier as the truck swung east and began to wind its way up an ancient dirt road toward the mountains in the distance. They bumped and jostled along the switchbacks, climbing out of the valley toward the poor village where his wife had been born, filling the three-hour drive with talk about what was happening in their country.

A group of men and boys flooded out of the mud brick dwellings when they arrived at the outer wall of the village. Aref stepped out and greeted the elders. When his wife got out moments later with their daughter, she had covered her head and lower face with a veil in deference to their strict religious and societal beliefs.

The women stood in their doorways as he escorted her to her parents' house. He saw her safely settled, brought in her things and showed her where he hid the cash in a cache beneath a rug on the hard-packed floor.

"You'll be safe here," he told her, taking her face in his hands as a wrenching sensation made it feel like his chest was being split apart. Her family and the rest of the villagers would hide and protect her and their daughter.

She stared up at him with frightened brown eyes, cradling their daughter to her chest.

"Stay out of sight until I come back for you." Hopefully within a few days. But he had to go now. It was him the Taliban wanted. He could not live with himself if anything happened to his family because of what he'd done.

"Be careful," she whispered.

He kissed her goodbye, filled with torment at having to leave her, then smiled at their daughter and placed a kiss on the top of her silky black curls. "God willing, we will be together again soon." He would be back for them when he had figured out how to get them out of the country safely. The Americans would finally have to honor their promise and help him now, provide safe transport and a home in the US.

Back in the truck with Gaffar, they headed back down the mountain and began the trek to Kabul. Encroaching darkness hampered their progress, and they arrived on the outskirts of the capital just before midnight. He'd no sooner unrolled his bedroll in the basement of the safehouse than he got a call on his cell phone. It was his father-in-law.

The man was breathless, his voice full of panic. "They're gone."

Aref sat bolt upright, his heart lurching into his throat. "What?" he croaked.

"A Taliban leader came and searched the village. He took them, would have killed us for trying to hide them if our elders hadn't intervened."

Cold sweat pricked his face and chest. "Where are they? Where did they take them?"

"I don't know. No one saw which way they went, but we heard gunshots a few minutes after."

Aref closed his eyes, nausea churning in his stomach. "They're dead?"

"I do not know, but… Yes. Probably. It was God's will—"

He ended the call and gripped his hair with both hands, a howl of agony building in his chest. The whole purpose for risking their lives in the drive up to the village earlier was because he'd been certain they would be safe there.

To know they had been taken at gunpoint, that his wife had almost certainly been abused and maybe defiled before her death was like a knife in his guts. And the thought of his innocent daughter paying for his crimes with her life…

A low, wounded sound wrenched free, echoing off the plaster walls.

His host rushed down the stairs moments later. "Aref? What is wrong?"

"Lila and the baby were taken," he whispered, a sob trying to wrench free. "They're both dead."

The man gasped and came over to lay a hand on his shoulder. "Surely not. There must be a mistake—"

"There's no mistake," he said bitterly, his voice wobbling. He felt like he was about to shatter, the pain ripping him apart inside. "The Taliban killed them because of me."

Swamped by his own agony, the crushing guilt, he didn't listen to whatever his host was saying. And soon his mind turned to revenge. The Taliban had innocent blood on its hands, but the Americans were just as much to blame for his family's deaths. They had come here to lay siege to his already suffering country, meddling and trying to impose their will. He had trusted them. Tried to help them because he detested the Taliban as much as they did.

In return, they had forsaken him and his family. Lied and then cowardly abandoned them to their fate.

Aref would avenge his wife and daughter. The people responsible for this would pay with their lives.

∽

CALLUM BREATHED in the salty tang in the air as he walked along Front Street on his way back to the office after grabbing some dinner, hoping to clear his head. He hadn't been sleeping well since Nadia had shown up on Friday night. He'd gone over everything in his mind so many times and was still torn as to what to do about their situation.

She was in Kabul now. She had texted him when she'd first arrived, telling him her location and sending pictures of her with some of the staff and children at the orphanage. Her bright smile in those photos was even harder to look at now.

The brick building that housed Crimson Point Security was just up from the waterfront, a heritage building that had been fully equipped with state-of-the-art security and fully wired with the latest technology required in their line of work. It was a perfect July day, all blue sky and puffy white clouds, with a cool breeze rolling in from the ocean.

He entered his passcode and fingerprints into the keypad outside the main elevator and stepped out onto the third floor. Jaia, the executive assistant, looked up at him from her desk. "Ryder's wanting to see you in his office right away," she told him in her crisp, British-Indian accent, her manner as efficient as usual.

"Did he say what about?" Ryder could have texted him if it was that urgent.

"No, but I think it's about a new contract that just came in."

"Okay, thanks." He bypassed his office and paused outside the door at the far end of the hall to knock.

"Come in."

Ryder was seated behind his desk, the large picture window behind him framing a view of the beach and the tide rolling onto it. "Hey, have a seat," he said, rubbing a hand over his short black goatee and mustache.

Callum shut the door and lowered himself into the leather club chair on the other side of the desk. "What's up?"

"New job just came in. It's big. My former boss handed it to us specifically. The name Andrew Wilkinson familiar at all?"

"Billionaire from Texas?"

"That's the one. He needs a personal security detail for an upcoming trip, so we need to get a team together."

"Doesn't he already have his own security?" All those billionaire types did, preferring to keep it all in-house, people they knew and trusted personally.

"He's got personal bodyguards that travel with him everywhere. But this job is beyond their scope."

Sounded juicy. "What's the job?"

"Afghanistan."

A spark of excitement leapt in him. He would never have thought he would be excited at the prospect of going back there, but he had a vested interest in going now. "Where?"

"Kabul. He's got high-level meetings with government officials there for a few days, something to do with military contracts, and I don't need to tell you how precarious the security situation is there right now."

Nope. He was clear on that. He'd lost sleep the past few nights knowing Nadia was in the midst of it. "What have you got on Wilkinson so far?"

"This." Ryder handed him a file that was a half-inch thick.

They went through the file together. Wilkinson kept two

bodyguards with him at all times. Their names and CVs were in there too.

"We need a small team to oversee everything there, from logistics to transportation and augmenting his personal security. Three people should be good. You'll need to decide who, but we're short on manpower at the moment—"

"I'll head the team."

Ryder blinked at him, closed his mouth for a moment before speaking. "You're sure?"

"I'm sure." He had the most experience over there of anyone on their payroll, and it would put him in proximity to Nadia, even if it was only for a few days. That was more than enough reason for him to go back to the country he'd hoped to never set foot in again. He wanted to see her in person, make sure she was safe and the place she was staying in was secure.

"I can give you a day or two to think things over. If you change your mind—"

"I won't."

"Okay, then the problem is going to be putting a team together for this," Ryder said. "I wasn't kidding when I said we're short right now."

The two guys who immediately jumped out at him were Walker and Myers. They had the qualifications Callum wanted for this job. But deploying them both to Kabul at the same time posed a big problem because of their family circumstance.

"I want Walker with me." Callum had worked with him before, back when he'd been deployed with the military. Walker was former military with a background in intelligence and was the best at logistics and intel gathering that Callum had ever seen.

"Good call."

"I'd love to have Myers with us too, but…"

"Yeah, that's gonna be too complicated. Anyone else?"

"What about Matthews and Abramson?"

"I just extended their contract in Paris for that same week."

"Yates?"

"Busted his leg mountain biking yesterday."

Damn. "Then that leaves Myers." He had come on board a month ago, recruited by Walker.

Both men were perfect for this job—former Special Ops military with a wealth of experience in Afghanistan. They knew the culture. The geography and topography. The complex social and political web that had resulted in the US withdrawal twenty years after putting boots on the ground there. But…

"Shae," Ryder said for him, stating the obvious. Myers' teenage daughter, but Walker was her stepdad and had mostly raised her.

"Yeah." Ryder rubbed at his goatee, deep in thought. Sending two parents overseas on the same job wasn't something the company would normally consider.

Asking them both to go wouldn't be Callum's first choice under the circumstances, but there was no one else suited for this detail available on such short notice. "I need Walker to work logistics on the ground while we're there. As for Myers, maybe it's something they would consider if we mitigated the risk for one of them."

"Maybe. I agree, they're the best candidates we have for this contract. But with Shae involved, there's an added risk. Only thing we can do is put it out there and let them decide."

They wouldn't know until they asked. "I'll call Walker now." He got up, pulled out his phone and dialed the number on the way to his office.

FOUR

Walker looked up from the stove where he was stirring a pot of his famous spaghetti sauce and smiled as Shae entered the kitchen. "Hungry?"

"Depends on what we're having. Do I smell your secret sauce?" She tossed her long brown hair over one shoulder, the makeup she'd just started using last year making her look like a grown woman instead of his little girl.

"Yes, ma'am."

"Then yes, I'm hungry." She perched herself on a high stool at the island and propped her chin on one fist. "Need a hand?"

"Why, do I look like I'm struggling?"

Her lips twitched. "No. But it's kind of pathetic that neither of us have more exciting plans on a gorgeous summer night like this, but I have an excuse since I just moved here and don't really know anyone yet."

"I like hanging around the house." He tossed her a grin over his shoulder. "Especially when I get to spend quality time with you."

She rolled her eyes in the way only an eighteen-year-old girl who knew everything could, but her little smile told him she was secretly pleased by that. "You don't have to hang around here just to keep me company. You should get out and do something fun."

"I'd rather spend time with you, but we can go out after dinner if you want, see that movie you've been wanting to go to."

"Dad," she said with a long-suffering sigh, shaking her head at him. "It's been almost four years. You're allowed to move on and live your life, you know."

There was no one he wanted to move on with, and he wasn't ready anyway. "I *am* living my life. And like I said, I'd rather be with you any night of the week."

"You're ridiculous," she told him and hopped off the stool to come stand next to him, the top of her head coming to his shoulder as she looped an arm around his waist.

A powerful wave of love swept over him, along with an edge of nostalgia. His little girl was all grown up, and the years had gone by way too fast. Shae might not be his by blood, but she was his daughter nonetheless. "How'm I doing, inspector?" he asked as he stirred the sauce.

"Dunno. Gimme that." She took the wooden spoon from him, dipped it into the pot before blowing across the surface of what she scooped out and taking a taste. "Mmmm, yeah. You've still got it." She handed the spoon back.

"Thanks. Grab some plates and we'll eat as soon as the pasta's cooked." The salted water was almost at a boil now in the other pot. He grabbed the box of spaghetti, paused when his phone rang in his back pocket.

Callum. "Walker," he answered, wondering what was up. Callum rarely called outside of work hours.

"Hey. You got a few minutes?"

"Sure." He poured the pasta into the water and set the timer for two minutes less than the package called for. Because mushy pasta was disgusting and a crime against cooking. "What's up?"

"New contract just came through. Heading up security for a billionaire named Wilkinson next week. In Kabul."

Ah, one of his least favorite places on the planet.

"It's going to be a small team because he's got his own personal bodyguards with him. He wants us to oversee everything, take care of the big picture and logistics while we're over there. I'm heading up the team. I want you with me, and we need one more. I know it's not normal procedure, and I know this will be complicated for you, but we're out of options, and I want to ask Myers as well."

He frowned. "Both of us?" He glanced at Shae.

She was mature for her age, legally old enough and completely responsible enough to be on her own when he traveled, if need be, but Kabul was going to shit currently, and he didn't like the thought of both him and Donovan being there at the same time. Shae had gone through enough pain and loss with her mother. Losing one or both of her dads would devastate her.

"Ryder and Danae offered to look out for Shae if you go. Danae's willing to come stay at your place if you guys want."

That was good of them, but it didn't mitigate the danger over there. "There's no one else besides Donovan?"

"Not with the qualifications we need."

Damn. "Let me talk it over with Shae and Donovan and I'll get back to you." Donovan might reject the idea outright. They'd never both been overseas at the same time before, let alone in harm's way together.

"Sounds good."

"Talk over what?" Shae asked when he tucked his phone away.

"Job offer came up for next week in Afghanistan. Callum wants me and Donovan on the detail with him."

"Oh." The tiniest flicker of unease passed across her face. "Isn't that… Things are pretty bad there right now, aren't they?"

"Yes." He'd never lied to her and wasn't about to start now, though he didn't want to scare her. "I'll talk it over with him, but I have to go even if he doesn't. Are you okay staying here on your own if—"

"Daaad, I'm eighteen. I'm fully capable of taking care of myself while you're gone."

"I know you are." It was hard for him to accept that, that she didn't need him the way she used to, but he knew she could handle this. "Danae offered to come stay here with you if I go."

"That's sweet of her, but I'm okay on my own. And I can always call her or Ryder if I need something. What, you don't trust me not to burn the house down or have a rager while you're gone?"

He stood there a moment, back to the counter with his hands braced on the top of it, reality hitting him hard all over again. Shae was getting ready to leave the nest and would be starting college in a few months.

Shit, he didn't want to think about that, or how empty his life would be without her when she moved out. Sometimes she looked so much like her mother it made his chest hitch. "I trust you completely. I just want to make sure you feel safe."

"I'll be fine."

He watched her a long moment. He could see the lingering worry in her eyes. "You're sure?"

"I'm totally sure."

Walker wasn't making this decision on his own. "I'll call Donovan, talk it over with him first and see what he thinks."

"Okay." She brought the plates over and set them down on

the counter beside him along with the silverware. "I think I'd actually feel better if you were both there together, because I know you'll watch each other's backs."

They would, but this was Afghanistan they were talking about. A place where things had a way of going south in the blink of an eye no matter how well they prepared for the mission.

∼

"NADIA."

She looked up from the small mountain of laundry she was folding to find her boss, the director of the orphanage standing in the doorway, and raised her eyebrows in question.

"We have another new little one," Homa said in heavily accented English. She knew Nadia spoke some Dari and a bit of Pashto, but still insisted on communicating in English—so there was no confusion, she insisted. "She just arrived. Can you come downstairs?"

"Yes, of course." She hurried after Homa down the narrow, pitted concrete stairs, the smell of lentil soup wafting from the kitchen in the back. The main floor was a hub of activity. Eleven young children ranging in age from three to ten were scattered around the largest room while four of their devoted Afghan volunteers played with them.

Nadia and Homa swept past it to the reception area where an old woman sat cradling an infant less than a year old wrapped up in a blanket. The child's large, dark eyes were wet with tears, shoulders quivering with the traces of sobs.

Homa began speaking to the woman in Dari, so fast that Nadia struggled to follow along. "Her name is Ferhana. She was found next to her mother." Homa's mouth twisted. "The Taliban shot her and left her to die on the side of the road. This woman's husband found them and risked a great deal to rescue the child and bring her here."

Nadia stifled a gasp, her gaze flying to the little girl. Jesus, the abject cruelty of the Taliban was horrifying. Every day there were more threats of Taliban raids as they approached the capital. New children were dropped off here almost every day.

Many times no one knew their circumstances or how they'd become orphans. If it weren't for the wonderful families willing to take in these poor children, this place would be overrun. They had to find homes for every child as soon as humanly possible before the deadline of the final US withdrawal in ten days' time.

She approached the woman and child, crouching down in front of the little one to give her an encouraging smile. "*Salaam alekum*, Ferhana," she murmured, glad for the two former soldiers stationed out front.

The little girl sniffled and rubbed her fists over her eyes, watching Nadia warily. Eight, maybe nine months old, and her whole world had been brought crashing down around her. The one blessing was that she was too young to remember the horrors of what she'd witnessed, and Nadia was glad of it.

"Are you hungry?" Those big, dark eyes stayed locked on her as Homa translated to the elderly woman. "Should we go find you something delicious to eat? Hmm?" She gave the baby another smile and held out her arms. "Will you come to me?"

The old woman handed her over. Ferhana let out a frightened wail and tried to twist away.

Nadia held her close and spoke to her in a soft, soothing voice as she carried her toward the kitchen. "You're safe here with us. No one's going to hurt you or frighten you again." A wave of protectiveness whipped through her, a sick feeling twisting in her gut when she thought of that poor mother. How terrified she must have been. How hard she must have fought to protect her child.

Several of the volunteers looked up as she passed by the next doorway. Nadia smiled at them, saw the sympathy on their faces as they looked at Ferhana.

They all treated Nadia with kindness and respect, but there was also a wariness about them when she was around. She was the outsider here, and her presence posed an added risk to these women if the Taliban came. She worried about that, would maintain as low a profile as possible while she was here.

"Let's see what we can find in here, okay?" she said to the baby. Ferhana had stopped struggling and was now fearfully staring straight ahead, her little fists clutching the material of Nadia's shirt.

The cook smiled at them and began to babble to Ferhana in Dari. A grandmother herself six times over, the woman had a wonderful way with children. She reached out one gnarled finger to stroke Ferhana's cheek and offered the child a spoonful of homemade yogurt.

Nadia cradled Ferhana while the cook spoon-fed her, smiling in awe of the resiliency all their children showed. Ferhana leaned forward for each bite, her mouth open like a little bird as she trustingly took the yogurt.

Their work here was critical. She would stay as long as she could, but it was becoming more obvious every day that there was going to come a point when she would have to leave to ensure she didn't bring danger to these people with her presence as an American—and to get out of this place alive.

FIVE

The smell took Callum right back the moment he stepped out of the plane into the dry afternoon air. Dry and dusty. Transporting him back to scorching hot days spent doing recon and clearing buildings and freezing cold nights waiting to go after an HVT in a mountain village.

Of firefights and calling in airstrikes. Faces of the guys he'd served with and lost here flickered through his mind like a film reel on high speed.

He held out a hand to stop Wilkinson's bodyguard from stepping out onto the metal stairway with him beyond the aircraft door and waited until Walker and Myers brought the vehicles around. Two black SUVs, armor reinforced with bullet-resistant glass. It wouldn't save them from a direct hit by an IED implanted in the road, but it afforded them an extra layer of protection while on the move.

Walker pulled the second vehicle up to the base of the stairs and kept the engine idling. "Let's go," Callum said, not expecting any trouble here at the secured airport but ready for it anyway.

He led the way down the steps, paused at the bottom to scan

around them at the aircrews refueling and performing maintenance on other aircraft. The two bodyguards hurried down the stairs with Wilkinson safely tucked between them.

Callum was in the zone now, and it was actually a relief after thinking about Nadia for too much of the flights here. Here he knew his role. Knew exactly what he was doing. In a weird way, it was almost comforting.

He opened the rear door of the vehicle Myers was driving. One bodyguard ushered Wilkinson in and slid in beside him while the other rode shotgun up front with Myers.

Callum took one more good look around and studied the gate at the far side of the tarmac before getting into the lead vehicle. The moment he shut the door, Walker started for the gate. Two US Marines guarding the inside opened the gate and waved them through.

"Straight to the hotel?" Walker asked, his Mississippi drawl filling the silence of the interior.

Callum nodded. "Take the alternate route."

They were both silent on the way into the city. Security checkpoints had been set up at regular intervals to check the ID of everyone coming in and out. They passed through without incident, Callum constantly scanning their surroundings. His role was to anticipate and avoid problems before they happened.

Their hotel stood in the center of the business district, more upscale than most of the others, catering to international business people. That made it an auspicious target for anyone wanting to make a political statement with an attack, but Wilkinson had insisted they stay here for at least the first night so he could meet with the military contractors in the conference room first thing in the morning.

Callum had made it clear they were only staying here for

one night and going elsewhere as soon as the first meeting was over.

At the lobby doors he got out and went inside to check everything out. It was a modern building, built of concrete and steel, its exterior painted bright white. Satisfied it was secure for the time being, he checked them in, then strode back to where Myers had pulled up behind Walker.

He signaled to the bodyguards, who immediately got Wilkinson out of the vehicle and rushed him inside, taking the stairs to their rooms. Not five or even four-star quality, and no doubt far less luxurious than Wilkinson was used to, they were clean with modern furnishings and en suite bathrooms. Callum had his own room. Wilkinson was directly across the hall, his bodyguards on one side of the billionaire and Walker and Myers on his other.

Once everyone was settled, Callum called Ryder. "We're at the hotel. The boys are showering up, and then we'll start looking at where to stay next." More than a night here was just asking for trouble.

"Great. How's the weather?"

"Oh, fantastic. Thinking of checking out a time share while I'm here."

Ryder's low chuckle filled the line. "Lemme know how that works out. Danae just popped by to check on Shae, by the way. She was fine, and alone. No boys, house still standing. All good."

"Thanks, I'll let the guys know." They had taken an additional risk by agreeing to be on this detail together. Callum owed them both.

"She said to tell them to stop checking on her all the time. She's fine."

"Don't hold your breath on that one."

"I won't, but I promised to deliver the message. You need anything else from me right now?"

"No. I'll let you know our new location as soon as I have it."

"Sounds good. Have a good night."

"Will do." He ended the call, downed a bottle of water and waited a bit to give the guys more time before going across the hall to their room.

Walker answered the door, ran a hand through his short black hair that was turning silver at the temples. "Come on in."

The bathroom door was shut and the shower was running. Callum dropped onto the couch. "Danae checked on Shae. She's doing great."

Walker was a stoic kind of guy. Quiet and watchful, never missed a thing and had the calm, cool, collected thing down to an art. He concealed his emotions seemingly without effort, but Callum saw the way the man's shoulders eased now. "Thanks. Glad to hear that."

He nodded. "You found any other places we should check out?" Walker was practically a wizard when it came to working intel and logistics. In deference to their situation and to mitigate the danger of something happening to both him and Myers, he would stay behind at the hotel to provide additional security for Wilkinson while Callum and Myers went out to do some recon.

"Just one. I'll text you the info. My contact's asking what time you want to meet him."

A former SEAL now doing security contracting work in Kabul. Callum glanced at his watch. "Forty minutes."

Walker texted the guy. "All set." He looked up, deep blue gaze direct. "I'll keep monitoring the situation on the ground and update you as needed."

"Perfect."

The bathroom door swung open. Myers strode out with a

towel around his waist, drying off his damp brown hair with another. "Give me two minutes," he said to Callum on his way to the open suitcase lying next to the closet.

Five minutes later the two of them exited the lobby onto the street, while Walker tracked them via their phones on his laptop. Callum slipped his shades on against the glare of the sunlight glancing off the windows across the street. A steady stream of older vehicles wove by, pedestrians making their way along the sidewalks amidst the honking and traffic noise.

It felt different this time. A new sort of tension in the air, a heaviness he could feel settling over him. People shot him wary glances as he and Myers passed by.

"Good old Kabul," Myers commented wryly on their way up the block.

The deadline for withdrawal was in less than a week. Things were going to be very different here after that, and it was always the innocent civilians that got caught in the crossfire. And the ones who had aided western forces were going to be at most risk.

Touring the area on foot gave him and Myers a better look at the real situation happening on the ground. But their upcoming meeting would give them even better intel.

The former SEAL, Jefferson, was waiting for them in the lobby of the hotel his detail was based out of. He shook their hands and stood with his arms folded across his massive chest. "You boys just arrived in country?"

"Little over two hours ago. Anything changed in the past twelve hours that we should know about?"

"There are reports coming in about Taliban ransacking villages up in the Kush, and some are saying they're sending patrols farther west, toward Kabul. Basically, they're licking their chops and rubbing their hands, just waiting for the moment we pull out. Then this whole country will go back to the Stone Age."

It was depressing as hell after all the blood spilled to try and change things during the war. "What's the current security situation like in this area?"

"Stable, for now. Locals are pissed though. They know what's coming and it hasn't exactly endeared us to the population."

No, and Callum couldn't blame them. It was also another reason he was worried about Nadia becoming a target here. He was so close to her now. Only a few miles from her. "Will local forces hold against attacks until the evacuation?"

Jefferson shrugged his massive shoulders. "Maybe. Like I said, they're mad as hell at us. There's this one guy, a former translator for a US unit, raising hell because apparently his wife and kid were taken by the Taliban and probably killed. He was here earlier demanding answers from another American contractor staying here. Not the first time it's happened either. It's not pretty."

No. War never was, and these people had been living in the midst of it for generations now. "Got a list of addresses we're looking at as a base of operations. Any of these raise any red flags with you?"

Jefferson studied the list on Callum's phone. "I'd steer clear of the third and fifth ones. Rumors going around that those areas are already infiltrated by Taliban and their informants."

He took the phone back. "Good to know. Appreciate it."

"No worries. Good luck." Jefferson strode away without a backward glance.

Callum reported the news to Walker, then he and Myers began scoping out the remaining addresses. Two hours later, they both decided the fourth option was the best. For now, anyway.

The situation was extremely fluid. They had to be ready to adapt at a moment's notice. To minimize risk and make it harder for anyone to target them, they would move around and vary their schedules for the duration of their stay.

"I'll let Wilkinson's people know," Walker said. "First meeting's scheduled for oh-eight-hundred. You guys headed back here now?"

"In a bit," Callum answered. "There's one more place I want to check out first."

Myer's eyebrows popped up over the top of his sunglasses as Callum put his phone away. "Where to?"

"Orphanage a half mile from here." He'd accomplished what he needed to do for now in an official capacity. Now he wanted to make sure Nadia's location was secure. "I'll drop you back at the hotel first."

"What am I, your date?" Myers teeth flashed with his grin. "I'm coming with you."

Not bothering to argue, Callum strode for the door. He'd memorized the exact location of the orphanage days ago and had studied the area around it using satellite images in his downtime. His feet took him there automatically.

He stopped across the street and studied the building. Three floors high, built of concrete with white paint peeling off the façade in the baking sun. Two Afghan men wearing khakis and polo shirts flanked the door, looking bored out of their minds, one of them half-asleep.

Callum wasn't impressed. He could personally have taken them both down without a weapon before either of them realized what had happened. Window dressing security wouldn't keep anyone in that building safe, let alone Nadia, who stood out as an obvious Westerner. And he still thought it was criminal that her org had sent her here in the first place.

He crossed the street, Myers right next to him. The two men

"guarding" the door suddenly snapped to attention, moving forward to intercept them. "What do you want here?" one of them asked in heavily accented English.

"To see a friend," he answered in Dari, and the man's eyes widened. "Nadia Bishop. Is she here?"

The men looked at each other, and the taller one pulled out a radio. He spoke in rapid Dari to someone, received a reply moments later. He gave Callum a wary look. "What is your name?"

"Callum Falconer."

The guard reported it, seemed surprised by the response. "All right," he said, not sounding happy about it. "You can go in."

Myers was right behind him as they entered the building, ducking their heads beneath the low beam across the doorway. "Who's Nadia Bishop?" Myers murmured.

"A friend," he repeated, not wanting to get into it. He felt insanely protective of her. And a little territorial, too, if he was honest.

They stopped in the reception area. Two women carrying children rushed across a hallway on the other side and disappeared into another room. Urgent whispers floated toward them, the women's fear palpable.

Footsteps sounded above them. A moment later a long, flowing green skirt appeared. His heart rate picked up as more of her became visible.

Then Nadia stood framed in the narrow stairway holding an infant. Her whole face lit up when she saw him. "Callum, you're really here!" Her joyous smile pierced him.

An intense ache filled his chest, proving beyond a doubt what he'd suspected for a while now.

He was hopelessly fucking in love with her.

SIX

Something inside Nadia went weak at the sight of him standing there, so tall and strong and solid. She couldn't believe he was really here, how incredible it was to see a familiar face. And now that he was, an invisible weight lifted from her, the deepest part of her feeling so much safer with him standing in front of her.

"I really am," he said, his smile making her insides do acrobatics. A slightly taller man with chestnut-brown hair stood beside him, watching them with amusement.

She rushed down the stairs toward them cradling Ferhana to her. The little girl had been frightened at first, but quickly warmed to her and had chosen Nadia as her person.

"It's so good to see you." She stopped in front of him, resisting the urge to throw an arm around his neck and burrow into that sexy wall of strength, a wave of longing crashing over her.

The dynamic between them was all off, and she was still unsure of where they stood other than both of them wanting each other. "This is Ferhana. She just came to us the other day. They found her next to her mother's body. The Taliban…"

Callum and the stranger absorbed that in silence for a moment, then Callum focused on the baby and gave her a disarming smile that made Nadia's heart squeeze. "*Salaam alekum*, Ferhana," he said softly.

The little one stared up at him with worried dark eyes for a moment, then a shy smile curved her lips.

"How's she doing?" he asked. Sexy Viking was right. With his short red-gold beard and sexy-as-hell body, she was having a hard time speaking in full sentences with him so close.

"A lot better than she would be if she was a few years older. The first two nights were rough, but she warmed up to me fast. Now she won't let me out of her sight and sleeps next to me on my cot. Right, sweetheart?" She grinned into that sweet little face, received a smile and a pat on the cheek with one tiny hand.

It melted Nadia every time, that innate trust children had. She could almost feel the oxytocin flooding her bloodstream. It didn't seem to matter to Ferhana that Nadia's language was strange and none of the words made sense. She somehow understood that Nadia was trying to help her.

"This is Donovan Myers," Callum added, nodding to the dark-haired man standing beside him. "He's working this detail with Walker and me."

Nadia smiled at Donovan. He was good-looking too with gorgeous green eyes, and she was guessing former military as well. But in her opinion, he wasn't even in the same league as Callum. "Nadia. Nice to meet you."

"You as well." He shot a sideways glance at Callum, the hint of a smile playing around his mouth. "I'm just gonna head out. See you back at the hotel." He thumped Callum on the shoulder once and left.

Nadia darted a glance after him. "Do you need to go with him, or…?"

"No, he's fine."

She focused back on him, admiring the view. And wishing she could just walk into his arms and cling for a while, absorbing the feel of him. "When did you get in?"

"Few hours ago."

He'd barely had time to get settled and come straight here to see her. She couldn't help melting at that, and the proof that she mattered so much to him. The uncertainty between them and his reserved behavior toward her held her back from touching him again. "It's really good to see you."

His hazel stare sharpened, and even though he hid his emotions well, she could tell he was trying to read her.

Ferhana whined and squirmed in her arms, rubbing her little fists against her eyes. "You tired, sweetheart?" Nadia cuddled her closer. Ferhana protested grumpily. "She needs to go down for her nap."

His expression closed up. "Okay. I'll try to call you later."

Nadia blinked at his abrupt acceptance and willingness to leave. It told her just how little he believed she wanted him. She felt awful about that, a physical weight pressing down on the middle of her chest. "No, I meant—"

"Here, let me take her," said a heavily accented voice as Homa appeared out of nowhere and rushed down the stairs toward them. She smiled at Ferhana, then cast Callum a curious and slightly wary glance.

"This is Callum, a good friend of mine," Nadia explained. "And this is Homa, the director of the orphanage."

Homa gave him a polite smile and reached for Ferhana. Nadia passed her over in spite of Ferhana's protests and ran a hand over the baby's silky curls. "You need some sleep, baby girl. I'll be back when you wake up."

Homa turned and whisked the little one upstairs, Ferhana's unhappy cries drifting down to them. Feeling inexplicably nervous, Nadia turned to Callum. "You want a quick tour?" He was so big. So damn irresistible, and now that he was right in front of her, she was having a really hard time remembering all the reasons why a serious, long-term relationship between them would never work. He made it hard to think at all when he was this close.

"Sure."

She showed him around the facility, mindful that the other women weren't necessarily comfortable with an unknown western man in their midst and avoided the private areas. In the kitchen she stopped talking, noticing his gaze was focused on everything but her. "Something wrong?" she asked.

His mouth tightened and he shook his head, then followed her to the next room without a word.

The rest of the tour didn't take more than a few minutes. "So, that's everything," she finished when they were back in the entryway. He was still looking around them, taking everything in silently.

He met her gaze, and her entire body lit up. It had always been like that with Callum. A single look from those intense hazel eyes, a single touch, and she was rendered helpless. "Can you get out of here for a bit?"

"Yes." Her voice sounded a bit husky. "But not too long." She hurried back upstairs.

Homa was stretched out on her cot with Ferhana, who had fallen asleep. Nadia whispered that she was going out and would be back soon. Receiving a nod and an unreadable look in reply, she covered her hair with a headscarf and went back down to meet Callum.

He stayed beside and slightly behind her as they stepped out into the baking hot afternoon air. The two guards at the entrance gave him borderline hostile looks.

"I tell myself it could be worse, because at least it's not

humid," she teased as her mind continued to spin like crazy. There was so much left unsaid between them. Right now, it felt like an insurmountable wall separated them, and she'd been the one to pile up most of the bricks. Regret sat heavy in the pit of her stomach.

"There is that," he said, focused on something across the street.

"Where to?" she asked, turning to avoid a man pushing a load of bricks in a wheelbarrow. The street was crowded as usual, the cacophony of noise unmuted. People stared at them, Callum's red hair and their paler skin standing out amongst the locals.

"There's a place up here I thought we could stop at." He stuck right to her, and though he appeared totally relaxed, she knew his eyes were never still behind the lenses of his shades. Always alert, in protective mode. Strangely, it made her feel both safe and yet more anxious at the same time.

She fought the urge to reach for his hand and pushed back the twinge at wishing he would reach for hers. "What kind of place?"

"You'll see."

He led her several blocks west and then turned south, winding his way through a series of narrow side streets until she was thoroughly lost. "How did you even find this place?" she said on a laugh. She loved that he was so confident and comfortable in foreign places, even here where there was a definite heightened edge of tension hanging in the air.

"Saw it on my way to the orphanage," he said, shifting fully behind her to put a large hand against the small of her back as the street narrowed more.

The heat of his palm sank through the thin fabric of her skirt, his touch making her heartbeat quicken. Her body reacted to that simple touch as if he was stroking her naked skin with his fingertips, her nipples beading tight and a rush of desire sweeping through her.

Her mouth went dry, her thoughts scattering like dandelion fluff in a gust of wind.

Up ahead a group of people had gathered near a street vendor, a line stretching back for almost a block. She inhaled, picking up the scent of rich, sweet spices.

"This is it," he said, guiding her to the end of the line.

"A tea cart?" He was so close, his hand wrapped around her waist now. She felt every single indent of his fingers, and when he stroked his thumb across the hem of her shirt, she swallowed.

"Best *kahwah* in town, I'm told."

She'd had variations of the green tea beverage at the orphanage. Tea was incredibly popular in Afghanistan, and every family seemed to have its own recipe.

They didn't speak as they waited, and Nadia was once again conscious of all the stares they were getting. It felt strange and almost forbidden, being out in the city like this. She would never have gotten the chance without Callum to escort her.

Then Callum's thumb slipped under the edge of her shirt to stroke across a sensitive patch of skin at her waist and everything else faded out. Her pulse kicked wildly, every sense attuned to him and heightened.

A tide of memories flooded back, of his talented, gentle hands peeling off her dress that first time at the hotel in Qatar. Exploring her naked body with sensual reverence before his mouth followed, making her boneless and liquid with the decadent pleasure he lavished on her.

For three days they'd barely left that room. When they'd checked out and headed for the airport, she'd never felt so close to anyone in her life. Then time and distance had slowly made them drift apart. *She* had let them drift apart.

She'd never had a lover like him and knew she never would again. Now her throat ached with the pressure of the words she'd held inside for too long. About how much she missed him and still wanted him.

Along with all the fears that kept holding her back from making the leap with him. Things from long ago in her past. Wounds that had never healed that made her afraid to trust and give her heart away.

He dropped his hand as they approached the cart, and she felt its loss keenly. She stood back while he ordered them both cups of tea in flawless Dari, and she was struck anew by how incredibly intelligent and talented he was.

What the hell is wrong with you? a sharp voice in her mind that sounded a lot like Anaya said. *Why do you keep pulling back from him?*

She knew why. She just couldn't say it to him.

The vendor poured the tea from a large *samovar*. Callum paid for it and handed her a steaming earthenware mug.

She murmured a thank you and inhaled the fragrant steam, then sipped, savoring the hot, bitter edge of the tea mixed with cardamom, cinnamon and saffron, and sweetened with honey. "Mmmm," she murmured.

"Good?" he asked, watching her over the brim of his mug as he took a sip.

"Really good. Stronger than what the cook at the orphanage makes. You're right, this might be the best *kahwah* in town."

His eyes warmed in the hint of a smile, and the way he focused on her made it impossible to think. "Maybe the country."

"Maybe." They drank their tea without speaking again, and with him watching out for her she was free to relax somewhat and take in the atmosphere happening around them.

She loved to travel, loved to explore new places and be

immersed in new cultures. It was one of the reasons she loved her work so much, and why she'd joined the Peace Corps right after college. The people of Afghanistan had suffered so much throughout history, yet their culture was so strong and vibrant, it fascinated her.

When she'd finished Callum took the mug from her, thanked the vendor and placed a hand against her lower back again. "Ready to head back?"

She didn't want to. This felt like stolen time together, it was too short, and she wished they could have kept exploring the city together for hours. Days. But she had responsibilities. Ferhana needed her, and Callum had work to do too. "Sure."

He took a different route back, and she had the feeling that he did it partly to show her more of the city as much as he varied the route for their safety.

An undeniable sense of anxiety built as they reached the main street she recognized and started toward the orphanage. Callum was right beside her, yet she could feel him slipping away as the seconds ticked past. She had damaged their relationship by pulling away before. If she didn't do something to stop this drifting, she was suddenly afraid she would lose him forever.

The jagged bolt of panic that sizzled through her at the thought was all the motivation she needed. "Callum."

He must have sensed something in her tone, because he stopped and looked down at her. His unreadable expression was magnified by his eyes being hidden by his shades.

Suddenly, she didn't know what the hell to say. But they were almost out of time. It was now or never. "I…can we talk?"

After studying her for a long moment, he nodded. "Okay." He reached down, his long fingers closing around her hand as he turned them and strode back the way they'd come. Just past a carpet shop, he tugged her down a narrow alley.

A wonderful coolness hit her as the shadows swallowed them, the sun too low to penetrate this small space. He guided her up and around a sharp turn and stopped, completely hidden from view from anyone passing by on the street a few dozen yards behind them, giving them total privacy.

Her heart was racing when he pushed his shades up on the top of his head and ensnared her with the full force of that magnetic stare. "What do you want to talk about?"

Talk, Nadia. She licked her lips, nerves buzzing in the pit of her stomach. "Us."

His stare never wavered. He had such amazing eyes. From a distance they looked an indistinguishable hazel, but up close they were mostly green with flecks of gray and blue close to the pupils. "What about us?"

It really shouldn't be this hard for her to speak her truth to him from her heart. But it was. "I don't want to lose you," she blurted, saying the first thing that came to mind.

"Lose me how," he said, an edge to his voice as he measured her with those miss-nothing eyes.

She hurried on. "I understand why you think I've been giving you mixed signals, but I swear that wasn't my intention."

He folded his arms, the powerful, well-developed muscle pulling the fabric taut across his chest and arms. "So what *was* your intention? Because from where I'm sitting, this is a pretty one-sided relationship."

She stared up at him helplessly, worrying the folds of her skirt between her fingers. "I'm... How can we make this work? We'd be apart all the time, and I can't give up my work for you—"

"Stop." He shook his head, frustration bleeding into his expression. "I can't keep doing this, Nadia."

Her heart sank like a rock. "Doing what?"

"This," he bit out, gesturing between them. "Chasing after

you like some pathetic idiot who doesn't know when to quit, never knowing what kind of reception I'm going to get, and then constantly waiting to hear from you when we're not together."

Oh, God. The anger and hurt radiating from him pierced her like a blade. She prided herself on being a good person, a kind person, and here she'd hurt the man who meant the most to her. "That's how I make you feel?" she forced herself to ask.

"Yeah. Because every time I try to make this work, you pull back. Why? What are you so afraid of?"

I'm afraid you'll leave me. She choked the words back, horrified by the sudden sting of tears burning the backs of her eyes. "I'm not afraid." *Liar*, a voice accused in her mind.

"Then what the hell is it? If you don't want me, just say it. Say it and let me go once and for all. But don't keep putting me through this. It's goddamn cruel." The pain and anger in his eyes crushed her.

She shook her head, horrified at the pain she'd inflicted, and reached for his shoulder. Desperate to hold on to him. To fix this, stop him from leaving. "Callum, of course I want you—"

Her hand had barely made contact when he went rigid. His jaw tensed, his eyes blazing with a frustrated, molten heat that shoved the breath from her lungs. "*Dammit*," he muttered, then his hands were on her.

Pulling her close. Tugging the headscarf away. Plunging into her hair, his long fingers gripping the strands tight as his mouth came down on hers.

Nadia whimpered and grabbed the back of his head, plastering herself to him as fire raced through her. Callum pushed her back against the wall, pinning her there with the length of his body. He wedged his hips between her thighs and lifted her, bringing his erection flush against her groin.

Need slammed into her, dragging a soft cry from her throat.

Callum absorbed it, his tongue tangling with hers. Simultaneously easing and fueling the desire tearing through her.

The rough brick caught at the fabric of her top while he took complete possession of her. The kiss was wild and untamed, the edge of desperation to it mixing with the taste of cinnamon and cardamom.

She clung to his broad shoulders, rolling her hips for more friction while the kiss shifted. One arm locked under her ass, the hand in her hair eased, stroked and caressed, his tongue teasing hers. She melted in his hold, something deep inside her chest twisting.

The way Callum held her, the combined power and tenderness and skill, turned her inside out. The rest of the world fell away. There was only him, anchoring her against the cool brick, his teeth nipping so gently at her lower lip before he nibbled his way across her jaw to her neck, finding the exact spot that sent an electric thrill through her.

She gasped, twisted, wanting more. He stilled. She opened her eyes, turned her head to meet his gaze. The torment there was unbearable, layered with a longing echoed inside her.

Slowly, he eased his hold and lowered her until her feet touched the ground. They stared at each other, unmoving, both of them breathing hard.

She would have given anything to be alone with him in a private room with a lock. Then he would have no more doubts about whether she wanted him.

"I better get you back," he said, pushing away from the wall.

"Callum."

He stopped, shoulders bunching as he looked back at her with a wary expression.

"I meant what I said. I don't want to lose you. I've never felt this way about anyone but you." Saying that to his face was hard enough. She was way too afraid to say the L word. What if he didn't believe her? And he hadn't said it yet either.

His gaze softened and the tension in her gut eased slightly. "Me neither, butterfly."

The endearment and his admission sent a rush of warmth through her. He said he called her butterfly because she was beautiful and flitted around from place to place. He'd called her that for the first time on their second day in Qatar.

A smile spread across her lips, a measure of relief sliding through her. He wasn't mad anymore. But things still weren't settled between them, and she didn't know where to go from here, or how to bridge the long absences that would keep them apart more than they could be together.

And there was also so much more she needed to tell him. Things about her past, her secret fears that she hadn't told anyone except Anaya.

"Come on," he said, lifting her headscarf back in place and then reaching out a hand.

Her heart sang as they walked hand in hand back up the street toward the orphanage. She no longer cared about the stares. She was proud to be beside Callum, the feel of his grip reassuring. With him next to her, she felt completely safe.

All too soon they stood just down from the entryway, the two guards out front watching them. "I get the feeling you're not too impressed by our security," she murmured to Callum.

"It's pathetic," he said without pause. "So bad I don't want to leave you here." He swiveled to face her, his shades hiding his eyes.

"How much longer will you be here?"

"A few days, maybe a bit more." He lifted his free hand, stroked a finger down her cheek. "I'll call when I can. And I'll see you before I leave, don't worry."

She breathed a sigh of relief. "Good." She ached to kiss him again. Wrap around him right here and kiss him in front of everyone. But that was a definite no-no here. "I miss you already," she whispered.

A grin softened his features. "Good." He squeezed her hand, and she could feel his gaze delving into hers behind the dark lenses of his sunglasses. "See you soon, butterfly."

He waited until she was safely inside before walking away. Her throat and chest ached as she watched him leave, a crushing sense of loneliness hitting her. And that gnawing fear that said there was a chance she might not see him again.

Feeling empty, she glanced up at movement from the top of the stairs. Homa was there holding Ferhana, who was rubbing her eyes.

The baby blinked, saw her, and a big smile covered her face. "Na!" she cried, because she couldn't yet say Nadia, reaching out her arms.

A bittersweet ache replaced the painful one as she rushed up the steps to scoop Ferhana up and squeeze her tight. This was why she couldn't quit this kind of work. Not even for Callum.

SEVEN

The battered truck rattled up the rough mountain road, a thin trail of dust kicking up from the tires. Ahead in the beam of the headlights, the small village appeared at the top of the next rise.

Aref drove straight for the gateway, fully prepared to face the risks for coming here again. His friends had warned him not to. His sister had begged him to reconsider.

He ignored the warnings. How could he not when he still didn't know the fate of his wife and daughter? But someone in the village must, and he wasn't leaving until he got answers.

Two men dressed in traditional Pashtun clothing of loose linen trousers, long tunics and vests stepped through the mud brick gate holding rifles as he climbed out of the truck. "It's Aref," he said in a hard voice. "I want to see my father-in-law. Now."

One maintained his position at the gate while the other escorted Aref into the village. More and more lights filled the windows as word of his presence spread from house to house. Men began spilling out of the houses into the dusty common area in front.

He spotted his father-in-law straight away and strode for him, jaw and fists clenched. "Have you heard anything?" he demanded, uncaring that he was being rude. He didn't have time for stupid social rules of conduct and didn't care if he offended anyone.

Ghaazi hesitated a moment as he glanced at the others standing behind Aref, then shook his head. "What have you found out?"

"Nothing," he answered, his voice cracking. "Nothing." It was unbearable. Four days he'd been searching for Lila and their daughter. Interviewing people in other nearby villages. Following the trail all the way back to Kabul and demanding audiences with anyone he thought might have information.

There were plenty of rumors flying around. Stories about how the Taliban had shot them both dead by the side of the road not far from the village and left them there. Others saying they had been kidnapped and taken somewhere deeper in the mountains to hold for ransom. Yet no one he'd spoken to had actually seen the bodies to confirm the first story, and no one knew for certain what had happened to them.

Maybe it was only the prayers of a desperate man, but Aref stubbornly clung to the hope that there was still a chance one or both of them were alive. Even if his mind and heart told him otherwise. He wanted to hold onto that chance. Needed to.

His father-in-law extended a hand, grasped Aref's upper arm and tugged. "Come inside."

Despondent, Aref followed him past the heavy rug covering the front doorway. His mother-in-law was by the fire with a kettle. She looked up at him, her face and hazel eyes haunted, reflecting the same grief that tore him apart day and night. And she reminded him so much of Lila it was hard to look at her.

He and Ghaazi sat on a rug in the center of the room while

the older man poured them both tea. "Drink," he said in a low voice.

Aref did, but he didn't taste it, and the heat didn't penetrate the ice coating his insides. He felt dead, even though he was still breathing. Couldn't understand why his heart continued to beat with this pain tearing him apart.

They were both silent for a long time. Aref stared down at the steaming cup in his hands, fighting to stem the trembling in them. "It's my fault," he rasped out into the quiet.

"No."

"Yes, it is. I should never have helped the Americans. I knew they couldn't be trusted."

The old man grunted. "They don't have the stomach for war. It's not in their blood the way it is in ours."

Aref agreed to a point, except he had met many American soldiers who were warriors to their bones. Brave men he had come to know and trust. Only to find out too late that their promises to him about protecting him and his family meant nothing. They were powerless to do anything, and their government didn't care what happened to the Afghans who had assisted them at such huge personal risk. He also knew deep down that he wouldn't get to America now after all. And without his family, he didn't have much to live for anyway.

"I knew the danger," he said. "I just never imagined my family would pay the price for my actions."

Ghaazi looked away, the working of his jaw the only crack in his stoic façade. He hadn't liked that Aref had aided the Americans, but he had accepted it. "There has been some talk in the village today," he began, his words halting, as if he didn't want to say them.

Aref stilled, focusing on him. "About Lila?"

He nodded once, a spasm crossing his deeply tanned, weathered face. He was a hard man, a proud warrior in his day against the Russians, but he had loved his daughter and grandchild with a rare affection and accepted Aref as a son. "Some are saying the Taliban knew you were coming here that night."

His heart seized. "Someone betrayed us?"

Ghaazi nodded once, face grave.

A torrent of rage erupted, instantly cutting through the ice. "Who," he ground out, his blood pulsing in his ears. "I want the traitor's name."

"No, Aref. It will do no good—"

"Who?" he said sharply.

A long pause followed. "It's…Mostafa," he said finally, face twisting with pain.

Everything funneled out around him, a deadly, seething anger building like a bomb in his chest. "What?" he whispered.

Lila's uncle by marriage had become a religious hardliner over the last five years or so. He had never approved of their marriage because Aref wasn't Pashtun and had also made his disgust with Aref aiding the American military against their people plain.

Ghaazi took a shuddering breath, tears dripping into his gray beard. "He hasn't been seen since the night you came."

Aref was on his feet without even realizing it, his upturned cup spilling tea onto the prized rug between them. "Where is he."

"Aref, no. You mustn't—"

"Where *is* he?" His voice cut through the room like a whip.

Ghaazi's shoulders sagged, and he named a village seven miles away.

Aref whirled and stormed out of the house, stalking toward his truck, a killing rage taking hold. Ghaazi shouted behind him, dozens of curious eyes watching his progress.

Aref didn't stop, jumping into the truck and turning the

engine over with a roar. He paused only when the passenger door wrenched open and Ghaazi scrambled in.

Without a word he sped back the way he'd come, taking a switchback three miles down the road that would take him up to the remote village. The security presence was more visible here. More sentries posted along the ridge of the crest.

Aref didn't care how many saw him coming. There only one man here who should fear his presence.

Men poured out of the darkened houses to see what was happening as Aref stalked through the village. Ghaazi shouted for the others to let them through, and for Mostafa to show himself. He knew Aref wanted answers.

A figure stepped out of a house near the end of the first row. Aref froze, his hackles rising as the man stepped into the glow of the light coming through the open door.

Mostafa.

A decade older than him, the man stood there wearing a cold, arrogant expression in the light of the lantern he held. "How dare you show your face here, American-loving dog."

"You traitorous bastard!" Aref charged him.

Before Mostafa could move Aref had him on the ground, his fist pounding into the bastard's face. He welcomed the pain shooting up his hand and wrist, punched again and again until two men dragged him off.

Aref staggered back, chest heaving. If Mostafa had sold them out, Aref would kill him. He swore it upon his wife's and daughter's souls. "Where are they?" he screamed, tearing free of the other men's grips.

Mostafa staggered to his feet, holding a hand to his nose and mouth. Blood dripped from his beard, spattering his light tunic. "Who?"

"You know who!" He punched him in the gut.

Mostafa doubled over, retreated a step and fought to get his breath back.

"Answer me!"

"I don't know," he wheezed, not bothering to protest his innocence.

"*Where are they?*" He took a threatening step forward.

Mostafa shrank back. "I don't know! I swear it!"

Aref was shaking so hard he could barely breathe, itching to tear this pathetic bastard apart. "You betrayed them, didn't you?" The accusation hung in the air like a death threat.

"They threatened to come after me if I didn't give them information on you," he gasped out, his whining tone grating on Aref's nerves.

"Who?" he shouted.

"The Taliban." A murmur went up from the crowd, but Aref remained totally focused on his enemy as Mostafa continued. "I…I told them when you were coming, and they must have told their Mullah."

"What is his name," Aref growled, shaking, the hunger for violence seething inside him.

Mostafa lowered his bloody hand, swallowed audibly. "Mullah Baasim."

Aref sucked in a breath, every muscle in his body jerking taut. A terrible silence engulfed the village, the collective horror palpable.

Aref had heard of Baasim. Everyone in this region had. His name meant "smiling," and he had a ruthless and sadistic reputation. He was known for twisting certain verses of the Quran to justify his heinous actions and sanction his favorite pastime.

Killing.

A wave of dizziness made Aref weave on his feet. He caught himself, shifted his stance as he stared at the man responsible for all of this.

The chance that Lila and the baby were still alive were almost zero. Baasim could have killed them both in cold blood to make a statement. "Where were they taken?" he asked, reining in the desire to land another blow.

"I don't know," Mostafa ground out.

"Are they dead?" He could barely get the words out. He thought of Lila's gentleness. Their daughter's musical laugh. Missing them was a constant ache deep in his chest.

"I don't know," Mostafa repeated, and it was clear from both his tone and expression that he didn't care. Didn't feel a single qualm about the innocent lives he'd destroyed. And there was no doubt that he had done it to punish Aref for siding with the Americans.

The hatred burned like fire inside him. "You...evil bastard," he whispered shakily.

Mostafa glanced past him at the others gathered around, mostly elders, then straightened and lifted his chin in defiance. "It's God's will that they were taken. And your reckoning is coming soon enough," he spat.

"Not as soon as yours, traitor." Aref drew the American pistol from the back of his waistband and fired two shots at the chest as he'd been trained.

Mostafa's eyes widened in horror as he toppled sideways and sprawled facedown in the dirt, a growing pool of blood gleaming in the lamplight.

Staring at him, Aref felt nothing. Not triumph. Not relief. Nothing.

An empty hole sat in the center of his own chest as if he'd been the one shot as he turned and started back to his truck, Ghaazi hurrying after him. No one said a word or tried to stop him.

Female cries of anguish split the night as he climbed into

the cab, probably Mostafa's wife seeing his body. Her grief didn't touch Aref. Nothing could now.

He would find his wife and daughter. If they were dead, he would give them the dignity of a proper burial. Then he would hunt down their killers, everyone responsible for this unbearable loss.

He pushed those thoughts from his mind, unable to accept it yet. If their bodies hadn't been seen, then there was still a chance they were alive.

I will find you, he vowed, Lila and their daughter's faces appearing before him in the darkness as he drove in silence down the winding dirt road. Lila gazed at him somberly, her hazel eyes filled with fear.

He didn't care about the danger anymore. Because if they were dead…

Joining them would be the greatest blessing God could bestow upon him.

EIGHT

In Callum's experience, jobs, as in ops, rarely went as planned. So it was a pleasant surprise when the morning meetings at the hotel happened without a single hitch and wrapped up on time. He'd ordered everyone to be packed up and ready to go first thing this morning, then he, Walker and Myers had moved their gear to new accommodations while the meetings took place.

He had just finished securing everything when Wilkinson called him. "Falconer."

"Callum." Wilkinson's booming voice with its Texas twang filled the line. "Come over to my room, will you? Need to talk to you about something."

"Be there in a minute." A sense of foreboding started up as he strode down the hall for Wilkinson's room.

One of the bodyguards opened the door. Behind him, Wilkinson was seated on the small sofa in the sitting room with the collar of his shirt unbuttoned, tie strewn across the low table before him. "Have a seat," he said warmly.

Callum did, wanting to see what was up. "What can I do for you?"

"I'll be honest, this last meeting didn't go the way I'd hoped. The company I'm dealing with is holding tough even now with all of this going on." He waved a hand to indicate their surroundings, which Callum took to mean the general tension and chaos unfolding within Kabul itself and beyond. "So I added something to my offer to sweeten the deal, and they've agreed to more talks."

"When?" They had a tight timeline. With Wilkinson's private jet unable to get clearance to land due to the current security situation, it had been hard enough securing another flight out for the five of them.

"One more meeting on Thursday. And another Friday morning."

Callum stared at him. Thursday was three days away yet, and Friday was the deadline for withdrawal.

Wilkinson grimaced, then grinned. "I know it's not ideal, but you fellas are the best for a reason, so I need you to work your magic and change our flights to Friday."

"We're leaving Wednesday night."

The man's smile slipped, annoyance simmering beneath his polished surface. "I need you to change the itinerary."

"I can't."

Wilkinson scoffed. "Of course you can. You said yourself Walker is a whiz with logistics. He can—"

"No."

He blinked at Callum, at first looking shocked, then confused. "I'll pay a bonus, of course. Double your fee."

"I don't care about the money. My job is to get you and the others out of here safely—" A familiar ringtone came from his pocket, cutting him off.

"That'll be your boss," Wilkinson said, setting one ankle on the opposite knee and leaning back into the couch with a satisfied look on his face.

He'd already talked to Ryder about this? Setting his jaw, Callum got up and answered, striding across the room and keeping his back to Wilkinson. "Hey."

"You hear the latest?" Ryder asked.

"Just."

"What do you think?"

"I think leaving past Wednesday is a big risk."

"That's what I told him." Ryder sighed. "It's your call. If you don't want to stay past Wednesday, you pull the boys out and come home. If he still wants to stay, Wilkinson and his people can figure it out."

Callum rubbed his forehead. "Finding five seats on a flight for the last day is going to be next to impossible."

"I know. Jaia's been digging around and can't find anything. Walker might have better luck with one of his contacts."

Any commercial flight was going to be overbooked. There was a chance Walker could find them something on an American military transport to Europe, but even that possibility was slim at this point.

Even as he considered it, he thought of Nadia. She was still here. Her organization still hadn't finalized her flight out, and it worried the hell out of him. "I'll talk to the guys, see what they say." He would look into finding a flight for Nadia himself, just in case.

"All right. But it's your call. I'll support your decision either way."

Callum wasn't surprised. He knew Ryder cared about his people and would have his back. "Thanks. I'll let you know." He ended the call and turned back to Wilkinson.

"I need to stay for these meetings," the Texan said, all signs of arrogance gone, replaced by weariness. "But I'd feel a damn sight better with you boys here watching things."

"I'll talk it over with my guys. See you in the lobby in thirty minutes." He exited the room and strode straight to Myers and Walker's room.

They watched him impassively as he told them, laying it out matter-of-factly. "I haven't given him a decision yet. I wanted your input first."

Myers and Walker glanced at each other, and Callum knew exactly what they were both thinking about. Shae. And he one hundred percent understood. Wouldn't blame them for saying hell no and insisting they pull out on Wednesday as the original contract stipulated.

Myers's gaze shifted to Callum. "He's really willing to double our fee?"

"That's what he said." That kind of money was probably nothing to him.

Myers raised his eyebrows at Walker. "Between the two of us that'd pretty much cover the rest of her tuition and a good part of a down payment for a place for her when she decides to move out."

Walker frowned, either unsure of his answer or hating the idea of Shae moving out. Or both. "Maybe one of us should still leave Wednesday."

"Not an option," Callum said. "We either stay put or pull out together. It's all or nothing." He glanced at his watch. "Talk it over, think about it a while longer, and let me know by the time the next meetings wrap up at the new place." In another few hours. "See you out front."

He walked out, heading for the lobby for a drink. His phone buzzed. He grabbed it from his pocket, hoping to find another message from Nadia. They'd texted back and forth a few times since they'd seen each other.

It wasn't Nadia this time, but Boyd. *Just checking in.*

All good, Callum responded, appreciating him reaching out.

His former captain was a great guy, and an even better leader. Callum would walk through hell for him any day.

It was the biggest reason Callum had decided to get out as soon as his last enlistment ended. He couldn't continue to serve their country when it would do something so heinous to one of its best and most loyal soldiers.

How are things there?

Status quo.

Callum smiled. *You love status quo.*

I do. Travis popped the question last night. She said yes.

Kerrigan was a sweetheart. *Congrats! Does this mean you're gonna be a grandpa soon?*

Three dots appeared. *Up yours*, came the response, accompanied by an emoji middle finger.

Callum smirked. The idea of Boyd as a grandpa amused him to no end. *Just think of all the things you could teach the kid.*

Two middle fingers popped up. *Carry on and watch your six.*

Will do, Cap. He tucked his phone away and jogged down the stairs to the lobby. There weren't many people left at the hotel, and the staff was down to only a handful.

With nothing to do for the moment but wait, he ordered himself a drink and a snack in the hotel restaurant and allowed his thoughts to drift back to Nadia. He wondered what she was doing right now. Probably still caring for that little girl he'd met the other day, since the baby seemed really attached to her.

She was incredible with kids. Didn't matter where she was in the world, or that she didn't speak their language, they naturally gravitated to her. She had a way of earning their trust and making them feel safe that awed him. He'd been drawn to her the same way when they met, her openness and warmth so opposite to him.

He'd also never thought much about having kids of his own before, but he could definitely picture having a family with Nadia. Not that he was going to tell her that. She was skittish enough of committing as it was, and it drove him nuts that she couldn't or wouldn't tell him why.

He wanted to see her again, hopefully tonight if he got some downtime once everyone was safely in their rooms for the night, though he would still be on call in case anything came up. If Walker and Myers opted to stay until the deadline, he would get Nadia a seat on their flight out as well. One way or another, he would make sure she had an alternate way out, just in case.

If she took her organization's booking, he would deal with it. Though leaving without her was going to be hard enough. Leaving without clearing up everything between them once and for all might kill him.

But that kiss in the alley a few days ago. The way she'd poured herself into it, as if she couldn't get close enough. And the look on her face before it. The clear distress that she'd hurt him, that she might lose him… It gave him hope that things would change between them for the better.

His phone vibrated, yanking him back to the present. He found a message from one of Wilkinson's bodyguards. *On our way down.*

Roger, he answered, and messaged Myers and Walker to be ready with the vehicles.

Three minutes later the electronic display above the elevator began moving down from the fourth floor. Callum alerted his guys and was standing in front of the elevator when it opened.

Wilkinson stepped out with his bodyguards, doing up the button on his suit jacket. He tossed Callum an easy smile as if their earlier conversation hadn't happened. "Where are we off to now?" he asked cheerily.

The upcoming meetings must have the potential to make him a shit load of money, because he couldn't see much else that would make a man smile about staying in Afghanistan an hour longer than necessary. "Not far." Callum strode toward the automatic doors, stepping outside just as both black SUVs pulled up. "You ready?"

"Yes."

He waited until Wilkinson was secured in the back seat of the second one before getting into the first one next to Walker and said, "Take route Charlie."

Walker expertly maneuvered them through the tangle of vehicles, carts, pedestrians and mopeds, heading for the second alternate route they'd mapped out earlier. They arrived without incident at the next location, a smaller, newer hotel Callum had reserved under an alias at the last minute for added security, though they all clearly stood out as westerners.

He jumped out and handled the check in for their group, taking note of the handful of people in the lobby. Partway through the process, he turned around at the sound of raised voices coming from the far corner.

A man who looked like a local but wearing western clothes was arguing with two men who looked western, gesturing agitatedly. The westerners both took a step back and held up a hand.

"Calm down," one of them said in a distinctively American accent.

Callum tapped his earpiece to activate it. "Stand by," he murmured. "Possible situation in the lobby."

"Roger," Myers replied.

The local got louder, his expression and movements more

agitated. "No, *listen* to me!" he yelled in perfect but accented English, and shoved the chest of the man in front of him.

The guy stumbled back, looked for a moment as if he was going to lunge at him, but his buddy intervened. "Hey, come on, man. Let's not do this. Let's just go."

"Yes, just go," the local sneered. "Run like the cowards you are!"

The two men spun around and stalked for the elevator wearing identical pissed off expressions and muttering to each other.

"That's it, run!" the other guy taunted. Then his gaze cut across the room and met Callum's.

They both froze. Callum knew the face but couldn't remember the name.

Before he could move, the man was rushing across the lobby at him, his expression desperate. "Falconer," he said, almost running now.

Callum didn't move, ready to go for his concealed weapon. He scanned the guy, spotted the slight bulge at his waistband.

He lunged forward, stripped him of his weapon and stepped back to aim it at him in one smooth motion. An American-issued Glock 19. "Hands up and step back," he growled.

The man's dark eyes widened. He raised his hands and slowly took a retreated a step. "You know me. I translated for your unit once." He tentatively placed one palm on his chest. "Aref."

"You got any other weapons on you, Aref?"

"No." He shook his head, his eyes burning with frustration. "But I need your help."

"My help with what?"

He nodded emphatically. "My wife and daughter are missing."

Callum lowered the weapon, satisfied Aref couldn't have

anything more on him than a blade. Whatever was going on, it was obvious the guy was in serious distress. Perspiration gleamed on his forehead and his eyes held a glint of panic. "What happened?"

"The Taliban took them hours after I dropped them at my wife's village a few hours from here in the mountains."

A pang of empathy hit him. "I'm sorry to hear that."

"The villagers said they heard shots, but no one has seen their bodies. I found out last night it was Mullah Baasim."

Callum's insides tightened at the name. Baasim was an evil, sadistic bastard who called himself a holy cleric, but in reality was just into twisting his religion in order to torture and kill anyone he deemed the enemy. Adult or child, it didn't matter. Callum's unit had once been given secret orders to take him out if they saw him.

"You know of him, yes?" Aref pressed.

"Yes." Unfortunately.

"Then you will help me."

Callum blinked, caught off guard. "Help you how?"

Aref looked like he was going to come closer, then changed his mind. "You have resources here. Contacts I don't. People in the military and working for your government. Someone might have satellite or drone footage of where the attack happened. Someone will know about Baasim. They will be watching him, and maybe they know what happened."

"I'm not military anymore. I'm a civilian now."

Aref's face twisted, his eyes gleaming with tears. "Please, I need to find them. I need to know if they're alive. And if they're dead, I need to at least give them the dignity of a proper burial."

Callum shook his head, unwilling to get involved any deeper in this. "I can't help you, I'm—"

"You have to at least try!" He grabbed at his hair, squeezed as a sound of anguish tore from him. "Your government promised to protect me and my family. They promised they would get us out of Afghanistan if your forces pulled out. But they lied! You abandoned our people, you're abandoning our country to the Taliban, and now my wife and daughter might be dead because I helped you—"

"All right," he interrupted, feeling for the guy. "I can make a few calls."

Aref shut his mouth, the hope in his eyes making Callum bite back a sigh. If Baasim had taken the wife and daughter, the chances of them still being alive were near zero, and Aref had to know it. Baasim would probably have killed them outright and left them someplace visible as a warning to others who had helped the American forces.

He kept his tone level and calm. "I'm working right now, but if you leave your number and your wife's and daughter's names and ages and any other relevant information at the desk, I'll pick it up after and see if I know someone who can help." It was the best he could do under the circumstances.

Aref lowered his hands, his eyes filling up. "Do you swear?"

Callum hid a wince. He didn't blame Aref for being suspicious. It was fucked up and inexcusable that the US government would abandon men like him who had risked so much to assist them over the course of the war.

He didn't like being in this position, but the least he could do was talk this over with Walker and make a few calls on Aref's behalf before they pulled out. Whenever that was. "I swear."

Aref held his gaze. "Shake on it." He stretched out a hand.

It said a lot about him that he still thought there was any real weight in a handshake. But it still meant something to Callum, and maybe Aref knew it.

He clasped Aref's hand in a firm grip. Giving his word. "Leave me everything at the desk, along with a number to contact you at. I'll get in touch by tomorrow afternoon, but I can't make any promises about finding answers."

"Thank you," Aref breathed, closing the distance to grab Callum in a desperate, sweaty hug. "*Thank* you."

Callum stiffened and clapped his back once awkwardly. "Sure."

Aref let go and stepped away, his whole body sagging as he closed his eyes on a sigh and dragged a hand over his face. Callum checked the chamber of the pistol he'd confiscated, ejecting the magazine just to be safe before handing it back. "You got more mags for this somewhere?"

"Yes. I'll leave the information now."

"You do that." While Aref rushed for the desk and started demanding a pen and something to write on, Callum put the mag in his pocket and tapped his earpiece again. "Okay, we're clear."

"Roger," Myers answered.

A minute later Myers and the bodyguards walked in, flanking Wilkinson as they hustled him through the lobby. Callum followed them up the stairwell and checked the principal's room personally before allowing him inside. Then he rushed back down and out front to get in the second vehicle, following Walker into the underground parking garage.

Walker stepped out of his vehicle, eyeing him. "What the hell was that all about?"

"Long story. I'll fill you in later tonight. Everything still on schedule?"

"Yeah. Did you know that guy?"

"Sort of. We met a few times on my last tour over here. He was our translator on a few ops."

In the lobby Aref was bent over scribbling madly on the pad

of paper the desk clerk had given him. He glanced up, his face brightening when he saw Callum, and gave a thumbs up.

Callum nodded and kept going, not wanting to engage with him again. The chances of finding any solid intel for him were slim. "You got any contacts in country keeping tabs on Mullah Baasim?" he asked Walker as they hit the stairwell.

Walker shot him a sharp look at the name. "Maybe. Why?"

"Because I promised I'd look into something."

Walker grunted. "By the way, Myers and I are in until Friday."

Callum glanced at him in surprise. "You're sure?"

"Yeah."

He was saved from responding by his phone vibrating. His heart rate kicked up a notch when he saw the message from Nadia. *Just thinking of you. Ferhana says hi.*

She sent a picture of the two of them. Ferhana was on Nadia's lap. They were both smiling at the camera, flashing peace signs. *Hope to see you soon. xo*

Everything about it tugged at him, the *xo* most of all. He slid his phone away without answering, wanting to wait until he had privacy, now more impatient than ever to get the rest of today's meetings over with. He wanted to see her tonight.

Right after he tried to find out if anyone knew the fate of Aref's wife and daughter.

~

WALKING down the sidewalk toward the hotel, Aref almost missed Falconer as he exited the lobby doors. It was twilight now, the shadows lengthening across the road. He'd spent the past few hours searching for anyone he thought might be able to help him, but he hadn't found anyone who would even listen to him except Falconer.

Falconer's red-blond hair gleamed in the streetlights as he turned the opposite way up the sidewalk and headed northeast. Aref followed at a distance to see where he went. But the longer he did, the hope he'd been nursing all day slowly turned to annoyance and suspicion.

Falconer had said he was working, and Aref had accepted that was why the former soldier couldn't step in and help him right away. But Falconer clearly wasn't working now. Where was he going?

Aref followed, keeping back and making sure to blend in with the rest of the foot traffic. Falconer was wary and watchful, glancing around and behind him every so often, once almost spotting him.

It wasn't easy following him unnoticed. Falconer and the rest of the men in his unit had been the best soldiers Aref had ever worked with during the war. Every single one of them were incredibly skilled. Deadly shots. Calm and cool under pressure, even in a firefight. The things he'd seen them accomplish were astounding.

Falconer and their captain had once saved Aref's life, yanking him back an instant before automatic fire peppered the wall he'd just been standing in front of. Aref had felt safe with those brave men. He'd trusted them.

But in the end, he'd merely been a tool they'd used and discarded when the mission was over. Today was yet another reminder of that. He'd remembered Falconer's name, but Falconer hadn't remembered his.

They must have walked for almost three miles before Falconer crossed the final road and approached a small, peeling building facing a main street. The two guards out front spoke to him briefly, then let him through the door.

Hidden in the encroaching shadows, Aref had a perfect view

as a woman appeared. A light-skinned woman with long brown hair.

She broke into a happy smile when she saw Falconer, then rushed forward to throw her arms around his neck. Falconer embraced her, holding on tight as the door shut behind him. The last glimpse Aref had of them was Falconer dropping his face into the woman's neck.

He stood without moving on the other side of the street, disappointment and a fresh wave of bitterness flooding him. Falconer hadn't been meeting a business associate. And that wasn't the sort of hug a man gave a female relative or friend. Whoever she was, she and Falconer were romantically involved.

It made him miss his wife even more. He would have given *anything*, including his own life to hold her one more time.

Aref dropped into a crouch with his back against the building, dragging a hand through his hair in despair. If his wife and daughter were still alive somewhere, every minute that passed diminished the chance of their survival.

Falconer had promised to help him. Had given his word and sealed it with a handshake. And yet instead of working on it now that he had finished work, he had chosen instead to meet this woman.

Or maybe he'd lied too. Maybe he had no intention of doing anything and had merely told Aref what he wanted to hear to get rid of him.

He shoved to his feet, despair tearing at him as he made his way down the street. Falconer wasn't going to help him. Once again, he was on his own.

No. He needed help. Refused to take no for an answer.

His jaw tightened, raw anger pulsing through him. If Falconer wouldn't help him willingly, then Aref would force him to.

A plan began to take shape as he strode through the city that would fall to the Taliban within days of the Americans pulling out. He couldn't trust anyone to help him now, so he would do what he must to get what he needed.

With Lila and their baby missing, he had nothing left to lose.

NINE

Nadia handed the two young elementary-aged children over to the organization volunteers waiting at the aircraft doors. A brother and sister, both of them wide-eyed and holding hands as they cast an uncertain look at her over their shoulders. They'd never been to a big city like Kabul before, let alone on a plane.

Their father had been killed by an airstrike last year, and their mother had fallen ill and passed away several weeks ago. Someone had brought them to the orphanage five days ago. Nadia and Homa had worked quickly to track down a surviving relative in Germany and arranged transportation for them prior to the deadline.

"It's all right," she told them in Dari, giving them a reassuring smile. This was her third trip here today, and each time the situation at the airport seemed more disorganized and frantic.

It was almost dinnertime. She was tired, stressed, and couldn't wait to get back to the relative sanctuary of the orphanage for the night. "Greta is going to take good care of you, and when the plane lands you'll get to see your auntie."

The middle-aged German volunteer put an arm around each child and led them into the plane. They were being flown to Munich, where their mother's youngest sister would take charge of them. It would be a huge culture shock for them, but they would be safe and well cared for, get an education and have a brighter future than if they'd stayed here.

On her way back to the van she glanced around this part of the airport. A heavy, palpable tension hung in the air along with the constant noise of jets, ground crews and the thousands of people crowded around the perimeter fence.

There had already been reports of security forces firing on the crowd to maintain order as people had frantically tried to rush through the gates to get to a waiting aircraft. Desperate people wanting to escape the Taliban and the threat of more violence, especially those with ties to the American military. Razor wire had been installed all along the top of the chain link fence several days ago to prevent anyone from scaling it.

A shiver of foreboding slid up her spine as she hurried to the waiting van and got in the back. The young male driver glanced at her over his shoulder and said in heavily accented English, "We go?"

"*Baleh*." *Yes*. It said a lot that she felt far safer at the orphanage in the middle of the city than she did here.

He slowed behind the line of vehicles already waiting inside the checkpoint at the main gate. Crowds of people barricaded on either side of it were shouting, jostling for position, arguing for the guards to let them through so they could make a run for one of the planes sitting on the tarmac.

Nadia swallowed and looked away, her heart rate kicking up. With only two days left until the final deadline for US withdrawal, the situation was critical, and things were quickly coming to a head here in the capital. She was due to leave on the final morning, and what her organization had sent her about her travel arrangements so far made her anxious as hell because too many things were still up in the air.

Out in the countryside and remote villages, the Taliban continued to take over territory left unprotected by the American troops pulling out. Moving into position to await the final withdrawal before taking over the large cities, especially Kabul. A constant flood of refugees kept pouring into the city, more and more people desperate to get out while they still could.

Looking at the situation around her right now put her stomach in knots. This was different from anything she'd dealt with so far, felt much more dangerous than even Aleppo. Everyone was on edge, and she had the constant feeling that things could turn ugly at any moment.

Her phone rang, jolting her from her thoughts. Her heart skipped a beat when she saw Callum's name come up. "Hey," she answered, glad for the distraction. They hadn't seen each other since he'd come by the orphanage four nights ago, and they'd both been so busy with their respective work there hadn't been time to meet up again. They'd only had around thirty minutes together. Just enough time to tell each other about their day and sneak in a cuddle and a few kisses. It had been harder than ever to watch him leave.

"Hi. Sounds noisy there. Where are you?"

The sound of his voice reassured her. Knowing he was still in the city helped too. His contract had been extended until the deadline, but when he flew out on a different flight than her, she was going to feel horribly alone. "Just leaving the airport after dropping two more kids off. Things have taken a turn here over the past few hours."

"I know. Are you safe?"

"Yes." For now, anyway. "Where are you?"

"New hotel across the city."

He had been moving them around from place to place every day they'd been here. "All done for the day?"

"Just about. We're still trying to figure out flights. Have you got a final itinerary yet?"

He'd asked her that every day this week, concerned the organization wasn't doing enough to ensure she got out in time. "The latest is they're trying to arrange a spot on a military transport to Germany, but if that falls through, they're going to bus me across the border into Pakistan and fly me home that way."

"What?" His voice was flat. Hard.

The thought of being stuck here on a bus heading through Taliban-occupied territory made nerves buzz in the pit of her stomach. Things were so chaotic, everything her organization had planned for her extraction initially had fallen through. She was the only one they had to make plans for here. "I'm trying not to think about it, honestly. I know they'll get me out one way or another, and until then we still have kids needing to be looked after."

"I'm going to get you on our flight."

"You don't have to do—"

"I'm not leaving you here, Nadia." Absolute steel filled his words.

She let out a breath, able to admit to herself that she was scared. And increasingly pissed off at her organization for not doing more to look after her and ensure her safety. She'd taken a big risk in coming here, had made the decision in good faith. It didn't feel like that faith was being reciprocated at the moment. She took such pride in what she did, but this whole thing was making her question her loyalty toward them. "Thank you."

He paused. "Have you eaten yet?"

"No, and with this traffic I won't be back to the orphanage for another hour at least." Her stomach grumbled in protest.

"What time will you be off?"

"I have to get Ferhana settled and off to bed, then do some paperwork—"

"Still haven't found her relatives?"

"No, but we're following up a potential lead. We were told she came from a village up in the mountains. Without anything more to go on, it's challenging, and everything's such a mess right now."

Time was running out for all of them, and it twisted her insides to think of leaving and abandoning Ferhana to an uncertain fate. "She'll go down by seven or so, then I need to lie with her until she falls fast asleep. I should be free soon after that. What about you?" She liked being able to talk to him about her day, ached to see him again. Had been thinking about him constantly. "Because I miss you." She didn't feel as vulnerable saying it now.

"I miss you too," he said in a way that made her toes curl. "Have dinner with me later."

She smiled, the heavy weight in her chest easing. She'd been afraid they wouldn't get to see each other before he left. "Love to."

"Good. I'll text you later to verify the time, then pick you up and bring you back after."

"Can't wait." She always looked forward to seeing him, but this time a hundred times more so. The deteriorating situation here was weighing on her mentally and emotionally. Callum would transport her away from all of that while they were together. "I—" She jerked, swallowed a gasp as sharp cracks rent the air.

Glancing left, she saw the crowd surge and swell near the fence line, people scattering in all directions.

"*Nadia*." Callum's voice was sharp, and she realized he'd been repeating her name.

"Someone's shooting," she said in a choked voice, a chill sliding through her as she ducked down in her seat. The van couldn't move. They were trapped here.

"Get down on the floor. Now. Flat on your stomach and don't move."

She wrenched her seatbelt free and scrambled to the floor as the driver cowered in his seat up front. More gunfire ripped through the air, followed by terrified screams. The van bounced and rocked as the crowd surged around it, jostling the vehicle.

"Nadia. What's happening?"

Her heart was in her throat. "I don't know. Someone's still shooting—"

An explosion ripped through the air. She saw a flash of light, felt the thud in her chest and the van rocked on its tires. "Shit," she breathed, her insides congealing.

"What was that?" he said sharply.

"Something just exploded near the gate," she whispered, fear pulsing through her.

"Stay down."

"I am." She was too afraid to move. Was suddenly terrified for the poor children she'd just put on that airplane and prayed they got out of here safely. "I can't see anything. We're trapped in traffic, and the crowd is swarming the area."

"Are the doors locked?"

"Yes."

"Stay still and keep out of sight." His low voice was strangely calm. Her heart rate slowed slightly in response. "I'm right here."

She sucked in a breath, squeezed her eyes shut and clung to the sound of his voice, wishing he was with her. Shit, she hated this. Knowing the city was dangerous was totally different from witnessing it firsthand. She was starting to have serious second thoughts about coming here. "Callum…"

"You're going to be okay. Keep still and tell me what's happening."

"I—I don't know." The driver suddenly hit the gas. She threw out a hand to brace it against the back of the seat to stop from plowing into it. "We're moving."

"That's good. Stay down."

"I am." The driver was muttering to himself in rapid Dari, saying words she'd never heard before.

The van lurched back and forth as it started and stopped in a jerky rhythm. She jumped when the horn sent out a continuous blare. Shouts and cries came from outside the windows. Something bounced off the side of the van, then they shot forward and picked up speed. "We're going faster."

"Don't move yet."

She stayed huddled on the floor until the sensation of forward momentum became more continuous and the exterior noise died away. Nadia glanced up at the driver, his profile visible between the split in the front seats.

"Okay now," he said, eyes wide, face tense.

Slowly she pushed up enough to risk a cautious peek through the side window. Sirens wailed from somewhere close by and the crowd by the fence line had dispersed. Emergency vehicles were rushing to the scene.

"I think we're clear," she said to Callum before sliding back up onto the seat, her hands clammy and heart still thudding against her ribs. A plane was just lifting off the far end of the runway. She recognized the paint on the tail as the one she'd put the children on. *Thank God.*

"You're sure?"

"Yes."

"Okay. Now close your eyes."

"What?"

"Close your eyes."

She did, trusting him. "Okay." Her chest was tight, her breathing suddenly shallow. "Closed."

"Take a deep, slow breath. Good. Now another."

The air stuttered in and out of her lungs, her muscles starting to tremble. "Th-that w-was…"

"I know," he said quietly. "But you're doing great, butterfly."

The nickname made her eyes sting. "No, I'm really not."

"Yes you are. Keep taking slow breaths and talk to me. Do you remember what I was wearing the night we met?"

The question threw her, but she understood he was trying to get her to focus on something besides her fear. "Y-yes. D-dark blue shirt and ch-charcoal…p-pants," she finished. She hated the way her voice shook and her teeth chattered. She felt cold inside even though it had to be at least ninety degrees in the sweltering van.

"And what were you wearing?"

"A d-dress."

"Not just a dress. A gorgeous, flowy dress and sexy high-heeled sandals. You wore your hair down with a flower pinned above your left ear. A pink hibiscus."

She blinked. How had he remembered all that?

He continued to talk to her, forcing her to focus on shared memories. When she thought back to that first night, the most vivid images were the way he'd shielded her outside the hotel without hesitation, covering her with his body to protect her, a total stranger.

She remembered how heavy he'd been on top of her. How his weight had blanketed and warmed her, shielding her from harm. "Wish you w-were on t-top of me again right now."

He laughed softly. "Me too, believe me."

He kept talking to her as the van wove through traffic and headed back to the city. It took a while but eventually her breathing and pulse slowed, and the tremors eased. "Thanks," she said when she got herself together again. "I feel better now."

"Good. I'll stay on the line with you until you get back safe."

"Okay." God, she was desperate to see him now.

Finally, the van pulled up in front of the orphanage. "I'm here," she told him, hating for their connection to end.

"Security out front?"

"Yes." Two guards, vaguely familiar. Nadia got out, nodding as she showed them her ID badge. They let her in. She shut the door behind her, locked it. "Okay, I'm in safe and sound." Her body sagged against the door.

"Good. Hang in there, butterfly. I'll see you soon, okay?"

Not soon enough. "Okay. Bye."

Homa shot her a relieved look when she walked into the activity room, seated on the floor reading a book to two elementary-aged children. Then her expression changed to alarm. "What's wrong?"

"There was an attack at the airport."

Homa paled. "The children—"

"Were already safely aboard the plane, and the attack happened outside the perimeter. They're okay."

Hearing her voice, Ferhana gave a glad cry, stood and took a few toddling steps toward her, arms outstretched. "Na!"

Just like that, all the lingering tension and fear was swept away. "Hey, you." Nadia scooped her up, hugged her close and pressed smacking kisses to the baby's neck.

Ferhana shrieked in delight and giggled, making Nadia grin. As scary as things were here, this child's laugh reminded her why she was doing this.

"I am glad you are okay," Homa said.

Nadia nodded, equally glad, but now even more concerned about everyone's safety here. "One last time—are you sure I can't convince you to leave before the deadline? Or to come with me when I go?"

What if the hired security didn't stay? Homa and her few remaining local volunteers were female and would be completely defenseless against the Taliban once they took over. And they would take over, probably within days.

Homa's expression hardened. "This is my home, and I will not run from those Taliban dogs." She said the name like a curse. "There will be more children coming in the next few months. I have to help them."

Guilt slammed into her, pulling her stomach tight. She'd thought she'd been brave to take the assignment here, but she'd been wrong. Real bravery was people like Homa staying here no matter what, determined to keep helping children and making a difference in spite of the extreme dangers they faced. They were heroes.

Nadia went and crouched next to her, setting Ferhana down for a moment to hug her new friend. "I wish you'd come with me when I go. But I understand. And I admire you so much."

Homa smiled and gave her a motherly pat on the arm. "And I am grateful to you for coming here to help us. You are wonderful."

Ferhana crawled into Nadia's lap, demanding attention. Nadia scooped her back up and stood, receiving as much comfort from the cuddle as the baby. "I'm going to feed her, give her a bath and put her to bed. Is it all right if I go out for a while after I finish up the files?"

Homa lifted an eyebrow. "Is your American friend coming for you?"

"If that's all right."

"Of course." Homa smiled to herself and picked the book up. "Enjoy yourself."

I will. Heat rushed into her cheeks as she carried Ferhana into the kitchen, mentally counting down the minutes until she saw Callum.

TEN

The dark SUV arrived out front at ten minutes after eight. Nadia was watching the street from inside and quickly slipped out when the security guards opened the door for her. She didn't recognize either of them. They seemed to be changing their staff every day now.

A big smile spread across her face when Callum leaned over and popped the passenger door open. "Hi," she said breathlessly as she got in.

He smiled back, melting her insides. He looked so good in the deep green button-down shirt and dress pants. "Hi." One hand came up to cup her cheek.

In the faint light from the nearby streetlamp his hazel eyes searched hers for a moment, then he reached out and drew her to him, his heavy arms coming around her and holding tight. "You okay?" he murmured against her hair.

She nodded, hugging him back, her face buried in the side of his neck. He smelled good, soap and something spicy and male, and his hold made her feel secure on the deepest level. The airport incident had shaken her pretty badly, and she was even more worried because she didn't have a solid evac plan yet. "Better now."

He held her for a few more seconds, then squeezed once and released her, capturing her hand as he checked his mirrors and pulled away from the curb into the sparse traffic. With more and more people fleeing the city, the shift in atmosphere felt strange without all the noise, hustle and bustle she was used to. "Did you eat?"

"No." She curled her fingers around his, savoring every moment of being with him. "Did you find out what happened at the airport?" She had been busy with Ferhana and other duties and hadn't had time to check the news.

He nodded once, shooting her a sideways glance.

"It's okay. I want to know."

He changed lanes before answering. "Militant attack, trying to get them to close the airport."

"Was anyone killed?"

"Four people. Nineteen wounded. How's Ferhana?"

The abrupt change in subject was a welcome distraction, letting her avoid thinking about the reality of her situation for a little while. "She's so sweet. And trusting. She has these huge dark eyes, and I swear she can see right into your soul. I'm so in love with her already. It's going to be hard to leave her."

"Hopefully, you'll find her family before then."

"Yes. Where are we going, by the way?"

"Hotel I'm staying at. It's got a restaurant that serves awesome kabobs with roasted veggies."

"Oh, I *love* kabobs."

He glanced over, and the smile he gave her sent heat spiraling through her. "I know."

She smiled back at him, her heart full to bursting. How in the hell had she made it an entire year without seeing him?

Being able to touch him? "I'm so glad you're here," she murmured, her voice rough with emotion.

"Me too." He raised her hand to his lips and pressed a kiss to the back of it, his short beard brushing her skin, sending tingles skittering up her arm.

It had been so long since they'd slept together. But her body remembered everything. The memories flooded back now, the deep ache of longing blending with the sharper edge of desire. Every breath she took made his scent swirl in her head. Every moment this close to him made the need burn hotter.

They didn't speak for the remainder of the drive. The silence allowed all her senses to sharpen, becoming more and more focused on him. The caress of his thumb on the back of her hand sent shivers up her arm, making her nipples tighten and heat pool between her legs.

By the time they reached the hotel, her entire body hummed with anticipation, every single nerve ending hypersensitive. Callum parked in the underground lot and quickly guided her into the stairwell, his arm around her waist. "Hungry?"

Food could wait. "Do they do room service?"

He stopped, met her gaze, and the molten heat in his eyes ratcheted the need higher. "Yes." He snagged her hand and tugged her toward the stairs.

The trip up to his room was a blur, every step making her heart pound harder. She couldn't think. Could hardly breathe as he let her into his room and locked the door behind him.

She wrapped her arms around him from behind, unable to keep her distance a moment longer. He spun around and took her face in his hands. "Nadia," he whispered, the tortured edge to his voice echoed in the tension she could feel thrumming in him.

Yes.

She grabbed hold of his muscled shoulders, fingers

squeezing tight as she lifted up on her toes to meet his lips. A shockwave of desire punched through her. His hands were in her hair, stroking, tugging, holding tight while his tongue delved inside to tease hers.

She plastered herself against him, every inch of her on fire and he was the only one who could douse the flames.

The kiss turned wild in the space of a few heartbeats. Callum's arms banded around her, a rough sound coming from his throat. He picked her up in an effortless show of strength that made her stomach flip, his tongue stroking hers as he walked her over and laid her on the bed.

Yes, hurry. Hurry. She dragged him down on top of her, desperate for the contact, and moaned in mingled relief and need when his warm, solid weight pressed her down into the bed.

She'd craved this for so long, but now it wasn't enough. Not nearly enough. She wanted everything. All of him, that deep-seated fear that this might be their last time making her frantic.

Her heart raced, making her fingers unsteady as she reached for the buttons on his shirt. He lifted up off her enough to allow her to undo them, still kissing her like he couldn't get enough, hands locked in her hair.

She pushed the halves of the shirt apart, ran her hands over the sculpted planes of his chest and stomach, greedy to touch him everywhere. It had always been good with him, but this was another level, the intensity of it shaking her.

A big, warm hand pushed the bottom of her T-shirt up too slowly. Impatient, she peeled it over her head and dragged her bra off. Callum eased back to stare down at her bare breasts, her nipples tight and aching. He cupped one in his palm, a low groan coming from him as he lowered his head to suck the tight point into his mouth.

Oh, God. She sucked in a breath, one hand sinking into his hair as her eyes fell closed. His mouth was so warm, the feel of his tongue so sweet as it stroked her sensitive flesh.

Hungry for more, she reached for the elastic waistband of her skirt and started shoving it over her hips and thighs. He stopped her from peeling off her panties by curling his long fingers around her wrist and making a low negative sound.

"Callum," she whispered. "Hurry."

He shook his head, kissed his way across to her other breast. "Slow down."

"Can't," she panted. "Please, hurry—" Her words dissolved into a broken moan when his lips closed around her other nipple, his tongue flicking, flooding her with more heat.

He refused to be rushed, ignored all her babbled protests and pleas while he took her apart with his talented hands and mouth. Teasing and then pleasuring. Turning her mindless with the need to ease the unbearable ache between her legs. She rolled her hips against him, seeking relief.

Callum pushed up on one forearm to sweep his gaze down the length of her body, naked except for her panties. His expression was taut, absorbed, the heat of his hand burning her skin as he skimmed it up and down her thigh. First one, then the other, his heated gaze zeroed in on the strip of fabric between her legs.

He brushed a fingertip down the center of it. She bit her lip and rolled her hips, trying to reach for the waistband of his pants. *Please, please…*

"Slow down," he whispered against her stomach, catching both wrists and holding them on either side of her hips, his upper body wedged between her knees and his face inches from where she was slick and throbbing.

The muscles in her stomach jumped when he lowered his head and nuzzled her there, his beard prickling and tickling at the same time. He kissed the spot above her navel. Then on either side of it. And beneath it.

Then lower. Slowly working his way down until she felt the heat of his breath through her panties.

"Callum," she choked out, trying to free her hands so she could touch him.

"Shhh," he whispered, his lips finally making contact. Kissing her through the damp fabric, his tongue flicking over the swelling bud of her clit.

She stilled, her eyes slamming shut, every ounce of her concentration on the hypersensitive bundle of nerves he was teasing. She was so wet. So damn needy for him. No man had ever made her body come alive the way he did. And better yet, he knew exactly how to please her.

When she was squirming and whimpering, he finally released her wrists and tugged her panties off. That bright hazel stare locked on the swollen folds he revealed, making her wetter. Hotter.

"I've been wanting to do this for so fucking long," he ground out, the intensity on his face making her insides clench. Then he lowered his head.

Nadia plunged a hand into his hair and held on, her breathing erratic. His lips touched her naked flesh, his tongue flicking the spot that ached so badly and a long, liquid moan rolled from her throat. Pleasure drenched her, pulling her belly and thighs tight while his tongue delved, stroking and caressing with single-minded intent.

One hand glided across her thigh to slide between them, then eased two fingers inside to soothe the empty ache. "Oh my God, oh…" She was going to come already, sensation gathering like a thunderstorm about to break.

He stroked the sensitive spot inside her with unerring skill, his tongue driving her to the brink of madness. She tugged at his shoulders, tried to protest that she wanted to come with him inside her, but he refused to be budged.

He stayed exactly where he was, one hand locked on her hip, the other between her legs as he licked her right to the edge of release, then slowed. Drawing it out. Making it twice as intense.

She bucked against his mouth, crying out as the waves rushed through her, pulling her whole body taut. He softened his tongue, kissed her gently before easing his fingers from her.

Gasping for breath, Nadia half sat up and reached for him. He came willingly this time, crawling up to lie fully on top of her, the bulge of his erection settling between her thighs.

She grabbed a fistful of his hair and brought his mouth down to hers, her other hand sliding down his back to his muscled ass. He groaned and rocked into her, her taste tangy on his tongue. She loved the heightened sense of intimacy it gave them.

He'd taken the sharpest part of the edge off for her, but she still wanted more. Needed them skin-to-skin.

Needed to show him exactly what he meant to her, because she wasn't ready to say the words yet.

THE ACHE IN his cock bordered on pain but it had been worth it. Going down on Nadia, making her come with his mouth satisfied a primal part of him that desperately wanted to bind her to him forever. The attack at the airport had reinforced just how easily he could have lost her. Now that he had her naked and underneath him, he never wanted to let her go again.

Her hands pushed at his open shirt. He sat up and peeled it down his arms, threw it aside then caught his breath, his fingers sliding into her hair as she planted her palms on his chest and stared up at him with hungry brown eyes. His fist squeezed, and the way her pupils dilated sent another wave of lust rushing through him.

He tugged her up for another kiss, her hands sliding down to undo his pants. He growled into her mouth when her fingers curled around his aching length, hips rolling to get the friction he craved more than his next breath.

"Lie down," she commanded. He went willingly, rolling onto his back, both hands plunging into her thick, luxurious hair.

The instant she had his pants off she sat back on her heels, giving him an unobstructed view of her insanely sexy body. Slender yet curvy, her firm breasts just large enough to fill his palms.

She licked her full lips, her gaze focused on his rock-hard cock as if she was already tasting him. He groaned as her grip tightened around him and she leaned down, those luscious lips parting an instant before her tongue peeked out to lick at the weeping head.

Callum hissed in a breath, his hands contracting under the instant lash of pleasure. He didn't know how much he could stand, it had been too long and he was more keyed up than he'd ever been in his life. He hadn't been with anyone else since her.

Nadia didn't tease though. She parted her lips and took him into her mouth, all the way down to the base in one insanely erotic motion that had every muscle in his body standing out in sharp relief. A strangled groan tore from him, the urge to clamp his hands around her head and thrust into her mouth until he exploded making him shake.

She made a sensual sound in her throat and slid her mouth upward, her gaze locking with his for an instant before she dropped back down and sucked. He swore and held on, his heart trying to pound right out of his chest. Watching her go down on him, reading the pleasure on her face and knowing she was enjoying it was almost too much. Ecstasy spiraled up his spine, his balls pulling tight.

"Sit up and ride me," he commanded, his voice low and gravelly.

Heat flared in her eyes. She lifted her mouth off him slowly, pausing to swirl her tongue around the head, the naughty look she gave him pushing him to the edge of his control. He grabbed his pants from the edge of the bed and took a condom from his wallet, quickly sheathed himself.

She pushed his hands away and gripped the base in her fist, her eyes heavy-lidded with desire as she shimmied up to straddle him, her core poised right over the flushed, swollen head.

"Sink down on me," he rasped out.

They both moaned as she lowered her weight, taking him inch by inch into her silken heat. Callum gripped her hips, not knowing where to look first. She was the sexiest, most gorgeous thing he'd ever seen, poised above him with her long brown hair tumbling over her breasts, her tight pink nipples peeking out to taunt him, and the rosy bud of her clit visible at the top of her slick folds.

He cupped one breast, pinched one nipple gently, reveling in her gasp and the way her core clenched around him. Holding his gaze, she planted one hand on his chest and trailed the fingers of the other one down her throat, between her breasts, down her softly rounded stomach to the wetness between her splayed thighs.

She gasped softly, eyelids fluttering as she caressed her clit. He clenched his jaw, fought to stay still while her inner muscles rippled around him. And the sounds she made. Christ, those breathless, almost helpless moans as she started to rock her hips, every single motion stroking his cock…

"Callum," she whimpered, the raw need in her voice lighting up every territorial, possessive cell in his body.

His hand tightened on her hip, helping to steady her and

guide her motions. Sensation swamped him, the edge of ecstasy coming closer and closer. "Ride me, sweetheart. Ride me hard."

Her eyes closed. Her head tipped back. She rode him faster. Harder, her fingers stroking in tight little circles across her clit, lips parting, a soft sob spilling from them.

Her cry of release sent a wave of triumph through him. He watched her as the orgasm rolled through her, drank in the expression of ecstasy on her face while the pleasure built and built in him.

Then she opened her eyes and stared down at him with a look of pure satisfaction and hunger that destroyed him. Planting both hands on his chest, she started riding him again. Different this time.

Slower, a sensual undulation of her hips, her entire body arching with the motion.

"Come for me," she whispered.

He'd been riding the edge already. Her words and the sight of her like that set him off. He thrust up into her again and again and exploded with a guttural cry of pleasure, the orgasm ripping through him like a blast wave. Through it all he could feel her gaze on him, hungrily drinking in his every reaction.

When it finally ebbed, he dropped back against the sheet, panting. With a satisfied smile, Nadia hummed and leaned down to kiss him. Callum slid his hands into her hair, sinking into the mattress as he sank into the kiss, their tongues stroking, caressing lazily.

Then he pulled her down to stretch out on top of him and wrapped both arms around her, holding her tight. God, he didn't know how he was supposed to let her go this time. Or if he even could.

He loved her so fucking much, walking away again would break him. He'd taken a professional risk by bringing her back with him tonight, since he was never off the clock here. But he couldn't stay away.

Nadia nestled her head into the curve of his shoulder and cuddled in tight, sighing gently. "I don't want to live without you anymore," she whispered.

He stilled, his body tightening even as hope flared hot and bright in his chest. "You don't have to. Come with me to the airport Friday. I'll find a way to get you on our flight."

She pushed up enough to look down into his face. "Can you do that?"

"Yes." He didn't know how he would do it, he just knew he'd find a way. He wasn't fucking leaving her behind and didn't have an ounce of faith in her organization's ability to get her out.

Her eyes were shadowed with concern. "I want to try to make this work."

Oh, fuck.

He crushed her to him and closed his eyes, burying his face in her vanilla-patchouli scented hair. He'd wanted to hear those words for so damn long, he thought his heart might explode.

"We'll make it work," he whispered back, flooded with love and tenderness. The urge to tell her he loved her crowded his throat, took all his control to hold back. She wasn't ready to hear it yet.

Not yet. But soon.

She trailed a finger down the length of his nose, a smile playing around the edges of her mouth. "You've been extremely patient with me."

"Haven't I?"

She grinned. "Yes, and I want you to know how much I appreciate it."

"You're welcome. Wanna know why?" When she nodded, he continued, studying her face as he spoke. Feeling that bone-deep connection forging between them like links in a titanium chain. "Because there's no one else like you in this whole wide world, and I know I'll never find a woman like you again."

"Bet your sexy ass you won't," she said, giving him a mock scowl.

A familiar ring tone filled the air. He cursed inwardly and rolled to grab it from the bedside table. "It's Walker. Hey," he answered, keeping Nadia tucked against him with one arm.

He listened, relaxed as Walker told him the good news. "Got it. See you at oh-six-hundred."

"Everything okay?" Nadia asked as he set the phone down.

"Yes." He kissed the top of her head, loving the feel of her draped across him like a living blanket. All warm and soft and curvy. "We're leaving on a military transport Friday afternoon at three." A day and a half from now. With everything going on it was going to feel like weeks until he got her safely on that plane. "You're coming with us."

She looked up at him again. "Are you sure it's okay?"

He didn't care if it was okay or not. It was too dangerous for her to stay here any longer. "I'm sure. But you need to be there by two at the latest, because it's the last flight out transporting civilians. I'll come get you." It was against company policy, and he would probably catch hell from Wilkinson, but too bad. Her safety was more important than his professional rep any day.

"Don't do that. I can get there on my own and meet you there."

He frowned, not liking it. "How will you get there?"

"Our driver, Javid. He'll take me. And that will give me a bit longer to say goodbye to Ferhana."

He didn't like it, but it might be easier that way. "Okay, but contact me right away if there's a problem. There's no room in our window."

"I will." A smile crept over her face. "Thank you."

He snorted. "You don't need to thank me for that." He would do fucking anything for her.

Her stomach growled. He tipped her chin up to kiss her, relieved that they at least had a plan in place for her. In just two days' time, she would be beside him and safely on her way out of this place. "I promised to feed you. Let's order that room service."

ELEVEN

Aref drove past the front of the building cautiously, keeping watch of everything happening around him. He had to stay alert, couldn't afford any mistakes because this was his one and only opportunity to take the woman.

For the moment, it looked like luck was still with him. Only two security guards were posted out front. An older man who looked half-asleep as he leaned against the building, bearded chin drooping on his chest. The other one was younger, and distracted by whatever he was doing on his cell phone. The street was near empty, devoid of its usual traffic and pedestrians, making it that much harder to do this without being seen clearly.

He pulled in a deep breath, his resolve hardening. He'd waited as long as he could. The deadline for withdrawal was tomorrow. Either he did this now or lost his chance forever.

This was the only way to force Falconer's hand. The man had made a half-hearted attempt to help him, making some phone calls on his behalf that had resulted in someone with loose military connections reaching out to Aref yesterday morning.

It hadn't amounted to anything. The person had no information on Aref's family or Baasim. Had not been any help at all and had not given Aref any other contact to approach. Everyone was too wrapped up in their own circumstances to bother with looking for his missing loved ones. He had accepted now that his wife and daughter were most likely dead. He still hoped to find them so he could say goodbye and bury them properly.

Not being certain of their fate was unbearable. He had hardly slept, had barely been able to choke down food for the past few days. He was done trying to play by the rules. He didn't know where Falconer was, but that would take care of itself once he took the woman. Unless Falconer had already pulled out of Afghanistan like so many of his countrymen.

Aref shook the thought away. He couldn't afford doubts and distractions now. His mind was made up. He had to do this, at least try this last act of desperation to make someone help him.

He reversed into an empty alley and parked the truck. The pistol was hard and unyielding as it dug into the small of his back beneath the bottom of his T-shirt as he got out and walked toward what he'd learned was an orphanage.

His strides sped up, a steely determination hardening inside him as he approached the front entrance and the lazy guard. He couldn't believe he'd been driven to this. But he would either get the help he needed—or die trying.

∼

THROUGH HER GROWING FRUSTRATION, part of Nadia couldn't help but admire the fight Ferhana was putting up. It was impressive, really.

She took a deep breath, picked the baby up for the umpteenth time and laid her back down in the crib. "Bedtime," she said with a hand on the little one's back, keeping her voice calm even though her nerves were halfway to shot. It had been a long day for everyone, and they were all feeling the effects of the increase in anxiety.

Despite all their efforts, they still hadn't found any of Ferhana's relatives. There still wasn't a plan to get her out. Nadia couldn't bear the thought of walking away and leaving her here, not even with Homa.

When the Taliban took over, women's lives here would change overnight. They stood to lose most if not all their rights. It sickened and infuriated her, and without any family to protect her, Ferhana faced an even bleaker future here.

Outraged at being thwarted yet again, Ferhana squawked in protest, scrambled to her hands and knees to grab the wooden slats on the side of the crib and hauled herself upright with an indignant wail, her expression flat-out reproachful as she glared up at Nadia.

She studied that tear-stained face, the puffy, tear-drenched eyes, and her heart squeezed hard. Ferhana was beyond exhausted. She hadn't napped all day, she'd been out of sorts from about noon, and uncharacteristically fussy at dinner. Homa had commented that maybe she was picking up on everyone's tension.

Maybe it was true because Nadia had never seen her like this. She'd tried giving her a warm bath, some puzzles and books, but nothing had settled her down. It was almost as if she knew Nadia was leaving tomorrow.

Ferhana leaned against the side of the crib for balance and thrust her arms out, her little hands opening and closing frantically. "Na! Naaaa!"

Don't cave, she ordered herself sternly, almost giving into the urge to pick her back up and walk her around the room some more. She'd put on several miles already doing laps.

Every time she thought Ferhana was down for the count, the instant she put her in the crib, this happened.

"I'm right here," she said softly, and knelt beside the crib.

None of this was Ferhana's fault. Her entire world had come crashing down around her when she and her mother were kidnapped. She was missing her family, and though she loved Nadia, everything was still strange and unfamiliar here.

Ferhana's shoulders shook with each sad, hitching breath. Then, finally, after a few long minutes she dropped onto her bottom and sat there, staring at Nadia through the wooden slats as though she was a prisoner in a cell.

A wave of helplessness hit her. What was going to happen to this sweet baby after she left? The guilt was going to haunt her forever.

They were nearly at eye level now. "You need to sleep, sweetheart. You're overtired and cranky. Lie down and I'll stay here." She reached through the slats and patted the blanket spread across the mattress. "I'll even sing for you if you want, though I'm warning you now, it won't be pretty."

"Na," Ferhana said, her lower lip trembling.

Her heart squeezed. Oh my God, that face. "Yes, I'm right here. Lie down, baby." She patted the blanket again. "I'll stay with you."

For now.

More guilt seized her. She'd never been in this situation before. Didn't know how to handle it emotionally.

Ferhana gave a great shuddering sigh and finally laid down facing her, her shoulders still hitching, those dark, wet eyes fixed on her like she was afraid Nadia would disappear.

"That's it." Nadia settled her hand on the baby's shuddering back and held it there as she started to sing softly.

"Hush Little Baby." Her mother had sung it to all of them when they were little when she was trying to put them to sleep if they were sick or had had a bad dream. It was one of the few things she remembered about her mother that brought her peace.

On the third time through, Ferhana's eyelids began to droop. She curled up onto her side with her fists tucked beneath her chin, her back and shoulders hitching with tiny, residual sobs. Nadia kept singing softly and drew the blanket over her, waited until she was certain Ferhana was fast asleep before withdrawing her hand and rising to her feet.

She crept out of the room, her heart heavy and more conflicted about leaving than ever. But she couldn't stay. As a western, white woman, she would be an immediate target and pose a potential threat to everyone around her as well.

Homa stepped out of the other bedroom where she'd been getting the older children settled for the night. Two were leaving in the morning with adoptive families. That would leave only Ferhana and one other child here.

"She put up quite a battle," Homa said with a wry smile, her silver-streaked braid peeking over her shoulder from beneath her pink headscarf.

"Yes." She would kill for a hot bubble bath and a big glass of wine right now. "I feel like she knows I'm leaving tomorrow."

Homa gave her a sympathetic smile and squeezed her arm. "She'll be well looked after, I promise."

"I know." But that didn't make her feel any better.

"Come downstairs, we'll have tea."

Tea wasn't wine, but it was hot and might help soothe her nerves a bit. Nadia followed, still torn. She felt like she should be stretched out on the floor beside Ferhana right now, spending as much time as she could with her now that their final hours together were ticking away.

"Have you heard from your American friend?"

Her lips twitched at the avid interest in Homa's pretty golden-brown eyes. "Just a few messages. He's been really busy with his work." She planned to call Anaya later tonight though. It had been days since they'd spoken, and Nadia missed her like crazy. Almost as much as she missed Callum.

He'd been on her mind constantly since that night in his hotel room. Saying goodbye when he'd dropped her off just before midnight had been hard, but she was proud of herself for opening up to him more and saying she wanted a relationship with him. He might not think so, but for her that was huge progress.

Homa patted her hand. "You'll see him in less than a day."

"Yes." Javid was going to take her to the airport before two o'clock, so Callum wouldn't have to change any of his plans or be put in the awkward position of including her on his job.

She was looking forward to being with him, and as guilty as she felt about leaving this place, she also couldn't deny she would feel a lot of relief once that plane took off. Things had shifted so quickly here. The street out front was eerily quiet tonight. It felt like half of the city was deserted and the other half was hunkered down to await the coming uncertainty.

Suddenly the silence was shattered by the unmistakable sound of gunshots close by. Two quick ones in a row, sounding like they were right outside.

Nadia grabbed Homa's arm, jumped when something thudded hard against the wooden front door a moment later. Homa immediately ran for the room she'd just come out of, shouting for the other two staff members to hide.

Only one thought filled Nadia's head.

Ferhana.

She whirled and raced back up the stairs, fear driving her. She flew into the room, shut the door behind her and was almost to the crib when the front door crashed open below.

Frightened screams from the women made the hair on the back of her neck stand up. She snatched Ferhana from the crib, bundling her quickly in the blanket and pressed the baby's face to her chest to smother Ferhana's tired whimpers.

"Shhh, shhh," she whispered as she gently bounced her, heart in her throat. *No sound*, she silently ordered Ferhana. *Don't make a sound.*

A man's voice rang out below, speaking Dari. "Where is she? The American woman!"

Ice flooded her. He wanted *her*? Was he Taliban? Had someone leaked her location?

She whirled around, frantically searching for a place to hide. There was nothing except a small closet, and she would never fit in it.

"Answer me!" the voice thundered.

The only chance at escape was a small window high up the wall beside the crib. She didn't know where it led to or if she could even fit through it, but she couldn't stay here and wouldn't leave Ferhana unprotected.

With grim determination she strode for it. She was two steps from the wall when she heard the thudding footsteps coming up the stairs. The door flew open, crashing against the wall.

Nadia spun around, holding Ferhana tight to her as the baby jerked and began crying. "Shhh, shhh," she whispered frantically, not knowing what the hell to do.

A thirty-ish man with dark hair and a short beard stepped through holding a gun in his hand. He didn't look Taliban in his jeans and T-shirt, but she couldn't be sure.

He froze when he saw her, his expression hardening, his gaze flicking down to the bundle in her arms before coming back to her face. "You are coming with me," he snarled in accented English, advancing on her with a menacing look on his face.

"No," she said, darting away to the other side of the room. There was no escape. The only way out now was past him through the door, and that wasn't happening. But she wasn't going to just surrender either.

His bearded jaw tightened. He raised his hand, the barrel of that black pistol pointed right at her. "Yes. Now," he snapped.

She could only cringe and try to shield Ferhana as he stalked forward and seized her by the upper arm. "*No*," she shouted, ripping free and lashing out at his face with an elbow.

He dodged it, seized her around the waist and shoved the muzzle of the gun to her temple.

Nadia froze, every drop of blood in her body draining to her feet. A wave of terror crashed over her. "You will do what I tell you," he said in a low, menacing growl that carried over Ferhana's crying. "Or I shoot the baby and then you."

Nadia sucked in a breath, a sick horror flooding her. "Let me leave the baby here." Her voice was high. Desperate. "She's not—"

"No. Both of you. *Now*." He gave her a hard shake and marched her forward.

Nadia dared not resist. Dared not scream or try to escape, too afraid that he wasn't bluffing. She passed through the doorway, Ferhana's cries filling the air. Who the hell was this guy? "What do you want with me?" she managed past the restriction in her throat.

"You'll find out soon enough," came the ominous response.

Through the open doorway to the left she saw Homa huddled on the floor in the other upstairs room with the three other children huddled in her arms, staring up at her with terrified eyes. "Nadia," she croaked.

"It's all right," she blurted, not wanting anyone to get hurt. "Stay there." At the top of the stairs, she wrenched her gaze to the shattered front door below. There was no sign of the security guards she'd seen out front earlier. Had this guy killed them?

Her legs were numb and weak. She couldn't feel them as she somehow made it down the stairs, past the two other staff members cowering in the corner by the kitchen door and outside into the hot night air.

She sucked in a breath when she saw the bodies of the security guards lying on the sidewalk, a pool of blood forming around them in the lamplight. The street was empty. There was no one to see her. No one to call out to for help.

Ferhana's cries had lessened to whines now. Nadia nestled her closer and thought of Callum. Would have given anything for him to be here to protect her now. He wouldn't know what had happened to her. No one would be able to give her family any information.

"Go," the man snapped, forcing her forward, the muzzle of the gun digging into her temple.

Having no choice but to comply, Nadia kept going, carrying Ferhana into the darkness and toward whatever fate awaited them.

TWELVE

Aref's pulse thudded out of control as he steered down the deserted side street in the middle of the city. He'd made the right decision in forcing the woman to take the child with them. He wouldn't kill a woman or child, but she didn't know that. And it was clear from her actions that she wouldn't risk doing anything that might jeopardize the child's safety.

"What do you want with me?" she asked, pressed up against the passenger door as she cradled the now sleeping child to her like it was her own. Shielding it while looking at him like he was a monster.

A sharp blade of guilt sliced through him. "You will see when we get to our destination," he answered tautly.

"Which is where?"

"Not far." He kept his eyes on the road, his mind churning. This had to work.

They reached the poor neighborhood at just before eleven o'clock. There were only a few lights on in the jumble of shabby houses crowding both sides of the street like a mouthful of crooked teeth.

He parked in a spot between two sheds and got out,

hurrying around to open her door. "Get down." He motioned impatiently with the pistol.

She did as he said, her face pinched. He felt a twinge of guilt at what he was putting her through, but there was no other way. She and Falconer both had to fear for her life, or this would never work.

"Come," he ordered, and put her in front of him, guiding her up the narrow path to the small dwelling that bordered an alley. A friend's cousin owned it and had agreed to let him use it on short notice. Aref hadn't told him what for.

He could feel hidden eyes on them as they walked to the front door. People peering out at them from windows on either side.

It was a dangerous time. The city was crawling with Taliban and their informants. In this area people were so poor, the reward money offered up to report on anyone opposed to the Taliban was too great a temptation to pass up.

He dug the key out of his pocket and let them in. The woman stepped cautiously inside. He wrinkled his nose at the smell. Stale air, with a hint of overripe garbage left in the heat to rot.

"Over there," he told her, gesturing with the pistol toward the half of the room opposite the tiny, cramped kitchen. He drew the shade on the window facing the street and flipped on a light, the dingy lamp casting a sickly yellow glow around the shabby, dirty room.

The woman sat on the small, worn sofa with the child, watching him with a wary expression and hatred in her dark brown eyes. Time to get this moving.

Just as he opened his mouth to speak, the baby woke and started fussing. The woman shifted on the sofa and bounced it gently, murmuring in decently accented Dari. It was obvious she wasn't completely fluent, but she knew at least some of their language. That surprised him.

"I'm going to make a call," he told her, "and you're going to tell the person everything I say."

The baby fussed harder, its cries growing louder. The woman shifted it and the blanket fell away from its face.

Aref stared, his gaze glued to the baby as his heart did a painful roll in his chest. No, it could not be…

The baby turned its head, and he clearly saw her face.

Without thinking he dropped the pistol on the chair and rushed across the room. The woman's eyes widened. She shot to her feet and wedged herself in the corner, face set as she snatched something from the small table next to the sofa. A candlestick she brandished at him.

"Stay back," she warned, teeth bared.

Aref paid her no attention. His sole focus was on his daughter. "Ferhana," he breathed.

The woman stilled, lowered the candlestick slightly and kept cradling Ferhana to her, staring at him suspiciously. "How do you know her name?"

He stalked over and wrenched his daughter from her arms, speaking to her in a low, soft voice. Ferhana stopped crying and looked up at him, and a huge smile of recognition spread across her face. His heart cracked open, joy and relief mixing with a suffocating wave of guilt and grief. Her mother was gone, taken forever by those animals poised to control their war-torn country.

"My little one," he croaked in Dari, falling to his knees there on the ragged carpet, rocking her back and forth. "My precious little one." He couldn't believe she was here, safe in his arms. It had to be a miracle.

"She's yours?" the woman said in a shocked voice.

He raised his head and nailed her with a hot glare. "Where did you take her from?" he demanded.

She paled and shook her head vehemently. "I didn't take her. She was brought into the orphanage just before I got there."

"*Who* brought her?" His voice cracked through the empty room.

Ferhana whimpered. He held her closer, his heart at once full and on the edge of breaking. Now he knew his wife's fate for certain. Lila was dead. There was no other explanation. His wife would have died before giving up their daughter. "Answer me!"

The woman shook her head again. "I'm telling you the truth," she said quickly. "Someone found her on a road beside…her mother."

"Her mother was dead?" he said in a hollow voice. He needed to know. Needed the closure.

The woman nodded. "That's what I was told."

Hearing it confirmed was like a knife being driven into his chest. He hugged his baby girl to him and buried his face in her neck, rocking on the carpet as pain twisted cruelly inside him. "Lila," he cried, his voice breaking. "Lila, I'm sorry…"

Something clinked softly. He looked up to see the woman had replaced the candlestick on the table. She shot an anxious look at Ferhana, then met his tear-blurred gaze. "I'm sorry for your loss," she murmured.

His jaw flexed, that deep, burning rage beginning to take hold again. "This is your government's doing."

A frown twitched her eyebrows together. "What do you mean?"

"I helped them. Translated for your military many times, and they promised to get me and my family out if the time came. But no one helped us when I asked for it. I took my wife and child into the mountains where I thought they would be safe. Instead, they were betrayed, taken by the Taliban and left for dead on the road as a warning. And then you take *my* child, the only person I have left—"

"No, that's not true," she argued, shaking her head. "She was brought in as an orphan and we've been trying to find her family ever since."

"No! Whoever brought her in knew her name. Knew what had happened to Lila. They would have known I was still alive."

Her face was pale. Strained, like her voice. "I don't know anything else. No one we contacted knew anything about you."

Ferhana was crying in earnest now, his anger and raised voice frightening her. He forced himself to calm down, take a deep breath. He soothed his daughter, but she twisted in his arms and held her hands out to the woman. "Na," she cried, reaching for her. "Na!"

His gaze shot to the American woman as a stinging sensation lit up his chest. It was clear that Ferhana had grown attached to her already. And when he remembered how she'd shielded his daughter, how protective she'd been in the face of his threats, he softened somewhat.

He stood, retreating a few steps. Ferhana protested, straining in his arms, her whole being reaching for the woman. "Na!"

"What is your name?" he asked her, not ready to let go of his daughter again.

"Nadia." She swallowed.

He nodded and looked down at Ferhana, overcome with love, and sadness for his wife. "Her name means One Leading a Comfortable Life." Bitterness swelled inside him. "My wife and I chose the name together."

The strain showed on Nadia's face. "What do you want with me? You have your daughter now."

He looked back at her. Couldn't help but admire her strength and composure. She didn't know him. Didn't know what he was capable of, or that he wasn't going to actually harm her. And he realized he did owe her for the care and devotion she had showed Ferhana, a complete stranger.

Pulling out his phone, he brought up Falconer's number and held it out to her. "You're going to call your lover."

She stilled, shock filling her expression. "My lover?"

"Falconer. I saw you together at the orphanage one night. He promised to help me, but he didn't mean it. If he wants to save you, he'll have to help me."

"What do you want him to do?"

His expression hardened. "I want him to honor the promise your government made to me. I want safe passage to America for my daughter and myself." It was their only option for safety now. He did not want his daughter to stay in this country any longer.

He nodded at the phone impatiently. "Call him."

She jerked a little when it suddenly rang in her hand. Her dark eyes met his. "It says Ghaazi."

His father-in-law. Ghaazi had come with him to Kabul and was waiting across the city.

Aref snatched the phone back and answered. "I have Ferhana. She's all right," he said in a thick voice.

"God is great," the old man breathed in relief. "But you are not safe there."

Aref stilled. "What?"

"The Taliban know you are going to Kaamil's house. And they know you are bringing the American woman. They are coming for you both. Someone from the village just called me."

For a moment the room swam before him as the implication hit home. He had been betrayed a second time.

He shoved the phone into his back pocket, wrapped Ferhana

up in the blanket and grabbed the pistol, pointing it at Nadia. He couldn't even trust his own people. This new betrayal made him more determined than ever to get his daughter safely to America. "The Taliban are coming for us. We must leave now."

He herded her back to the truck, the back of his neck prickling with each step. Jumping into the cab, he reluctantly passed Ferhana back to her and quickly drove away, praying Ghaazi's warning had given them enough time to escape.

~

"CALLUM."

He looked up at Walker. "What's up?"

Walker shook his head once, his expression full of regret. "Just got word…the orphanage was attacked a little over an hour ago."

Everything in him stilled, except his heart, which went into double time. "What?"

"Lone gunman took out the security guards, burst inside and took a hostage." His face was grim. "It was Nadia."

Fuck!

"Apparently he came for her specifically. He took a baby with them too."

"Where did he take her?" His whole body was strung taut as a tripwire.

"No word yet. The owner of the orphanage called it in."

With the deteriorating security in the city, the police sure as shit weren't going to be bothered looking for an American woman right now. "Stay here and keep tabs on any possible intel. Myers, you're with me. We're going to the orphanage." If Wilkinson didn't like it, too fucking bad.

He raced out of the room, Myers right behind him as he slid

his weapon into its holster and dialed Ryder. He launched into the explanation as soon as his boss picked up.

"Jesus Christ," he swore softly. "Have you got any backup?"

"Myers. Walker's staying here to work intel. Wilkinson is secure, but—"

"I'll handle Wilkinson. If I can do anything on my end, let me know. I hope you find her."

"Me too." He ended the call just as they hit the door to the underground parking garage. This time he jumped behind the wheel while Myers rode shotgun and tore out of the lot into the darkness.

"Walker's in contact with the State Department," Myers said, texting a reply.

"Even if they decide to put manpower on this, it's gonna be too little, too late," he muttered, racing down the dark, quiet streets. It was as if the whole city was holding its breath now, waiting for disaster to hit.

He pulled up outside the orphanage, immediately spotting the ruined door and the bloodstains on the sidewalk. Myers was right next to him as they approached the police, showing their IDs. The cops let them inside.

A sixty-ish woman with a long braid stiffened fearfully when she saw them.

Callum held up his hands. "I am a friend of Nadia's. Can you tell me what happened?"

She relaxed somewhat but wrapped her arms around her middle, face pinched with worry. "He burst in and took them. Nadia and Ferhana. He had a gun to her head."

The image made him want to drive his fist through the wall and howl. But he reined in his emotions, locking them away. Anger and fear wouldn't help Nadia. He needed to be clear-headed, make good decisions and figure out how to find her. Fast. "Tell me everything exactly as it happened."

The woman, Homa, explained everything, then took them into a back room that served as an office. He caught a whiff of vanilla and patchouli and grief twisted hard in his guts, Nadia's scent hanging hauntingly in the air.

"Do you have any security footage?" he asked urgently.

Homa nodded and went to an ancient laptop on the desk. "Here," she said as she brought it up.

He and Myers stood on either side of her watching the screen. She reversed the video, paused when an older model silver Toyota pickup roared up out front. Shock hit him like a sledgehammer when the driver drew his weapon, and the cameras caught his face.

"Aref," he snapped.

"That's the guy who came at you at the hotel that night, right?" Myers said.

Callum nodded, jaw clenched. That motherfucker. He'd kept his promise, had tried to help him, and in repayment Aref had just kidnapped Nadia at gunpoint.

"You know him?" Homa asked urgently.

"Yes." He pulled out his phone and called Aref's number. His muscles drew tighter and tighter as the seconds passed, the rings droning in his ear.

It went to voicemail.

Cursing in his head, he tried again. Same result. Then he called Nadia's phone. A faint ringing came from the other room. He glanced up.

"Nadia left her phone in the kitchen," Homa explained in a sympathetic tone. "Before she went upstairs to tend to Ferhana. I didn't think of it until now."

Hanging up, he dialed Walker, instructing him to relay the intel to whoever would make the best use of it, in Kabul and

D.C. But the sinking sensation in his gut told the truth. Whatever contacts they had left here were useless at this point.

"I'm on it," Walker vowed.

"I'll update you if I hear anything else. I'm bringing Myers back to the hotel, then I'm going looking for her. If I'm not back by noon tomorrow, you have my permission to get Wilkinson and his guys to the airport. I'll meet you there."

"Roger that."

"Fuck that, I'm going with you," Myers said as he ended the call, giving him a hard look.

"No. Your contract was to provide security for Wilkinson. Not to rescue someone else."

Myers raised a dark eyebrow in challenge. "Yeah, and I'm still going with you."

Reading the determination stamped into his face, Callum nodded once. "Okay." He turned and headed back out to the SUV, the scent of vanilla and patchouli lingering. But he had to face the hard truth.

Finding Nadia in this city was going to be next to impossible. The only thing to do now was throw money at anyone who might have intel, and pray it led him to her in time to get on that flight tomorrow—because it was their only way out.

THIRTEEN

What the hell was happening now? Nadia cradled Ferhana in her lap, a fresh wave of fear flooding her as the man raced them away from the house. "What's going on?" she finally blurted, unable to stand it.

"Someone must have followed me," he muttered, speeding down the narrow road.

It was doubly terrifying since Ferhana didn't have the protection of a car seat. Nadia had looped the shoulder strap around the baby's back for at least some protection if they stopped sharply or hit anything, but it was flimsy and could injure her if it pulled too tight.

"Why?" she pressed, anger beginning to take hold. This asshole had taken her at gunpoint, threatened to shoot her and Ferhana before he'd recognized his daughter.

"I told you. Because I helped your military," he snapped.

"How do you know Callum?" She didn't see a way out of this. Her phone was at the orphanage. Assuming Callum would eventually find out she had been abducted, he had no way of tracking her. And while she felt a little more confident that her kidnapper wasn't insane, and that he seemed to want to keep her alive—for now at least—that could all change once he got what he wanted. "And if you kill me, you'll never get asylum in the US."

He didn't answer right away. Waited until he'd taken a hard left turn that had her bracing her shoulder against her door before speaking again. "I translated for his unit."

This entire situation was nuts. But if he thought Callum could help him get asylum, she wasn't going to argue and risk angering him more when he had a weapon on him. "Let me call him," she urged. The sooner she did, the sooner he could start trying to locate her and forming a rescue plan. Her family would likely be notified that she'd been kidnapped. They would be worried sick.

He hesitated for a moment, then reached down to dig his phone out of his pocket. "Tell him Aref has taken you hostage. Then repeat exactly what I—" He cut off abruptly when a bright light appeared behind them along with the sound of a high-pitched engine.

She twisted around and saw what looked like a motorbike speeding after them. Her heart lurched.

"Hold on," Aref warned, and floored it.

Nadia crushed Ferhana to her, tried to quiet the baby when she woke and started fussing, protesting the rough way Nadia was holding her. She resisted the urge to shut her eyes as they flew through the darkness, zigzagging down various side streets at a bumpy, nauseating pace.

They had almost reached the next intersection when another bike suddenly zipped around the corner ahead and came at them. She bit back a cry as Aref hammered the brakes. She darted a look behind them, stomach knotting when she saw the other bike coming on fast.

They were trapped.

Cursing, Aref kicked the truck into reverse, swung the big

vehicle around in a tight arc that clipped the mirror on her side with a metallic shriek and shot up another side road. Clothes pelted the hood and windshield from the multiple clotheslines strung across the narrow alley.

She clung to Ferhana, scared out of her mind. Were the people chasing them Taliban? She didn't even want to think about what would happen to them if these guys caught them.

She jolted and sucked in a breath when something punched into the bed of the truck. Ducking down, she saw sparks fly up out of the corner of her eye when another hard thunk sounded from the rear.

Oh my god, they're shooting at us!

A hard hand landed on the back of her head and shoved. "Down," Aref commanded.

She crouched as low in her seat as she could, bent over Ferhana, who was now starting to struggle. "No, baby, stay still," she whispered, trying to keep the terror out of her voice.

The sound of the motor behind them grew louder, rising in pitch. She shut her eyes, every muscle in her body drawn tight. Two more shots rang out in quick succession. A cry escaped her as the bullets punched through the rear window of the cab a foot above her.

Aref grunted and swerved, cursing. "Brace yourself," he bit out.

She had no time to wonder what he would do. The next instant, he hammered the brakes again. There was a sudden screech of tires behind them, then a violent impact with the back of the truck. A heartbeat later Aref shot forward again, racing up the street.

"What happened?" she asked, afraid to sit up.

"He hit us."

"Is he down?"

"Yes, but I have to get us off this road."

She tentatively sat up a bit and looked around. They were alone now, houses flying past on either side.

No sooner had Aref started to slow to make a turn when that high-pitched engine noise came again. She tensed as the second bike appeared out of a side street just as they crossed it and opened fire.

Nadia screamed as bullets raked the cab. Aref grunted and wrenched the wheel hard left. The violence of the movement almost wrenched Ferhana from her arms.

She held on with all her might as the truck spun in a hard half-circle. Another solid thud sounded as something bounced off the back end. A second later she heard a metallic crunch as the bike hit a wall somewhere to their right.

When she peeled her eyes open and glanced over her shoulder, there was no one behind them. But her heart wouldn't slow down, the fear still coursing through her. There might be more people chasing them out here.

Aref continued driving, but slower now. More erratic, and his breathing was funny.

She glanced at him. In the faint light coming from a house they passed, she saw the wetness on his shirt. Blood, soaking the front of it.

Nadia bolted upright in her seat and automatically began checking Ferhana over. Her pulse slowed only a fraction when she saw the baby was unhurt yet crying in earnest now.

"It's okay," Nadia murmured, not knowing what the hell else to do to help her right now. Aref had acted out of sheer desperation and had just been shot. She was torn between sympathy and fear. "It's going to be okay, baby." God, they'd both come so close to being shot along with Aref.

His breathing was raspy now, and he seemed to be growing weaker every second. She didn't know how to help him. The truck kept slowing. Eventually he lost his grip on the wheel. The vehicle turned slightly and ran into the brick wall on the right side of the alley with a bone-jarring thud, then stopped.

Nadia risked another look behind them. There was no one back there, but that didn't mean they were safe yet.

"T-take this," Aref said hoarsely, and she looked down to see his phone in his hand. He showed her the passcode, his hand shaking. She grabbed it, hesitating for a second. If she called for an ambulance after she got out of here, could they track her?

Blood bubbled from his lips, making a hideous froth in the faint light seeping from the road ahead into this end of the alley. And she knew an ambulance would never get here in time to save him.

She swallowed hard, edging away from Aref, the iron smell of it twisting her stomach. She'd never had to watch anyone die before. Frightened as she was of him, he had risked everything to try and get his daughter out of here. Any parent would do the same.

His eyes swung to Ferhana. And the grief-stricken look on his face made her suck in a breath. "I l-love you," he forced out, struggling to say each word. "Allah…b-be with you." He lifted a shaky hand, fought to reach out and cup his daughter's cheek for a moment before his arm fell and he collapsed back against the seat with an agonized groan.

"Take…h-her," he wheezed, clutching at his chest now, his hand, face and lap all slick with blood. His face twisted with pain, and not just physical. He knew he was dying. Knew he would never see Ferhana again or make it out of here. "Pl… Please," he begged. "G-get her…out…"

Nadia nodded, then scrambled to unstrap herself. She wanted out of this vehicle and as far away from it and Aref as possible. People had already followed him, might have reported the plate number. She felt a stab of regret at not being able to help save him.

Reaching over, she fumbled with the door handle, more fear and adrenaline pouring through her. She shoved the door open and climbed out, Aref's phone clutched tight in her fist as she held Ferhana to her.

Stealing one last look at him slumped behind the wheel, she spun and ran around the back of the truck, heading for the end of the alley ahead of them. A wave of panic rose, threatening to drown her.

She shoved it down and ran to the next main street she came across, pausing there only an instant before making a split-second gut decision and heading right. She had no idea where the hell she was, but she needed help and had to find somewhere to hide her and Ferhana. At least the baby was quiet now, giving little sniffles as her tears dried.

This street was better lit and lined with small homes on both sides. Not knowing what else to do, only knowing that she couldn't stay exposed out here, she ran up to one and pounded on the front door. "Help," she said in Dari. She was cold now, shivers speeding through her. "Please help us."

An old man opened the door. His brows snapped together as he looked her over, but his suspicion quickly turned to concern when he saw Ferhana and the blood spatters on their clothes and blanket. "Come inside," he urged, waving her in as he stepped back.

Nadia rushed past him, repressing a shudder of relief when the door shut behind them, and praying she hadn't just made a huge mistake. The man called out two names. Moments later two women rushed into the room, their eyes widening when they saw her and Ferhana.

"What has happened?" the older one gasped as she crossed to Nadia.

"Taliban," she said, swaying back and forth to try and soothe Ferhana. "They shot her father."

The woman's mouth twisted in disgust, and she shook her head, tutting as she stroked Ferhana's dark curls. "There there, little one. Such a terrible crime those evil men have done." She gave Nadia a sympathetic smile and held out her arms for the baby. "May I?"

Shaky and weak as she tried to fight off the shock, Nadia handed Ferhana over. The younger woman, not much older than Nadia, ushered her to a sofa, sat her down and gently stroked her back. "Are you hurt?"

"N-no," Nadia said, trying to get hold of herself. *Breathe. Just breathe. You need to think.*

"I will call the police," the old man said, turning to exit the room.

"No!"

He froze, looked back at her in surprise. "You need help. I have to report what happened to the father."

She shook her head, a fresh wave of fear taking hold. "No, I do not trust them." She was an American, and too many organizations here were corrupt. They might turn her over to the Taliban to collect some sort of reward rather than do the right thing. "And the father is already dead."

He relented but didn't look happy about it.

The younger woman squeezed Nadia's shoulder. "I will get you some tea. Don't worry, you are safe here with us."

God, I hope so. Because it wasn't just her life at risk here, she had Ferhana to protect as well. "Th-thank you." She glanced down at herself, at the bloodstains on her skirt and top. She shuddered, knowing how damn lucky she was that none of the bullets had struck either her or Ferhana.

Across the room the older woman was murmuring softly to

Ferhana, cooing at her and bouncing her gently. The baby was quiet, staring up at her with sleepy, puffy eyes.

Nadia glanced down at her lap. Aref's phone was still clutched tightly in her hand. She tried to enter the passcode, a flare of panic hitting her when she couldn't remember the numbers.

Stop and think, Nadia. Closing her eyes, she fought to calm herself, took some slow breaths until the worst of the shakes had passed, and then tried to remember the code he'd shown her.

Her first attempt was wrong. As was the second. She swallowed, hesitating to try a third time. If she got it wrong again, she would be locked out and the phone would be useless.

No. She had to try. Callum's number was on here somewhere. She didn't know it by heart, so she needed this to contact him.

Her thumb trembled as she typed in her third guess.

It unlocked.

Breathing a slight sigh of relief, she began looking through Aref's contacts. But there was nothing under Callum. Nothing under Falconer.

She tried various spellings in case he'd entered it wrong. Nothing.

Text messages, she thought frantically. Maybe there was a chain still on here.

But when she pulled up the app, it was empty. She checked the call log next, but he had deleted everything there too.

"Dammit," she whispered, near tears with frustration and fear.

She needed Callum. But she had no idea where he was right now, and he'd told her they always used different names when checking into a place, so she wouldn't even know how to ask for him even if she managed to find the right hotel.

In desperation she dialed Anaya. Only to get a recorded message that the call could not be completed.

Shit! She blinked fast against the burning at the backs of her eyes and opened the web browser. It was late morning on the West Coast, on a business day. If she could find Crimson Point Security's number, she could call and get Callum's number from someone there.

Except the signal was so weak she couldn't get a connection to the Internet.

Out of options for now until she could calm down and think more, she shot off a text to her sister, praying it would go through somehow.

911. Need Callum Falconer's number. Crimson Point Security. Help!

She hit send, sent up a prayer that it would go through.

"Tea," the younger woman said, giving her a sympathetic smile as she set a steaming cup on the table in front of Nadia.

"Thank you." She reached for it with an unsteady hand, blew on the surface and took a sip. She couldn't believe what had happened tonight.

If the Taliban had come after Aref, they must have been watching and would likely know about her now as well. She had no idea if the motorbike drivers were dead. If not, they would report back to whoever had sent them. More people could be out looking for her right now.

What should she do? Going back to the orphanage wasn't an option. Any Taliban informants might be watching the place now. Her organization had been pretty much useless so far in terms of helping her here, and there was nothing they could do for her at this point anyway.

Trying to find an American agency to help her would be a waste of time, and she didn't trust the Afghan authorities not to betray her to the Taliban considering the country would inevitably fall to them in the coming days or weeks.

She jumped, sloshing tea on herself when a brisk knock sounded on the front door. The old man went to answer it, muttering under his breath.

Nadia shot up and quickly ducked out of view behind the corner of a nearby wall, holding her breath. The door opened. And when the caller spoke, cold slithered up her spine.

The Taliban had people in the area searching houses for someone. They were going door to door a block over and heading this way.

The old man thanked whoever it was and shut the door. He whirled and stalked toward her where she was peeking out from her hiding place. "Are they searching for you?"

"I don't know," she said, terrified that they were.

He pressed his lips together, staring at her for a long moment. Then he glanced at Ferhana and his face softened. "You cannot leave here tonight. It is not safe. Come." He waved her forward, then gestured to his wife and the younger woman. "We must hide them in the cellar."

A protest formed on her tongue, but she swallowed it. As afraid as she was to trust them and place her and Ferhana's safety in their hands, what other choice did she have? If she fled on foot now at this time of night, she would have zero protection and an increased chance of being caught.

As if sensing her turmoil, the younger woman walked up and gently grasped her hand. "It is all right," she said quietly, her face solemn, deep brown eyes kind. "We will not betray you. We hate the Taliban."

Nadia glanced from her to the elderly couple, who both nodded in confirmation with identical expressions of determination.

"Come," the old woman said with a reassuring smile. "God willing, this will soon pass."

Still clutching the phone, Nadia took Ferhana from her, the awful tightness in her chest easing the moment she had the baby in her arms. Ferhana turned into her with an exhausted whimper and melted against her shoulder. Nadia's heart squeezed hard. Ferhana was truly an orphan now. What was going to happen to her?

She followed the young woman through the trap door in the floor near the kitchen and down the stairs to the cool cellar, unable to shake the feeling that she was entering a prison cell. She thought of Callum, and how he would be waiting at the airport for her tomorrow.

And that she would be trapped and alone in this terrifying city if she didn't figure out a way to get there in time.

FOURTEEN

Nadia sat in the front passenger seat of the little car with Ferhana cradled in her lap, her gaze fixed up ahead at the huge crowd assembled along the fence ringing the airfield. Her insides tightened when she saw all the security vehicles in front of a roadblock leading to the terminal.

"What do you want me to do?" the old man asked, slowing.

He and his family had been so incredibly kind to her, and brave. They had hidden her in their cellar and lied to protect her when two men had come asking about her just after breakfast.

They had fed her, helped take care of Ferhana. Even given her clothes, and found diapers and other things for Ferhana the daughter had put into a backpack.

Now this man had risked his life by bringing them here.

"Stop," she answered, not wanting to put him in more danger than he already was. If people were looking for her and spotted him with her, he would become a target as well.

He shot a glance at the feverish crowd to their right and shook his head, his mouth thinning. "This isn't safe. I don't want to leave you here. I will take you home again, and we can—"

"I can't. I have to get in there now, this is the last flight taking civilians." She had Aref's phone in her pocket, now fully charged. She hadn't turned it back on yet for fear that it was being traced by someone working for the Taliban. Her plan was to get here early and wait to switch it on here when it was safe.

Unless someone had been following Aref to the orphanage last night, it was the only way she could think of that he had been tracked. She was anxious to switch it back on now and see if Anaya had responded, then reach out to Crimson Point Security personally for more help.

She unstrapped when the old man slowed and threw her arms around his neck in impulse. "Thank you," she breathed. Callum always teased her about believing in the good in people too much. In this case, she was glad she'd followed her gut and knocked on their door last night.

He grunted and patted her back with gruff affection, then ruffled Ferhana's curls, his expression troubled. "God be with you both."

"And you." She quickly wrapped the headscarf around her hair and neck, securing the bottom tails inside the long, modest Islamic robe the wife had loaned her, feeling optimistic for the first time since Aref had burst into the orphanage.

This was it. Against all odds, she'd made it, and she was taking Ferhana out of here as well.

She exited the car and made her way to the crowd gathered along the fence, holding Ferhana close to her chest while the backpack bumped against her spine. But the rush of relief and optimism she'd felt quickly began to drain away.

Something was wrong.

Everyone was tense, fear and dread stamped into the faces before her. Trepidation coiled tighter and tighter inside her with every step as she approached. As soon as she got within earshot, she picked up little bits of the conversations going on around her. There was talk of security and militants shooting into the crowd earlier.

She lifted on tiptoe to see over the heads in front of her. Several planes were parked on the tarmac about a hundred yards away. All military, painted the same dull gray. One of them was her and Ferhana's ride out of here.

Over the buzz of worried voices and idling plane engines, she heard an unfamiliar noise in the background. A sort of grinding, hissing noise.

"My God, they're welding the gates shut," one man suddenly blurted, his gaze fixed on something to Nadia's left.

It was a like a shockwave rippled through the crowd. Nadia's head turned along with everyone else's toward the main gate leading into the airfield. Among the cluster of armed security personnel gathered there she clearly saw the glowing sparks coming up from the fence.

Her insides clenched.

"They're shutting us all out!" someone cried.

A palpable wave of panic spread outward from that epicenter. People everywhere began shouting and pushing, fighting desperately amongst themselves to get to the fence. The few who got to the front began to climb it, frantic to get inside the airfield and onto one of the remaining aircraft.

Nadia took a hasty step back, holding Ferhana tighter as she scanned the fence line, looking for another way in. Someone slammed into her back. She stumbled, barely caught herself in time to keep from hitting the ground. In this volatile crowd, falling meant being trampled.

Ferhana started crying, her little fists clutching at the front of Nadia's robe.

"Shhh, shh," she breathed, fumbling in a side pocket of the backpack to pull out Aref's phone while she skirted the back of the crowd and headed right where the lines were thinner.

Heart hammering, she switched the phone on, relief flooding her when she saw the message from Anaya giving Callum's number, along with over a dozen missed calls.

Please let me know you're okay!

But at the moment all she was interested in was Callum's number. He was their only hope of getting past this fence.

She pulled back from the crowd and kept going as she dialed his number, the ringtone barely audible over the noise of the crowd and the crying baby.

Please pick up, please pick up…

∽

CALLUM PLUGGED a finger in his free ear to hear what Ryder was saying on the other end of the phone and walked away from the lowered ramp of the C-130 sitting on the tarmac. The constant noise was getting louder and louder as the crowds swelled around the fence line.

"What's happening?" Ryder demanded.

Other than the two-thousand-plus people trying to get into this part of the airport any way they could? "They're welding the gates shut," he said flatly.

Ryder hissed in a breath. "Christ."

"Yeah. It's a total shit show." He'd barely been able to get Wilkinson and the rest of the team inside the barrier before it happened. Wilkinson had been successful in getting the business deal he'd wanted. Now he wanted to get the hell out of here.

Their entire timeline had been pushed up by three hours because things were going sideways in a hurry. He and Myers had still been out searching for any signs of Nadia when he'd gotten a call from Walker saying they needed to get to the airport ASAP or risk not being able to make the flight. He'd had no choice but to abandon their search and rush straight here.

As it was, they'd barely made it in time. All the roads in and out of the terminal were now closed indefinitely. There had already been two suicide bombings around the perimeter fence in the past few hours. Right after the second one, the local security forces made the call to weld the gates shut over his and others' protests.

He scanned the seething crowd all jammed against the chain link fence surrounding the airfield. "Anything more on Nadia Bishop?" He was running on fumes, desperate for any word on her since the trail had gone cold.

Just after midnight Walker had learned from one of his contacts that Aref had been found shot to death in an alley last night on the other side of Kabul. Whether Nadia had still been with him, no one knew, but when they'd raced over there, they had found no trace of her.

"Not yet." Her sister had called Ryder a few hours ago, relaying a desperate message to find Callum's number. They were trying to trace the phone it came from now. "We've got Ember working on it, so hopefully it won't be long now."

It helped to know Ember was on it. She was a pro with anything IT-related. His best hope was that she was still somewhere in the city, and that she would make it here by three. Wilkinson and the flight crew weren't happy about having to wait that long, but that's the time he'd told her the original departure time was.

He opened his mouth to say something else, but another call came through. "Hang on a sec." He checked the display.

When he saw the name Aref on screen, his pulse shot up.

Ignoring Ryder, he answered the new call. "Who is this?" he demanded.

"Callum!"

Everything in him stilled at the sound of Nadia's voice. He whirled, stalking farther away from the plane in the hopes of finding a quieter spot to hear her better. "Nadia! Are you all right?"

"No. Aref's dead."

"I know. Where are you?"

"Here!" She was shouting now, the noise in the background almost drowning her out.

"Where?" he demanded.

"The airport."

No. He stopped and whirled around, scanning the tarmac for her. How had he missed her? "I don't see you, where—"

"Look to your one o'clock."

A heavy ball of dread settled in his chest as he turned and stared at the far fence line. As far as the eye could see there was only a seething wall of people surging all along the fence. But no sign of Nadia.

"Here! I'm here!"

Then he saw her. Standing near the back of the crowd at that section of the fence, jumping up and down as she waved an arm over her head, holding Ferhana in the other.

Fuck, no...

He ran flat out, his boots thudding on the baking hot asphalt. He was vaguely aware of someone shouting his name behind him. He didn't stop. Couldn't look away from Nadia as she forced her way through the thinnest section of the crowd to the fence.

And then he was standing at the fence, curling his fingers around the wire links, chest heaving as they stared at one another.

She had Ferhana with her. And the fear in her eyes, that haunted look told him she knew.

She wasn't getting into the airfield. Not without getting shot at and sliced to bits on the razor wire on top.

He clenched the wire until his fingers went white, a roar of denial and grief building deep in his gut. Every muscle in his body bunched with the impulse to tear the fence down. Rip it open with his bare hands, grab her and run to the plane behind him.

"Ferhana is Aref's daughter," she said in a shaking voice. "He took me to force you to help him and died trying to protect her. He wanted you to help them get asylum in the States."

He looked away for a second, glancing in all directions. Searching for a way to get her inside. But everywhere he looked there were more and more security forces converging on the area. Already forcing the crowd back. No one was getting through that main gate, including him.

When he turned back Nadia was shrugging out of the backpack. She attempted to soothe the crying baby as she set the little girl into the largest pouch and zipped it closed to her neck, leaving just her head exposed. "There are diapers and food in here for her—"

"No," he forced out, his voice like sandpaper. He knew what she was doing. Couldn't stand it.

Her expression twisted, her eyes filling with tears. "Get her out. Please. You know what's going to happen here." Her voice was raw with emotion. "She has no chance of a future here now. No chance of an education, and no family to protect and love her. Please, take her."

Everything in him rebelled at the idea of taking the baby and leaving Nadia behind to an uncertain fate. But he knew how much the child meant to her. Knew everything she'd just said was true, and that he could save her here and now if he acted fast.

Just like he knew there was no chance of getting Nadia over or through this fence.

It ripped his fucking guts out to do it, but he managed a nod, unable to speak with a boulder-sized lump blocking his windpipe.

Shouting to the right drew his attention. The security forces were getting closer. Firing shots into the air to disperse the crowd. And guaranteed there were more shooters or suicide bombers mixed amongst the crowd. People screamed and ran.

"Hurry," he said to Nadia. They had only a minute or so to do this, then the opportunity would be gone.

He started climbing up the chain link. Nadia handed Ferhana to a young guy next to her and begged him to carrying the baby up. The guy slipped the backpack onto his chest and started climbing on the opposite side, mirroring him.

Two feet of razor wire separated them at the top. Callum braced his feet and lower body against the top of the chain link, then reached up and out. He grasped the closest strap of the backpack in one fist and hauled it upward, trying to protect its little occupant from the razor wire.

The wickedly sharp blades sliced at his hands and arms and caught on the bottom of the backpack. Ferhana was crying in earnest now, looking down at Nadia on the ground in terror.

One last tug and the pack came loose. He grabbed Ferhana and held her to his chest, slipped the straps over his shoulders and began his quick descent.

Moments later he was standing on the ground facing Nadia through the fucking mesh of wire separating them, blood dripping from his arms and hands. He didn't feel the pain, the agony inside him obliterating everything else.

Ferhana was wailing now. She twisted around in the backpack and strained toward Nadia.

Callum saw the moment Nadia's heart shattered, felt a sharp

pain in his own chest. He unzipped the bag a bit to free Ferhana's arm and the little one immediately reached a hand through the wire mesh. But Nadia forced a brave smile through her tears and twined her fingers around the baby's hand, then grasped one of Callum's with her other.

He'd thought he'd known what heartbreak felt like before.

Not even close. This was a sledgehammer blow to the chest. A splintering, crushing pain that made it impossible to breathe, a mix of rage and grief and despair howling inside him like a hurricane.

He held her tear-bright gaze, dying inside. They were separated by fucking inches, and he couldn't get to her. Couldn't protect or save her.

All his training. All his combat skills and experience. They meant nothing now. Even if he charged the gate and took out a few of the guards on the way through, he would be shot dead before he made it to the other side. And staying put wouldn't do her any good. They would never let him back out through the gate.

He was trapped. They both were.

"Cal!"

He forced his gaze away from Nadia, glanced over his shoulder to see Walker and Myers running flat out toward him. "Plane's about to taxi," Myers shouted, waving him forward. "We gotta go!"

He couldn't move. Couldn't take a single step away from Nadia.

"They won't let her through, man. We already tried arguing with them," Myers said.

Fuck that. He stubbornly held his ground and faced Nadia again, everything in his body refusing to leave her. But he had no choice. And they both knew it.

"Cal!" came another urgent shout.

He gripped her fingers harder, the backs of his eyes burning, chest so tight it felt like his heart and lungs were being crushed in a vise. "I'm coming back for you tonight, I swear it, Nadia."

She sucked in a ragged breath and nodded, trying to force a smile that was all the more heartbreaking given the fear in her eyes.

"I love you," he rasped out, needing her to know. Her face twisted but he kept going. "I love you so fucking much, and you have to stay alive. You do whatever it takes to protect yourself," he snarled, taking out his phone and shoving it through a gap in the wire to her.

A tear spilled down her cheek. She dashed it away and opened her mouth to say something, but Myers's voice cut her off. "Cal! Move it!"

She glanced past him at Myers and Walker. Squared her shoulders and pulled her hands free, stepping back out of reach.

No, he howled in silent agony. *Don't go! I can't do this. I can't leave you.* "Nadia—"

"I love you too," she choked out, taking another step back, her eyes locked with his.

He thought his heart would split open. He'd wanted to hear those words from her for over a fucking year. But not here. Not like this.

The frantic crowd swelled around her. Swallowing her within seconds. He lurched to the right, trying to follow her. Still desperately trying to figure out a solution to this nightmare. "Nadia!"

He couldn't see her anymore. And the security force was closing in.

"Cal, we gotta go *now*!" Walker yelled at him, closer now.

A second later Myers and Walker both grabbed him. For a second, he almost went at them, ready to rip apart anyone who stood between him and Nadia.

"She's gone, man," Myers said, as if reading his mind. "And you can't help her from here. We gotta go."

He knew they were right. Understood it on a logical level. But the pain in his chest was splitting him apart.

"Come on," Walker said, pulling him away from the fence.

There was still no sign of Nadia.

Sick to his stomach, he turned away from the fence and somehow forced his legs to carry him to the waiting aircraft, Myers and Walker half-dragging him with them. Wilkinson stood up when he entered, face livid, and opened his mouth to blast them, but stopped when he saw the look on Callum's face and the baby in his arms.

Without a word Callum handed Ferhana off to Walker and strode to the far corner of the aircraft. Away from the others he sank to the floor and shoved the heels of his hands into his eye sockets, only dimly aware of the tail ramp rising behind him and the aircraft's engines powering up to taxi them down the runway.

The haunted, resigned look on Nadia's face was burned into his brain. All he could think about was her outside that fence right now with no one to help or protect her. He swallowed back the bile that rushed into his throat, his stomach twisting hard even as he ordered himself to snap the fuck out of it and *think*.

She'd told him she loved him. And it damn well wasn't going to be the one and only time he heard it.

He had to have a plan in place by the time this plane landed in Delhi. Because the moment it did, he was coming back for Nadia.

FIFTEEN

"I'm going back for her."

The utter silence in the room during the few moments they waited for Ryder's reaction to Callum's announcement was heavy as hell. Walker knew what was coming. They all did.

"You know I can't sanction this." Ryder's voice was quiet through the speaker of the phone sitting on the coffee table in the middle of the hotel room, carrying over the noise of the traffic and constant honking six floors down on the street below. It was Callum's backup, since he'd given his primary one to Nadia. Six hours had already passed since he'd been forced to leave her behind, and it was killing him.

"I know," Callum answered. "I wouldn't expect you to. But I'm going back for her regardless."

Walker shot another look at him across the room by the tiny window overlooking the crowded urban sprawl and chaos of Delhi. Callum was quiet and grim-faced, had spent the entire flight here in a corner of the cargo bay away from everyone else, and they'd let him be.

He was taking the Nadia situation hard. Walker didn't know what the deal was between them, but he could guess well enough after what he'd seen today. Even for battle-hardened guys like him and Donovan, that scene at the airport had been fucking wrenching to witness. Callum was desperate to go back to Kabul to extract her, but their job wasn't done yet.

It put them all in one hell of a position. Walker was with him on this, however. They couldn't leave an American woman essentially behind enemy lines.

"Wilkinson's contract stipulates that we provide protection for him until he lands in the UK," Ryder said.

"And he'll have it. Just not from me."

"You're team leader."

Callum's jaw flexed, his eyes flashing. "If it was Danae trapped alone in Kabul right now with no way out, would you give a shit about a contract or title?"

Walker winced internally at the verbal punch, but Ryder only sighed. "No. I get it, I really do."

"I'm going back on the first flight out—"

"Look, Cal. I want to help you, and Nadia. But legally my hands are tied on this one. I can't break Wilkinson's contract, and I can't allocate company funds, personnel or equipment to this without going through the proper channels. Corporate would—"

"I understand, but I'm not asking. And I take full responsibility for what happens to me as a result of this."

"I'm not firing you, Cal."

Callum's shoulders eased only a fraction, the tension thrumming from him palpable. "I gotta go."

"What about Ferhana?" Walker asked. He and Donovan had taken turns looking after her on the flight. She was a handful, always moving, even in the vehicle on the way here, trying to squirm out of their arms. She'd finally passed out a few minutes before reaching the hotel, so they'd put her on the bed in between stacks of pillows to keep her from rolling off while they figured out what to do next.

"I've got a call in to Nadia's organization," Callum said. "Just waiting to hear back."

Oh, they were in for one hell of an ass-ripping when they returned the call. Leaving Nadia scrambling until the last minute to get out of Afghanistan was flat-out criminal. As far as he was concerned, they'd abandoned her. Whatever happened to her was on their heads, and he hoped her family would wipe them out with a major lawsuit over this.

"I called them too, and Jaia's getting me her boss's direct number now," Ryder said. "I'll let you know once I hear anything. But for now, she's your responsibility."

Callum met Walker's gaze, and he got the message. He hadn't counted on being a nanny on this trip, but Callum was in no fit state to look after a baby and would be turning around for Kabul tonight anyway.

Walker had missed out on those early days with Shae, but Donovan had some experience with it, and at least looking after a kid wasn't a completely foreign concept to them the way it was to Callum.

"What are you going to do?" Ryder asked.

"I need to talk to the others," Callum said.

Their boss made a frustrated sound. "All right. Let me make some more calls and see if there's anything I can do on my end in the meantime. Let me know what the plan is with Wilkinson ASAP, and then keep me posted about where you are and what's happening."

"Roger that." Callum ended the call, read a message on his phone and then folded his arms as he faced him and Donovan, his expression set. "Wilkinson's secured a Learjet and pilot for tonight. Leaves for Frankfurt at oh-six-thirty. He's dropping the London leg, so once that plane touches down in Germany our contract with him is over." He glanced at his watch, opened his mouth to say something else and stopped when an unhappy cry came from the bedroom.

"I'll get her," Donovan muttered, and strode for the door they'd left open a few inches. He emerged moments later with a tousled Ferhana who rubbed her eyes and stared at them all fearfully. Donovan wrinkled his nose. "She needs a change." His gaze swung to Walker.

Walker stared back and held his palms out. "Whoa. Never changed a diaper in my life." Shae had been a few years past all that when he'd come into her life.

Donovan gave him a sour look and picked up the backpack. "Fine."

Walker made a face as his buddy knelt on the carpet. "Are you really gonna change her out here in the middle of the floor?"

Donovan glanced up in exasperation. "Yeah. You got a problem with that, you're welcome to have at 'er yourself."

"I'm good." He could figure it out if need be, but he'd rather let Donovan do the honors.

"Yeah, that's what I thought." Donovan caught her around the waist, earning an outraged squawk. "FYI, floor's the easiest—and safest place to do this," he said, quickly laying her down and gathering what he needed from the backpack.

Not wanting to watch what was coming next, Walker turned his attention back to Callum. Their team leader's expression was far away, no doubt he was already planning the mission to Kabul.

"What are you going to do?" Walker asked. There was no way he could pull this off alone, not even with all his formidable skill set and experience as an operator. He needed backup.

Callum started texting someone. "Find her and bring her

home." He stopped, looked at the two of them. "But I could use some backup."

Walker immediately glanced at Donovan, who looked up from where he'd mercifully already finished the nasty part of the diaper change and met his stare. Walker knew they were sharing the exact same thoughts.

They couldn't let Cal do this alone, it was too damn dangerous. But they had the job to finish and Shae to think of too, and they'd already rolled the dice once by taking this contract. Going back to Kabul for seconds when the Taliban was poised to retake the country was just asking for shit to go sideways. They owed it to her to make sure at least one of them came home.

"I'll go," Donovan said before Walker could answer, doing up the fastenings on the new clean diaper.

Walker blinked, not having expected him to volunteer that quickly. "We should talk about it in pri—"

"Nothing to talk about. You're our logistics guy. You can help us just as easily from Germany as you can anywhere else. You can escort Wilkinson there, and that way Shae'll still have one of us if things go tits up in Kabul." He let Ferhana go and she immediately rolled to her hands and knees, then pushed to her feet.

Walker stiffened when she began toddling toward him, her big, dark eyes fastened on him. She babbled something and raised her arms with what sounded like a command. He reached down and picked her up, holding her on one hip while they stared at each other, and something started to melt inside him. Damn.

"Besides, this little princess has already chosen her knight in shining armor, and it ain't me." Donovan shook his head at her. "And after I just changed your stinky bum, too."

"It's only because I had her for most of the flight." Walker felt for her. She was still a bit leery of him, but her curiosity was winning out. One dimpled hand reached out and patted his short beard. "*Salaam*," he said, earning a big grin showing her four front teeth.

"Myers, you sure?" Callum asked.

Donovan nodded. "Yeah. Long as I know Shae's looked after, I'm good to go."

Walker was about to protest, but Callum's phone rang. He took the call, and Walker could tell by his clipped tone and lethal expression that it was Nadia's relief org.

Ferhana squirmed and demanded to be put down. The second Walker did, she took off, tottering unsteadily around the room to explore everything. Donovan followed her like a shadow, repeatedly saving her from toppling into or knocking things over as he listened to what Callum was saying.

Walker took the opportunity to talk to him while Cal's attention was elsewhere. "You can work logistics just as well as me for this op, and you hate Kabul."

"Everyone hates Kabul." Donovan shrugged and shot out his hands to catch Ferhana, saving her from falling headfirst into the corner of the coffee table. "You're the one with the background in intel, and your contact network's way wider than mine. It makes sense for you to go with Wilkinson."

Nope. That wasn't the reason. "Why you, Don?" Walker pressed. There was something else at play here. Something big, and he wanted to know what it was.

Another shrug, this one borderline defensive as he followed Ferhana toward the bathroom. "Because you're her dad, jerkwad."

Walker drew his head back in shock. "What?"

"She needs you more than me," Donovan muttered. "Of the two of us, I'm the expendable one."

What the hell? "*You're* her dad, Don. I'm just the guy—"

That green stare cut to him like a laser. "Just the guy she calls Dad, the guy who raised her who she trusts more than anyone on earth and spent most of her life with? Exactly."

Hell. Was that what was going on here? Donovan seriously still doubted his relationship with Shae? Yeah, he hadn't been there for her much when she was little because he was always overseas, but he'd put in a lot of effort in healing things between them over the past five years.

"Come on, man. Your relationship's great now, the best it's ever been."

"I said I'll go, so I'm going," Donovan said shortly. "End of discussion."

No, it fucking wasn't. This was long overdue. "You were twenty-one, and a different person back then," he said in a low voice, trying to keep the irritation out of his tone. "How long you gonna beat yourself up over it?"

Donovan shot him a hard look and didn't reply, but his answer was clear enough. He was planning to punish himself for it forever.

Callum got off the call. "Her org's useless as shit. They're useless, don't have a fucking clue how to get her out, and I'm not waiting." He eyed them. "You both sure about this?"

"Yeah," they both answered, though Walker didn't feel good about leaving him and Donovan behind while he flew off to safety in Germany.

Yet he understood that one of them had to escort Wilkinson and Ferhana there, and it was true he could work just as effectively from there as anywhere else. Better, probably, given how chaotic things were in Afghanistan. He could still work all his contacts, track them and handle logistics from there.

"Okay. Thanks." He gave Donovan a nod, then switched his attention to Walker. "We'll go with you to the airport, make sure everything's in order, then catch our own flight. You'll escort Wilkinson and the baby to Frankfurt. Someone from Nadia's organization is going to meet you at the airport and take her off your hands."

Okay, that helped a bit. "What about equipment?" Walker asked. "You're gonna need transportation, weapons and ammo."

"Three-man team would be better," Donovan said, now sitting on the floor while Ferhana played with the laces on his boots.

"Two's gonna have to do," Callum said.

"What about Boyd?" Donovan asked.

Callum shook his head. "He already volunteered, and I turned him down."

"Why?"

"He's just finally recovered from getting shot, and he's too far away. Nadia can't wait that long."

Walker mentally reviewed his relevant personal contacts. He didn't think anyone could help them on such short notice. Except for one person.

"Let me make a call." The other two stared after him as he walked into the bedroom and shut the door, searching up a contact he hadn't used in years.

With the touch of a button, he dialed Alex Rycroft.

SIXTEEN

"Peace be upon you, friend."

Gazing into Homa's kind, worried brown eyes, Nadia almost broke down. Her friend had taken a huge personal risk in coming here after Nadia's call when she'd left the airport.

"Thank you," she whispered, leaning into the hug the older woman offered. It was dark now, and Homa needed to get back to the orphanage because it wasn't safe out here for either of them. "Take care of yourself."

"And you."

She watched Homa walk away with a heavy heart, shifting the strap of the bag her friend had packed full of all her important belongings Nadia had left at the orphanage. People within the Taliban knew Nadia had been there and might be watching, waiting for her to return. So Homa had come to her.

Nadia took a deep, slow breath and looked up and down the tiny alleyway they'd met in. The streets on either end were all but deserted, the enveloping silence eerie after all the noise and movement she was used to here.

It seemed like half the city had evacuated, fleeing the

inevitable Taliban takeover. Those who had stayed mostly remained behind closed doors.

The weight of Callum's phone in her pocket was the only source of reassurance she had left. She'd ditched Aref's at the airport, but Callum's phone only had sixty-percent battery and she had nothing to charge it with. Which meant she had to keep it turned off most of the time and only periodically switch it on to check for messages.

Last time she'd used it to contact the US Embassy in Islamabad, Pakistan, giving her name, location and situation. She was sure Callum was doing everything he could for her on his end, but if he couldn't get to her, maybe someone from the Embassy could send someone to meet her at the border. She'd left a message on their voicemail.

For now, she was on her own in this hostile place. If all else failed, she would have to get to the border by herself. She wasn't going to waste precious cell battery to call her organization. They'd been worse than useless, and she no longer trusted them to help.

Pausing at the end of the alley, she checked up the street in both directions before turning on the phone. It powered up, showing a weak connection.

She started up the street, searching for better reception as she followed the instructions Homa had given her to the safe house she had arranged for her. Nadia would lay low until she figured out her next move.

A soft ding filled the silence. She stopped to read the new message, a painful burst of hope expanding in her chest when she saw Callum's text from several hours ago.

I'm coming back for you. About to board a flight. Afghan airspace closed. Conserve battery and check messages every few hours. I love you. C

Love you too, she replied, knowing how lucky she was to

have someone with his skills and background committed to pulling her out of here. *Can't wait to see you.*

There were a hundred other things she wanted to say, but she held back and shut the phone off after her message sent. Instantly she felt alone, cut off from the world.

When he'd told her he loved her through the airport fence, she'd almost lost it. Callum was the strongest man she'd ever known. The look on his face, that tortured, haunted look, and the raw emotion in his voice and eyes were seared into her memory. He'd stared at her like he was afraid it was the last time they would ever see each other.

It had felt like goodbye.

Stop. She shook her head at herself and kept walking, staying alert as she strode up the cracked asphalt. She had to stay positive. Think carefully. Believe that Callum would find a way to pull her out soon.

Homa's directions were clear in her head as she walked the unfamiliar streets of the residential neighborhood. Six blocks east. Three northeast. Another half mile north…

The ball of dread in her gut pulled tighter with each block. There weren't many people out and about, but they were all men, and though she'd covered her hair and lower face with a veil, as a lone woman out walking at this time of night, she still stood out.

Their stares made the back of her neck prickle. Made her feel twice as uneasy.

She picked up her pace, her pulse thudding in her ears.

The small, darkened house crouched between its neighbors near the end of a deserted side street. It belonged to friends of Homa's who had recently fled the city.

She found the key in a flowerpot under the front window as Homa had said. Quickly unlocked the front door, she stepped inside, breathing a tiny sigh of relief when she found it quiet and still. Bolting it shut behind her, she glanced around the small space.

Both windows overlooking the street had blinds on them. She pulled them down for extra security, then switched on a dim lamp in the corner and sank onto the small sofa. Her stomach growled, reminding her that she hadn't eaten since before leaving the elderly couple's home this morning. She checked the fridge and cupboards, but they were empty.

At the top of her backpack she found the food Homa had tucked inside for her. Tears pricked her eyes. She blinked them back and ate a bit, conserving the rest for later. She only had a little money. She needed to make that and her food stores last, because she had no idea how long she would be on her own.

It was still such a shock to realize that this is what her efforts here had come to. She should have listened to Callum and turned down the posting. And now that she'd had more time to process everything, she was furious with her organization.

They had begged her to take this posting. She'd trusted them. Had come here in good faith believing they would always do right by her and have her back. Instead, when things had become critical, they'd failed her. Abandoned her, essentially.

If she made it out of Afghanistan, the first thing she was going to do once she got home was give her notice. She would never work for them again.

Since dwelling on that would only make things worse, she turned her thoughts to happier things instead. Callum and her family. Her parents and siblings would all know what had happened by now. As rocky as her relationship with her mother was, she would have given anything to hear her voice right now. At least she'd texted Anaya to say she was okay for the moment and would contact her again later.

She also thought of Ferhana. Of all that the little girl had been through and suffered in her short life. Nadia wondered where she was right now, and who was looking after her. What would happen to her. She knew Callum would ensure Ferhana was protected as well. He would be such an amazing father.

She pressed her lips together as her throat constricted, thinking of all that had passed between them since the night they met. He'd stuck by her, had still wanted her even after she pushed him away. It made her realize that he loved her as she was, imperfections and all.

It also made her realize that she had loved him for a long time, long before she'd been ready to admit it to herself, and yet it had taken something like this to get her to say it.

She regretted that. Regretted holding back from him. Given another chance, she would do things differently moving forward. If—*when* he got her out of here, she would explain everything, and vowed never to hide the depth of her feelings for him ever again.

No more hiding. They deserved a future together.

Glancing around the empty room, one question kept tumbling through her mind.

Was it worth it? Was everything she'd risked in coming here, everything she'd done and gone through worth it now that she was stranded and alone in one of the most dangerous cities on the planet?

She needed to believe it was.

∼

CALLUM GLANCED IMPATIENTLY at his watch again, standing at the rendezvous point with Myers with the hot morning sunshine beating down on them. The meet-up time with their driver was only minutes away, but every second he was forced to wait pushed his frustration higher.

Nadia was brave and resourceful, but she had to be scared right now. Wherever she was, he hoped she was okay, and trusted that he would get her out somehow.

He'd exhausted every old military contact he had that he'd thought might be of any help, trying to find someone near Kabul who could get to Nadia before him. Boyd had been working his connections too. But their efforts had gone nowhere. Every military contractor still on the ground in Afghanistan had their hands full dealing with the shit show happening.

As of right now, he, Myers and their mystery driver were Nadia's best hope.

"Who's this driver coming to get us?" Myers asked, repacking his ruck.

"Not sure. Walker's contact said they'd be here at oh-nine-hundred." Callum knew of Alex Rycroft but had never met him.

The man had spent a celebrated career in Special Forces before becoming a legend with the NSA. In Delhi, Walker had reached out to him for help, and Rycroft had arranged transportation for them.

Walker's message from Germany had been vague: *Rycroft said he's sending you one of the best*.

Callum would have preferred a lot more intel than that, but he wasn't in a position to be picky and just wanted to get moving toward Kabul.

He and Myers had flown from Delhi to Peshawar last night, then taken a bus out of the city toward the Afghan border and come on foot to this place outside a small village right on the border. With Afghan airspace closed, their only way in was overland.

Except all the main mountain passes and many smaller ones were being monitored by Taliban forces. That meant their best bet getting in without risking attack was a narrow, ancient overland route used through the centuries that was going to make for one hell of a harrowing drive through the mountains.

Myers pulled out a detailed map they'd brought and unrolled it, placing it on the ground between them. "How many hours you figure it'll take to reach the valley floor?"

Callum squatted down and found the route with his finger. "Four if we're lucky. Then another two-and-a-half to Kabul." Myers was making a big personal sacrifice by doing this with him. Callum owed him big time and it took a weight off his mind to have him here.

"Does she know where to meet us if we can't get into the city?"

The situation on the ground was changing every hour, making up-to-date intel tricky. By the time he and Myers reached the outskirts of Kabul, there was a good chance all roads into the city would be blocked off by Taliban checkpoints. If that happened, Nadia would have to slip out and meet up with them somewhere.

"She hasn't responded yet." That worried him. She'd messaged last night saying she was at a safe house and sent the address. But his phone might have died since then. It hadn't been fully charged when he'd given it to her.

They both looked up at the sound of a vehicle approaching in the distance. After a few moments a filthy black Toyota pickup appeared at the top of the rise, its tires kicking up a cloud of dust into the bone-dry air.

He and Myers stood as the driver sped toward them and pulled to an abrupt stop twenty feet away, the angle of the sun glinting off the windshield making it impossible to see the driver.

The door opened and a thirty-something brunette with a chin-length bob hopped out wearing khaki cargo pants and a white T-shirt. "You Falconer?" she asked him, pulling off her sunglasses.

Callum blinked, noticed Myers was gaping at her. "Who are you?"

A grin broke over her face. "I'm Ivy. Rycroft sent me." She put her shades back on. "Hear you boys need a ride. Hop in."

Callum shot a look at Myers before grabbing his ruck and striding for the truck. Rycroft had sent a woman to go with them into Taliban-occupied territory?

He got in the front passenger seat while Myers climbed into the rear of the cab. "Where did you come in from?" he asked.

"UK." Ivy opened the other rear door and rummaged around in the bags back there. "Brought you guys some kit. Wasn't sure what you needed, so I brought lots just in case." She handed over tactical vests, pistols and ammo. "Got a few M-4s as well if we need 'em. Oh! I brought some snacks, too." Beaming, she handed out some bags of chips, popcorn and jerky.

Who the hell was this woman? "How do you know Rycroft?" he asked her, unsure what was happening. "You NSA?"

"No," she said with an amused snort.

"Then how?"

"Let's just say he's become sort of a father figure to me," she said evasively.

"You former military?" Myers asked from the back, already tearing into a bag of jerky.

"Not exactly."

"CIA?" Myers said.

"Nope."

Callum paused in texting Walker to glance back at Myers. His teammate was scowling now, his mouth full of jerky. "Do you have military training?" he asked.

She glanced up at Myers, amusement clear on her face. "Why, you worried?"

"Little bit, yeah."

She reached over and clapped him on the shoulder once. "Don't be. You're in good hands."

Callum whipped off the text to Walker. *Woman named Ivy's here to pick us up. Rycroft sent her?*

Three dots appeared. Then, *Affirmative.*

Ivy finished in the back and hopped in the driver's seat. "So, Nadia's a civilian?"

"Yeah," Callum answered, still trying to puzzle her out. Not former military, not NSA or CIA, and hadn't worked with Rycroft. So who the hell was she?

"Any training?"

"No. But she's smart." She would know to be careful, stay out of sight and cover her face if she went out in public.

"That's good. She's gonna need every last one of her smarts." Ivy grabbed a rolled-up map from inside the center console and tucked a lock of light brown hair behind her ear. "Most recent satellite images from a couple hours ago show this is still open. No Taliban for miles in either direction. Question is, can we get all the way through on that 'road.'" She used finger quotes on the last word.

Her map was far more detailed than theirs, and how did she have access to satellite images? Callum's phone buzzed in his lap. *Ivy's legit.*

He had so many questions but only asked the main one. *Who is she??*

A pro. Rycroft says not to worry.

Oh, well, if Rycroft said not to worry...

"When's the last time you had contact with her?" Ivy asked, helping herself to a rope of red licorice sitting in the cup holder.

"Last night, just before midnight in Kabul."

She nodded, stretching the licorice rope to bite off a piece, and took out her phone. "She was still at the same location as of an hour ago when I gassed up."

Callum looked at her sharply. "How the hell do you know that?"

"Because we've got the best in the business monitoring her phone."

What? "Who?"

"One of my sisters." She pulled up something on her sat phone, grunted in satisfaction and put on a headscarf to cover her hair. "Nadia's still at the same location. Just switched her phone on a minute ago."

As if on cue, Callum's phone buzzed again. This time with a text from Nadia. A thumbs-up in reply to his instructions about what to do if they couldn't get into the city.

Then another one from Walker. *All good?*

Maybe. He wasn't sure. But whoever she was, Ivy seemed on top of things, and he didn't have a choice but to go with this. *Yep*, he answered, then replied to Nadia. *Heading across Afghan border now. Will contact you in a few hours. Are you safe?*

Yes.

Some of the tension inside him eased. *Good.*

Have to turn phone off now. Not much battery left.

Okay. Love you. Pressure formed in his chest. He should have told her way before. Wished he had.

Hell, he wished so many things had gone differently for them. Once he found her and got her out of this, he was laying everything out on the table. They'd lost too much time together as it was, and he refused to lose any more now that she'd said she loved him back.

Love you too.

Ivy took another bite of her licorice whip, watching him. "So, you guys ready to get this show on the road?" She twisted around to look back at Myers, raised her eyebrows over the rims of her shades.

"Let's go," Callum answered, doing up his seatbelt. He hoped the hell Ivy knew what she was doing. But even if she did, they were in for one hell of a bumpy road ahead.

SEVENTEEN

Nadia squeezed as much water from her hair with the towel as possible and then plaited it into a single braid. She hadn't slept much last night, every little noise setting her heart racing.

She hated everything about this situation, all the uncertainty, the constant fear she couldn't shake. The only thing that helped was knowing that Callum was coming for her. Without that, she would have given in to tears and despair.

After changing she went into the kitchen/living room and ate the piece of bread and cheese left over from last night. It wasn't much but it would fill the hole in her stomach and buy her time before she needed to figure out something to replenish her food supply.

Her heart careened in her chest when a frenzied knocking suddenly came at the front door. Automatically she edged backward toward the hallway, then froze when a voice said her name. Female, speaking in a loud, frantic whisper.

"Nadia!"

Not trusting whoever it was, she crept to the window over

the sink and risked a peek through a gap between the edge of the blind and the windowsill.

A middle-aged woman wearing a headscarf stood on the doorstep. She paused for a moment, wringing her hands anxiously, then knocked again. "Naadiaaa!" she said a little louder, then cast a furtive glance around her as though she was afraid of being seen.

No way Nadia was answering the door. It could be a trap. Someone could be waiting for her just out of view, anticipating the moment she opened the door.

The woman unleashed a stream of urgent, rapid Dari, her voice unsteady. But Nadia caught the gist, and as the meaning sank in, the blood drained from her face.

Taliban. In the area and looking for her. They had offered money to anyone with information about her. The woman continued by saying Homa had asked her to warn Nadia if there was any sign of trouble.

"Please, you must go. Now, hurry," the woman finished. She waited another few seconds, cast one final glance at all the windows along the front of the house, and when Nadia didn't answer, she finally left.

Nadia had heard and seen enough to know what kinds of things the Taliban did to women they captured. Knowing she was actively being hunted by them made her skin crawl. She couldn't afford to gamble with staying here. She needed to get the hell out now.

Pulse thudding in her throat, she rushed for the bedroom and grabbed her few things, stuffing them all into the backpack. Her hands shook as she covered her hair and lower face with the headscarf.

She had no idea if the woman was telling the truth or not, but she couldn't risk staying here a minute longer in case this was real. Moving around in the daylight would leave her totally exposed, but it appeared she had no choice.

She took out Callum's phone, turned it on. There were no more messages from him. Her heart sunk a little, but she shot off a quick one of her own, hoping he would see it eventually.

Taliban in area looking for me. Have to leave. God, she didn't know where to go now. *What should I do?*

She checked the phone battery. Down to under twenty-percent battery already. Fear burst inside her. The phone was her only lifeline to Callum. Without it he'd never find her.

She quickly shut it off to conserve what was left and eased the curtain on the window aside an inch to look out back. The tiny courtyard behind the house was empty, crisscrossed by lines of drying laundry from the other houses sharing it.

Going out the front was way too risky. If she was going to make a break for it, fleeing through the courtyard was her only other option.

Cursing under her breath, resenting her organization for putting her in this untenable position, she slid the backpack on, pushed the window open and jumped up to throw one leg over the sill. Perched there for a moment, she paused and glanced around.

Seeing nothing, she swung her other leg through and hopped down. Her shoes sank into the dry soil of the garden bed hugging the rear of the house, the thorns of the rosebushes snagging on her clothes.

Five narrow footpaths radiated out from the courtyard. Picking the darkest one, she darted across to it and started up the walkway between two of the houses, having no idea what to expect when she reached the other side.

She'd never felt so scared and alone. Even when Callum had been forced to leave her at the airport, she had been able to connect with Homa. Now that connection was severed as well. She had only herself and her wits to get her through this.

Voices reached her as she neared the end of the pathway. She stopped, shrank back against the rough stucco wall of the house behind her, pulse tripping.

Men walked across the gap at the end of the path, speaking with some locals. They wore traditional tribal clothing. Had long, dark beards. Black turbans. One was carrying a rifle.

Taliban.

Fear choked her, cutting off her windpipe as she spun and raced as quietly as she could back the way she'd come. When she reached the courtyard she skidded to a sudden stop, a gasp tearing from her throat.

The woman who had been at her door earlier went dead still, a shirt she was pinning to the clothesline in her hands. Her eyes widened when she saw Nadia, her expression tightening in alarm.

She darted a glance left, then met Nadia's gaze, her face stiff with apprehension. "That way," she whispered, pointing right. "Hurry child, they are close."

Nadia broke into a run, going in the direction the woman had indicated because there was no other choice. This pathway widened into a small alley that twisted its way between a crowded section of houses. She kept going until a narrow street came into view up ahead.

She stopped in the shadows at the end of the alley, glanced right and left to make sure there were no Taliban anywhere in sight before turning the corner and hurrying up the sidewalk. Her skin prickled the entire time, every male voice she heard making her heart slam against her chest wall.

The few people she passed seemed to take little or no notice of her. Heartened, she crossed the street and hurried down another alley. Wound left. Then right. Left again.

She smelled the marketplace before she saw it. Spices and roasting meat.

Tugging the scarf tighter around her lower face, Nadia kept her head down slightly and skirted the edge of the market, watching all around her. Something Callum had once said to her triggered in her brain. About always walking with a sense of purpose because it drew less attention.

She forced herself to straighten and slowed her stride, even though it went against all her instincts.

To her surprise, no one seemed to give her a second glance. Better still, she didn't see anyone who looked like they might be Taliban.

She hurried on, afraid to stop. Afraid to look at anyone lest it draw attention to her and make someone notice her paler skin.

She walked for miles and miles, winding her way across the city. The bottoms of her feet were hot and sore by the time she stopped in the shadows between some shops in an area of the city she didn't recognize and chugged half the water left in the bottle Homa had given her.

Looking up, she noticed the sun was no longer directly overhead. Meaning it was past noon already, and that she'd been walking for almost four hours.

Dying for word from Callum, she took out the phone and switched it on. Her heart squeezed when a message from him appeared.

Keep heading east and keep the phone with you. Conserve battery and turn on only in emergency. We're across the border, heading to Kabul. Unsure whether we'll be able to get into the city, but we'll track you with the phone. You can do this. I love you.

She inhaled a shaky breath, the lump in her throat making it hard to breathe. East? She'd been going in zigzags all morning.

But she knew the sun had climbed to her left and was now sinking on her right.

Putting the phone away, she turned left and kept going, Callum's message giving her added courage. She could do this. She *would* do this, and then he would get her out of this place.

Traveling east to the best of her ability, she was forced to stop and hide off and on for several hours. It was dark before she finally reached what she hoped was a safe enough place and stopped for the night behind some businesses closed for the night.

She glanced around to make sure no one was around, then checked the phone again, wincing at the amount of light it gave off. No more messages from Callum, but hopefully someone on his team was monitoring her phone signal, would know she'd turned it on and see her current location.

Tired, footsore and afraid, she huddled in an empty doorway out of sight from the street and curled up, shivering against the chill. She was exhausted but too afraid to sleep. Dreading the approach of dawn, and praying Callum found her before daylight hit.

~

"LAST KNOWN LOCATION as of three hours ago was here," Ivy said, indicating the spot on the map she'd pulled up on her phone. They had made it through their arduous journey through the mountains and finally reached the outskirts of Kabul.

Callum studied the map from the passenger seat, anxious to get to Nadia *now*. No, desperate to.

He'd never been this emotionally invested in the outcome of a mission before. Had never been emotional about one period, because that had been trained out of him early on. But there was no getting away from it this time.

The woman he loved was trapped in harm's way and he would do whatever it took to get her out, even if it meant going into a Taliban stronghold on his own.

According to the GPS beacon in his primary phone, Nadia was right at the eastern edge of Kabul. Or at least she had been the last time she'd turned the phone on. Thank God all their phones had custom tracking systems on them, or they would have been running blind without a way to locate her. "We've got three hours tops until it starts to get light," he said. "We have to get to her before then." After that, the risk went up tenfold.

"Can't get in on the highways," Myers said behind him, leaning forward in the backseat. "Taliban have already choked them off and are having fucking parades with the tanks and other equipment we left them." His voice dripped with anger and disgust.

Callum didn't blame him. This entire pullout had become an epic shit show. "Walker says this route to the southeast might still be clear." He tapped the screen to show the thin, ragged line indicating a road that wound into the city. It would cost them more time, but it was their best option. "If it is, it won't be clear for long."

"Okay, so we go now," Ivy said, passing him the phone and starting the ignition again, tugging her headscarf into place.

Callum didn't know anything about her operational abilities, but she had won his respect as a driver. The "road" they'd taken through the mountains was some of the roughest terrain he'd ever traveled over. Ivy had gotten them through it with only a few scratches, a dented side mirror and one flat tire.

Nobody could have done better, including him.

"Agreed," he said. There was no point waiting to do more recon on the Taliban movements and positions. It was now or never, and with the enemy having already choked off several routes yesterday, they would begin all over again come daylight.

No. By the time the sun came up they had to have Nadia and be on the way south to the border.

Callum navigated for Ivy while Myers monitored comms with Walker. Ivy got them across to the route they'd chosen. Everything went smoothly until they hit a steady stream of traffic about five miles from the city and slowed to a crawl.

The closer they got to the capital, the more Callum's gut tingled. At least it was still dark out, helping conceal their appearances, but he may have to swap seats with Ivy soon in case they ran into any military checkpoints. Having a female driver would make them stand out.

For the moment, luck was with them. They didn't spot any checkpoints or Taliban patrols for the rest of the way into the capital.

Callum was aware of his pulse accelerating, a mix of hope and anticipation pumping through him. Nadia was out here somewhere, within a few miles of their position. Now it was just a matter of tracking her down.

"Turn right up here," he told Ivy, and sent another message to Nadia saying they were close, and for her to stay put. "Still nothing?" he asked Myers, who was monitoring Ivy's phone for messages from someone named Amber.

It meant Nadia hadn't turned the phone back on again. If she was out of battery, she might not be able to turn it on at all. Then how would he find her?

"Negative."

Ivy did as he said, following the winding street through a residential neighborhood that would lead them toward the area where Nadia had been. The next twenty minutes seemed like hours, but finally they reached an intersection close to her last beacon marker.

"Stay close," Callum said to Ivy, slipping in an earpiece as Myers did the same. They both got out, weapons in hand, and raced across the last three darkened blocks to reach the spot where Nadia's phone had marked.

She wasn't there.

Disappointment hit him hard, even as he forced it away. He hadn't really expected her to still be sitting here this many hours later, but a part of him had hoped she would be.

"Where now?" Myers asked.

"East and northeast. She has to be close." She would have done exactly as he'd asked. Would likely be hiding somewhere out of sight.

They split up to do a search of the area. The city was like a rabbit warren, a million little walkways and alleys all disappearing into each other.

After an hour without any luck, they met back at the truck. "Sorry, no more signals from her," Ivy told them. "Amber's all over this, trust me. Once Nadia turns the phone back on, Amber will lock her location." During their trip through the mountains, he'd learned that Amber was one of Ivy's sisters, and apparently a world-class hacker. Walker was incredible at his job, but Callum was grateful for the extra hand.

Shoving away the sinking sense of disappointment that they no longer had a lead on where to look for Nadia, Callum took out their map, put a line through the area they'd just searched, then drew a grid on the remaining areas adjacent to it. "We'll keep going east and northeast. Be ready and alert us of any potential trouble," he said to Ivy, then he and Myers left her to continue their search.

He strode through the darkened streets, scanning every nook and cranny he came across. Frustration mounted with every step. Nadia was out here somewhere, had to be close, and the dawn was coming fast. Too many things about this were out of his control. He hated it.

Where are you, Nadia? He would find her if he had to search every inch of this city alone. One way or another, no matter how long it took.

He wasn't leaving Kabul without her again.

EIGHTEEN

Walker handed Ferhana over to the German female aid worker outside the hotel with a sense of relief that this added responsibility was now off his shoulders. But when the baby cried out in protest and twisted around to reach back for him, something hitched in his chest.

"It's okay," he told her with a reassuring smile, stroking the hair back from her forehead. "She's going to take care of you now, take you to a safe place with toys and all kinds of food and other kids to play with." Not that she understood a word of what he was saying, but he felt the need to anyway.

Ferhana's lips trembled as she stared at him, her eyes liquid with tears.

Damn, that look would make even the hardest heart melt. She'd gone through things in her short life that no child should ever experience. But at least she was safe now, and on her way to a place where she could have a future. He had to stop himself from pulling her back for one last hug.

The relief worker whipped out a stuffed toy, smiling as she spoke in a happy but soothing tone to the little girl. Ferhana latched onto the toy but cast a few uncertain looks at him while the woman carried her toward the van waiting at the curb.

He stood there until the van pulled away, then walked back into the lobby as he dialed his boss. Ryder picked up almost immediately. "Walker. Did the orphanage send someone yet?"

"She just left, and Wilkinson's all settled in at the hotel. He's chartered a flight for tonight back to Texas."

"Good. What do you want to do? Stay there for a bit longer, or fly home?"

"I'm going to stay." He couldn't go home when Donovan and Callum were still over here. "Just wanted to update you."

"I appreciate it. Any word from Cal yet?"

"Last contact was a few hours ago. They'll be on the road now, heading down through the mountains." The terrain was rough, and the road was questionable. It was going to be slow going, and that was without running into any Taliban patrols.

"Also—who's this Ivy, anyway?"

"I don't know. Rycroft was weirdly evasive about it when I asked questions." Rycroft was a man of many secrets, and apparently Ivy had her own as well. The only thing that made sense was that she was an undercover operative of some sort.

"If you find out anything, let me know. I couldn't find anything about her, and no one I've talked to knows her either. Rycroft's a legend for a reason, and I trust his judgment with this, but my people are involved here so I want to know."

"Same." That bothered him. He would keep digging on his own. Right after he called his daughter.

After ending the call with Ryder, he dialed Shae. "Hey, sweetheart."

"Everything okay? Where are you?"

The blatant worry in her voice tugged at him. "I'm fine, all safe and sound in Frankfurt."

"And Donovan?"

"He's with Callum and another operative, on the way back to Kabul." As to what *kind* of operative Ivy was, he had no clue.

"He texted me yesterday and said there's an American woman trapped there."

"Yes. They're going back to pull her out. There's no one else to help her now."

"I'm glad he's doing it."

He smiled at the fierce pride in her tone. "Me too. Listen, the job I was working is done now, but I'm going to stay here until the others are out of Afghanistan, just in case they need me."

"I get it. I'm worried about him, Dad. The things I've seen on the news there look really bad."

He wasn't going to sugar coat it, but he also didn't want her to worry more than she already was. "They're going to be in and out. As soon as they find her, they'll leave. But maybe turn off the news for now."

She sighed. "You always said that when you got deployed somewhere, and it never works. I've tried not to look this time, I swear. But it's all over social media and everything, so I can't avoid it. And I *want* to know what's going on."

"I know you do." Their line of work was hard on her. It was why he'd taken the job with Crimson Point Security, so he was home with her more and didn't do much travel to hot spots. "I promise I'll update you as soon as I hear anything, okay? Just wanted to let you know I'm safe and going to be a few more days."

"Thanks. Who's the other person with them?"

"It's a woman."

"Yeah? Is she kickass?"

"That's what I hear." Rycroft had vouched for her personally, so that said a lot. But it made Walker damn uneasy that no one else knew anything about her, and she was currently embedded with two of his teammates headed deep into hostile territory.

"Is she American?"

"Not sure, to be honest." Another question near the top of his list.

Whatever digging he did would have to be done under the radar. If he was right about Ivy being an undercover operative, he had to make sure he protected her identity.

∼

DONOVAN SLID the to-go container of kabobs and fire-roasted tomatoes on a bed of saffron rice across the rental suite table and eyed Ivy as she worked on her laptop, deep in concentration. It had been a long day and they were both hungry.

"Thanks," she murmured absently, stabbing a fork into a piece of chicken while still looking at the screen.

It was just the two of them here. Callum was still out searching, probably wouldn't come back until morning. After spending the past twelve hours with Ivy, Donovan now had more questions about her than answers. "What are you looking at?"

"Intel reports from Amber."

Frowning, he shoved a bite of kabob into his mouth and leaned in over her shoulder to peer at the screen. They needed a break if they were going to find Nadia here. A big one. "Intel from where?"

"Her sources."

"What sources?" He scanned the text, his eyebrows rising. "This is top secret military intel."

"Yeah." She kept reading, scrolling down the page, as if

getting top secret reports was an everyday thing for her. Maybe it was, who knew.

The report detailed Taliban movements as recent as two hours ago. As expected, the Afghan military had pretty much collapsed and were mounting only sporadic operations against the enemy away from the capital. The Taliban had also already captured strategic points and US military materiel and were converging on the capital.

"Amber's your sister?" he asked.

"One of them."

"How many do you have?"

"Eight."

He blinked. "Your mom had nine kids?"

"No." She kept reading.

Getting information out of her was painful. She was so secretive. "You an undercover agent?"

"Nope. Better."

"Better how?" She sure knew her way around a computer.

She stopped reading and made eye contact with him, one side of her mouth kicking up. "I could tell you, but then I'd have to—"

"Don't even," he said darkly. He opened his mouth to say something else, but her phone rang. She picked it up and answered.

"Hey, I just read the report. Falconer's still out looking for our target, but I'll let him know. Anything else?" She paused, looked up at him through intelligent hazel eyes as she listened. "Got it."

She ended the call and set her phone down. "Mullah Baasim's in the area, last spotted about twenty klicks northeast of Kabul."

Nasty motherfucker. Probably drooling at the prospect of

torturing all the victims he would round up in the coming weeks and months.

"Recent intelligence confirmed that Aref and his wife were killed on Baasim's orders. And he's apparently just issued a fatwah for Nadia's capture due to her involvement with Aref and being an American. He's got patrols out looking for her now."

Damn. It meant their window was shrinking fast. "I'll call Cal." He whipped out his phone, was about to dial when it rang in his hand. The caller was unknown, but it was a Virginia number. "Myers," he answered.

"Donovan?"

He blinked at the unfamiliar female voice saying his name. A sexy voice, soft and clear. "Yeah. Who's this?"

"I'm Anaya, Nadia's sister."

"Hi," he said hesitantly, wondering how the hell she'd—

"Nadia texted me your number yesterday. I already tried someone named Walker, but he didn't answer."

He frowned. In all the missions he'd been on in his life, not once had he received a call from a relative of someone he was trying to rescue. "What can I do for you?" he asked as politely as he could manage. He wanted a solid piece of intel so he could help find Nadia, not be talking to her sister.

"Other than getting my sister out of there safely, I was hoping for an update," she said, and he appreciated that at least she got straight to the point. "My family is totally in the dark and all of us are worried sick. We haven't heard from her since she last messaged me yesterday morning after leaving the airport. Have you had any contact with her since then?"

"Some, but obviously I can't give details about an ongoing operation." That was not only standard procedure, it was common sense.

"I get that, but is she still okay? On the news it said the

Taliban are close to taking Kabul. She'll be a target if she's found."

She was already a target, because she was American and had been with Aref when he was killed. "Look, I can't tell you anything more." This whole conversation was weird and awkward, and he wanted it over with.

She made a frustrated sound. "Then what *can* you tell me?" Her voice was still sexy, but now it had an edge to it.

"That we're going to find her and bring her home," he answered, ready to wrap this up. Nadia was alive and on the run as of this moment. That was all they really knew.

A loaded pause followed. "All right. I guess that's the best I can hope for right now."

It was the best any of them could hope for. "I need to go. We'll contact you when we've recovered her safely." He ended the call, shaking his head.

"Who was that?" Ivy asked, forking up a bite of rice.

"One of Nadia's sisters." Anaya. She was the youngest of the six Bishop kids, he remembered from the file Callum had given him on Nadia prior to this mission. Nadia was closest to her, so he guessed it made sense that Anaya had been the one to reach out and see what was going on.

Ivy's hazel eyes widened. "She called you? Wow, that's—" She stopped, eyes snapping to her phone when it rang again. She answered it immediately. "Hey. Got something else?"

Her expression changed as she listened to whoever it was, he was guessing Amber.

"Hang on." She pulled up a satellite map on her laptop, zoomed in on a neighborhood in the southeast of the city, not far from their current location. "Okay, got it. Where's the patrol?"

A Taliban patrol?

Moments later she ended the call and looked up at him.

"Just got another signal from Nadia's phone. Here." She tapped a spot on the map. "It was fast, as if she turned it on, shot off a text and then turned it off. Maybe the battery's low."

Donovan nodded and texted Callum the location.

Ivy jumped up and holstered her weapon in a way that told him she'd done it thousands of times before. He hoped she was a good shot, because it looked like they weren't going to make it out of here without enemy contact. "There's a Taliban patrol half a mile from her. Amber said Nadia was moving southeast. Which means she's heading right for them."

Shit.

He dialed Callum as they raced for the door. They had less than fifteen minutes to find Nadia before the Taliban did.

NINETEEN

Now what the hell was she supposed to do?

Nadia sucked in a ragged breath and fought back a rush of tears under the crushing weight of disappointment and the anxiety grinding a hole in the pit of her stomach.

Callum's phone sat in her right pants pocket beneath the folds of her robe, stone dead and useless. The battery had drained faster than she'd anticipated. When she'd turned it on a minute ago, it had barely flickered to life before dying in her hand. She'd had just enough time to glimpse a text from Callum, hadn't even been able to read it before it disappeared.

Her lifeline had been cut.

He should have been here by now. Something must be wrong. Maybe he hadn't been able to get into the city. Maybe they'd run into the Taliban on the way.

Maybe he wasn't going to be able to help her.

Her vision blurred as her eyes filled. She blinked the tears away, struggled to think of what to do next. Based on the neighbor lady warning her the other day, Nadia assumed she was now wanted by the Taliban. Maybe because of her connection to Aref, or maybe because she was an American here after the deadline. The reason didn't matter.

Should she keep heading in the direction Callum had told her to go? Or stay put in case he had picked up on the signal when she'd turned her phone on?

It would be dawn soon and she hadn't eaten since that morning. She was down to one small piece of bread, hadn't slept more than a handful of hours over the past two days. Exhaustion made everything worse, pressing down on her like a physical weight and making it hard to think.

Deciding it was safest and smartest to stay put for now, she sank back down into the little alcove tucked between two buildings she'd been huddled in for the past few hours. It was quiet here and deserted.

She pulled the shawl Homa had packed for her tighter around her shoulders and curled up tight in an effort to keep warm. The temperature during the day was scorching hot but now she was chilled through, hungry and facing an unavoidable trip to a market at some point in the next twenty-four hours.

Her anxiety kept building. She wasn't sure how much longer she could keep this up on her own. She needed help desperately and didn't speak the language well enough to blend in with the locals.

When she heard the male voices drifting her way from the end of the alley she stiffened and sat bolt upright. It was still dark but if she moved and was spotted it would look highly suspicious for her to be out here alone at this time of night—well, morning. They might try to stop her to investigate.

She waited tensely, willing them to pass by. But they didn't. Instead, they came near enough that she was forced to get to her feet, her back pressed against the rough bricks behind her, heart thudding as she prepared to bolt from cover.

The footsteps kept coming. The voices became louder and clearer.

They weren't speaking Dari. Or at least not a dialect she could understand. Then the beam of a flashlight lit up the narrow street, bouncing along the cobbles.

Behind it were two men. They were going to walk right past her. No way they would miss her at this range.

The blood pulsed in her ears, the sound of her breathing overly loud in the enclosed space. For them to be out here at this time meant they had to be looking for something—or someone. Were they Taliban informants?

She was out of time.

Darting from her hiding spot, she cringed as the beam of the flashlight came perilously close to her. Panic licked up her spine, her brain screaming at her to run.

No! Don't run. Walk tall, head up, and don't look back.

She slowed. Drew herself upright.

The voices paused behind her.

Her muscles tightened. It took everything she had not to cast a furtive glance back to see if they were watching her, the back of her neck prickling with unease. *Keep going. Don't stop.* It could be nothing.

Rounding the corner, she saw the light filtering into the alley from the streetlamp across the road up ahead and faltered. She was trapped. If she kept going the light would give her away. But staying put wasn't an option.

She forced herself to keep moving forward, making sure her face was covered and keeping her pace sedate.

One of the men called out something behind her. She walked faster, unsure whether he was talking to her.

The man snapped something louder, and this time she understood what he said. *Stop.*

Nadia bolted down the street.

Shouts erupted behind her. Fear turned her limbs to ice as she ran, darting left around the corner. This road was wider, but empty aside from the few vehicles parked along the curb on either side. She raced across it and ducked behind a car just as the men burst out of the alley.

Swallowing, she peered under the vehicle and saw them clearly as they stepped into the light and looked around. Her blood chilled when she saw the pistols in their hands.

Not random locals. These men were hunting someone. Her.

They spoke to each other, then split up. One man walked up the opposite sidewalk from where she was hiding, glancing around. He had a cell phone to his ear.

Nadia didn't dare move. She stayed rooted in place, watching his every move. The other guy had already been swallowed by the shadows farther up the street in the other direction.

The man across from her began speaking to someone. She couldn't understand anything he said. While he talked, he switched the flashlight back on, sweeping it down each tiny walkway or alley he passed. He was almost directly opposite her now.

He stopped abruptly and swung toward her, aiming the flashlight across the street to check under the vehicles. She inched to the left, curled into as tight a ball as possible to try and hide behind the back wheel. Cringed as the beam of light swept under the car.

It paused there, inches from where she was huddled.

Nadia held her breath and dug her fingers into the cool rubber of the back tire. Ready to run for her life the instant she was spotted.

The beam moved past her. Sliding left to the next car. And the next, the man holding it muttering into his phone as he headed back the way he'd come, his back to her.

She released a slow, shaky breath, relief hitting her hard. Waited until he'd reached the alley she'd just run out of before rising to a crouch and slowly easing her way to the right, away from him.

Her heart stopped when another beam of light landed on her from the left. She whipped her head around to see the other man's silhouette appear out of the shadows there, flinched and threw up a hand as the light blinded her.

He shouted for his friend, ran toward her.

No! Nadia shot up and ran blindly to the right, panic coursing through her. The soles of her shoes slapped against the uneven concrete sidewalk. Her thighs burned, her lungs tight. She sprinted as fast as she could, desperately glancing around for a safe place to go.

Her toe caught an uneven edge on the sidewalk. She swallowed a cry, threw her hands out to break her fall an instant before she hit the ground.

Her chin slammed into the concrete, breaking the skin and clacking her teeth together sharply. The pain stunned her for a split second before she shoved to her feet and scrambled onward, the sound of the men's running footsteps coming ever closer.

She stumbled. Had just taken a lurching stride forward when one of them caught the top of her backpack. Her sharp cry ripped through the night as she was wrenched backward.

She whirled, lashing out with the heel of her hand, making contact with a bearded jaw. He grunted, reeled back.

Wrenching free of the backpack straps, Nadia left him holding it and took off across the street, her heart in her throat.

The second man was right behind her. So close she could hear his rapid breaths.

She pushed herself to go faster. Faster. But she was no match for him.

A hard arm caught her around the waist. She yanked against it, twisting even as she lashed out with an elbow. A low grunt answered when the point of her elbow slammed into his ribs. His grip loosened for a fraction of a second, but he didn't let go.

Nadia turned on him, teeth bared, and drove a fist at his face with every bit of her adrenaline-fueled strength. He dodged it, seized her wrist and wrenched it behind her, his other hand gripping her jaw.

Planting her feet to balance her weight, she drove a knee into his balls.

He let her go with a startled cry and dropped to the ground. Without pause she drove her knee into the underside of his chin, barely feeling the pain of the impact, and took off before he'd even toppled over.

A scream caught in her throat when she ran straight into a wall of flesh.

She bounced off him, stumbled, only to be jerked upright by two fists locked around the neckline of her robe. His hand flashed out. A sharp crack sounded as his palm made contact with her cheek, the stinging pain sending a rush of tears to her eyes.

She pulled back her right fist, drove it forward and hit nothing but air. A heartbeat later she was shoved facedown on the sidewalk, the rough edges digging into her throbbing cheek.

The man was kneeling over her now, straddling her, one powerful hand locked around the back of her neck while the other held her wrists behind her. Her struggles were useless.

Heavy treads thudded across the concrete, then the other man was there. He switched his flashlight on, deliberately aiming it right in her eyes.

She flinched, slammed her eyes shut. Over the frantic thudding of her heart, she heard him.

"It's her." They hauled her upright roughly.

"Let me go!" she screamed, trying to smash her foot into the side of the closest knee.

"Shut up, American bitch," one of them snarled in heavily accented English.

Pain sizzled along her scalp as a rough fist seized her hair and wrenched her head back. A second later a thick, twisted piece of fabric was yanked across her lips. She shook her head back and forth, struggling to get free, but they forced the gag between her lips and tied it tight behind her head.

"No!" she yelled, her voice too muffled to carry.

She went rigid when something came down over her head, sealing her in complete darkness. Disoriented, terrified, she let out another scream beneath the hood that barely carried beyond the gag and thrashed in her captors' hold.

A painful blow to the side of the head silenced her. One of them lifted her. A hard, bony shoulder jammed into her stomach as he started carrying her. His friend laughed, rained more blows down on her every time she tried to fight.

Her breath wheezed out of her nose, the frantic sound of her respiration amplified in the confines of the hood. It was so hard to breathe. Felt like she was slowly being smothered.

A vehicle door opened nearby. She bucked and kicked but got nowhere. The man carrying her tossed her onto the seat and climbed in beside her, pinning her flat with his weight.

"Tell Baasim we have her," he said, and the engine started.

A wave of terror rolled over her, more powerful than all the rest. She knew what Baasim was capable of. Knew he would want to make a statement with her to the rest of the world—especially the US.

Trembling, unable to move, Nadia squeezed her eyes shut as scalding tears slid down her cheeks. *Callum, please help me!*

"DOWN HERE." Callum raced around the corner and charged down the alley, Myers right behind them while Ivy was a block away with the vehicle.

After endless hours of stress and uncertainty, they were finally closing in on Nadia's location, but now they were in a deadly race against the clock. If they didn't find her before the Taliban patrol did, he couldn't even think about what would happen.

A short, high-pitched scream echoed through the darkness. Callum's heart seized.

Nadia.

He went rigid, the blood rushing in his ears as he turned in a tight circle, looking in every direction. "Where was that?" he demanded. The damn echo made it impossible to tell which direction it had come from.

"That way, I think," Myers answered, pointing toward a side street.

Callum took off, racing through the darkness, fear and rage fueling the rush of adrenaline pouring through him. *Hold on, baby. Please hold on. I'm coming...*

Another scream ripped through the air, the terror in it making the hair on the back of his neck stand up. He swore and ran faster, legs pumping, grip tightening on his weapon. Itching to kill the assholes who had attacked her.

The alley twisted right and disappeared into shadow. He ran straight into a dead end.

"Fuck," he snarled, spinning around to backtrack. It had cost him precious seconds he didn't have.

Another alley branched off to the left ahead. He took it, running flat out, Myers close behind him.

"Let me *go!*"

Nadia's voice. Shrill with panic.

Fear ripped through him like a blade. His boots thudded

against the ground, his muscles straining to go faster. The muted sounds of a scuffle came from somewhere up ahead.

The alley came to an abrupt end at a side street. He shot out of the end, glanced right and his guts constricted when he saw two men shoving a limp bundle into the back seat of a truck in the distance.

He whipped his pistol up to fire, a sick feeling of helplessness hitting him when the pickup tore away with its tires squealing. God *dammit*! "Ivy, get to—"

Their truck shot into view half a block up. He and Myers raced for it. Ivy threw open the doors. They dove in.

"Go, go," Callum commanded, ready to come out of his skin. Those evil, sadistic bastards had Nadia, and the thought of them hurting her filled him with a suffocating mix of horror and rage.

Ivy hit the gas. The truck screeched around in a tight arc in the middle of the street and then roared after the other truck. Callum scanned the road ahead, his heart about to explode. He couldn't see the truck. "Where is it?" he burst out.

"Ten o'clock," Myers said urgently, pointing to his left.

Callum braced a hand on the dashboard as Ivy hammered the brakes and veered sharp to the left at the next street. In the distance he could see the red taillights just before they disappeared around a bend in the road.

"Hand me a rifle," he told Myers.

Myers passed over an M-4. Callum readied it, prepared to fire the instant he was within range of the truck. The pitch of their engine rose as Ivy floored it.

Darkened buildings whipped past in a blur. They rounded the bend where the other truck had disappeared and—

Shit! A guarded roadblock was dead ahead. The truck carrying Nadia had just passed through and was speeding away on the other side in the darkness.

Ivy braked hard, laying down rubber as she turned hard right to get them out of the line of fire. "How many guards?"

"Five," Callum answered, wrenching his door open. There was no time to lose. They had to neutralize the threat and get through that roadblock. "Myers—"

"I'm with you."

They jumped out and used the edge of the building on the corner as cover. Callum ducked his head around it to check what was happening at the checkpoint. All three guards had their weapons up and were talking excitedly amongst each other, pointing at where Ivy had pulled the truck out of sight. There were more headlights farther away in the distance. Taliban backup.

"Ready?" he asked Myers, faltering when Ivy suddenly appeared around the back of the truck wearing an ankle-length robe.

"Ready," Myers answered.

"Ivy, stay down behind cover," he ordered, then made his move.

The instant he broke from cover he took aim at his first target and squeezed the trigger. The tango dropped and the others whipped around, wildly returning fire in Callum's direction.

He dropped back behind the wall, shifted his stance and waited until the firing stopped. "On three," he muttered. "One. Two. Three."

He broke away from the wall, turning and firing as he ran. Two more tangos dropped as bullets cracked over his head, slamming into the mortar and brick building.

Muzzle flashes lit up the darkness as he and Myers advanced on the enemy. Within seconds they'd taken out all five guards.

Callum rushed toward the prostrate forms, weapon up and

finger still on the trigger. The other trucks in the distance were pulling away.

Three of the men on the ground were already dead. The last two were dying. One of them had a radio on him. It crackled to life. "Muhammad. Muhammad, what's going on?" someone asked in Pashto.

Callum dropped to one knee beside the dying man and grabbed him by the throat. "Where is Nadia Bishop?" he growled in the same language. "Where are they taking her?"

The man's mouth opened. Only a gurgling sound came out, followed by a long, wheezing sigh, then nothing.

Myers looked up from where he'd been checking the pulse of the fifth man. He shook his head. "Dead."

"Let's go." The other vehicles were withdrawing. This was their only chance to follow Nadia.

He sprinted back to the truck. Stopped and looked around. Ivy was nowhere to be found.

"Ivy," he snapped. "Where the hell are you?"

"Track me," she said in his earpiece.

TWENTY

Ivy might not be as gifted an actor as her sisters Trinity and Kiyomi when the situation called for it, but she could hold her own when necessary. While Callum and Myers had taken care of the guards at the checkpoint, she had raced to cut off this truck as it retreated from the checkpoint.

She stepped out of the shadows directly in front of it, hands raised high. Her original intention had been to take them all out. Now she had a better idea.

The truck plunged to a stop in front of her. Two armed men jumped out.

"Don't shoot," she said in English, putting a quiver in her voice.

They gawked at her, weapons trained on her.

"They took my friend Nadia," she said in deliberately broken Dari. "We work together. Please, where have they taken her?"

One of them stalked toward her, his menacing expression exposed by the beam of the headlights. She couldn't see what was happening back at the checkpoint, but she'd heard Callum and Myers through her earpiece and knew they'd neutralized the guards. They should be driving through it any minute now in pursuit of Nadia's captors.

Ivy faltered and stumbled back a step, shaking her head at the enemy fighter striding toward her. "No, please. Just tell me where my friend is—"

He seized her by the front of her robe and tore her headscarf off, yanking her into the light. A chorus of disbelieving mutters followed. "What do we do with her?" the guy holding her asked in Pashto, having no clue that she understood every word he said.

"Bring her. Quick."

He dragged her to the truck, ignoring her struggles and cries of protest and tossed her into the back seat. The driver took off immediately, and while the guy in the back held her down, the one in the passenger seat made a call on his radio. "We captured another American woman. She said she works with the other one."

A few seconds of silence answered, then, "Take her to the warehouse. Baasim can decide what to do."

The men in the truck laughed. The guy leaning over her leered down into her face. "Baasim will find a creative way for you both to die tomorrow, American whore."

Ivy kept struggling, shouting at him in English. The stupid bastard hadn't even bothered checking her for weapons and her earpiece was still firmly in place, transmitting every word back to Falconer and Myers—and Amber.

She hid a smile of triumph. *Big mistake.*

∽

"WHAT THE HELL JUST HAPPENED?" Myers said from the passenger seat as Callum veered around the dead guards at the checkpoint.

"I don't know," Callum bit out, unable to believe what he'd heard. He'd tried to get her to respond several times and she was either ignoring him or couldn't hear him.

Track me? Track her how? And what the hell had possessed her to take off and surrender to another Taliban patrol? Now he and Myers had two hostages to extract, and their entire mission had just been blown out of the fucking water.

His cell phone rang on the dash. Myers grabbed it for him and checked the screen. "UK number."

"Answer it," he muttered, searching in vain for any sight of either truck. They had heard every word of the bizarre exchange between Ivy and her captors, and everything the assholes in the second truck had said to her. They were taking her and Nadia to some warehouse, but he had no fucking clue where, and both women's lives were in extreme danger.

Myers put it on speaker. "Who's this?"

"Amber," a brisk female voice said in an American accent. "I'm sending you a link. The beacon is Ivy. Follow it and you'll find Nadia."

"Wait, what?" Myers said. "How do you—"

"I'll be monitoring everything on my end too." The call ended abruptly.

"Jesus Christ," Myers muttered. "This is insane, and how is she doing all this?"

"Is there a link?" he demanded. He didn't give a shit who Amber was at this point, who she worked for, or how she was doing anything. He just needed to know where the hell he was going to get Nadia and Ivy back.

"Yeah. It's…" He studied the screen for a moment. "Got her. They're moving northwest."

Callum hit the brakes and took a sharp left at the next street. He'd been going in the wrong damn direction for the past two minutes, costing them time they didn't have. "Where now?"

Myers navigated, following the dot on screen. It was almost dawn now. The city was beginning to wake up, the early risers coming out with their vehicles and carts. Callum swerved past an old man with a cart and donkey, missing them by inches, and laid on the horn to narrowly avoid colliding with the front end of a delivery truck.

"Left here," Myers said urgently as they roared up to an alley. "Too much traffic up ahead."

Callum made the tight turn, shot out the other side and had to hit the brakes to keep from ramming into a bus. He swerved around it, ran the next light and ignored the blaring of horns everywhere as he shot through the intersection. "Where are they now?"

"Four miles ahead and gaining."

He ground his teeth together. "Any more checkpoints we need to worry about?"

"Can't tell. Keep going."

Oh, he wasn't stopping. Not until he got Nadia and Ivy back.

By the time they reached the road both trucks had taken past the outskirts of the city, they had lost almost fifteen minutes lead time. The entire way they could hear everything the bastards holding Ivy were saying. Including the unspeakably brutal execution Baasim had ordered for Nadia tomorrow—and presumably now for Ivy as well.

Callum's stomach lurched. He'd seen some horrific, fucked-up shit in his tours over here, but death by stoning was unspeakably cruel.

"They've stopped," Myers said, enlarging the on-screen map. "They're at the warehouse."

His heart raced frantically. No matter how hard he tried to shut down his emotions, it was impossible with Nadia's life hanging in the balance. "How far out are we?"

"Not quite four miles."

Callum's hands clenched around the wheel and drove as fast as he could through the waking streets, prepared for the looming battle they would face once they reached the warehouse.

TWENTY-ONE

Ivy estimated that about twenty minutes had passed since her "capture" until the truck drove into the open bay door of the warehouse. Ivy was counting on them having brought Nadia here too.

The guy holding her to the seat finally eased up, shoving a hand between her legs just to be an asshole and laughing at her outraged screech before seizing her by the hair and wrenching her upright. "Don't worry. I wouldn't touch your diseased American pussy for a million dollars," he sneered.

If they'd been alone, she would have cut his throat for that and left him to bleed out. But he would die soon enough. Every one of these assholes would.

The other men in the warehouse called out to them. "We captured another American woman," the driver told them triumphantly.

They spent a few minutes joking amongst themselves, then the front passenger reported their arrival to someone over the radio. "Take her to the holding room and put her in with the other one," he said to the guy holding her. He was clearly the one in charge of the others. "But tie her hands first. I don't trust her."

He also seemed to be the only one with any brains at all.

Her captor muttered to himself but did as he was told, grabbing her wrists and securing them behind her with a few rounds of duct tape.

Ivy winced as he dragged her out of the backseat, almost pulling a fistful of hair out of her scalp with his rough movements and stumbled as he shoved her forward. She got a good look around on the way to a door marking what she assumed was an office of some sort on the back wall in the center of the large space. Three more men were sitting around a table near the open side door to her left, and she spotted two more standing outside with weapons.

"You wanted to see your friend?" her captor taunted in Pashto. "Here she is." He wrenched open the door and shoved her inside. "You can spend your last few hours alive together."

Ivy pitched forward, managed to catch herself before doing a face plant as the door slammed shut behind her. The blinds on the windows were drawn, but there was still enough light seeping through the slats for her to see the interior of the room. A figure lay sprawled on the carpet against the far wall, hooded, hands bound behind it.

She hurried over and crouched beside her, keeping her voice low in case anyone was listening on the other side of the door. "Nadia, can you hear me?"

The figure twitched and sucked in a sharp breath. Then the head nodded.

As far as Ivy could tell she didn't seem badly hurt at least. "I'm Ivy. Callum's coming." Should be arriving any minute now. They weren't sure what the hell was happening, but it couldn't be helped. There'd been no time to give them a heads up when the opportunity had presented itself. "We're going to get you out of here. Understand?"

Another nod.

"Good. Hang tight." She swiveled around so her bound hands were near Nadia's head, reached back to grasp the hood and tugged it off.

Nadia blinked up at her, face streaked with tears, and Ivy's jaw tightened. Those fuckers had gagged her as well, her chin was bleeding like crazy, and she might have other injuries elsewhere.

She stilled at a voice right outside the office door. "Baasim wants pictures of them."

Ivy rolled to her side and maneuvered around until she could slide her hands down the backs of her legs and over her feet. She had intended to free Nadia first but now there wasn't time. "Just lie still," she whispered to her, rising.

Facing the door, she braced her feet apart, brought her hands up high over her head and then wrenched them down toward her stomach, pulling apart with all her might. The duct tape split with a ripping sound.

She shook out her wrists and wiggled her fingers to restore the circulation, then reached up and repositioned her earpiece. "Falconer. You in position yet?"

"Are you okay?" Callum demanded.

"Yes, and I'm with Nadia in the back office," she answered calmly. "Are you in position?"

"Affirmative."

His voice was rock steady, no hint of emotion, telling her he was in full operator mode. "Good. Stand by."

"Stand by for what?"

Ivy reached down to draw her blade from the sheath on her ankle, then grasped the grenade that her captors had failed to notice in a hidden pocket near the hem of her robe. "Fire in the hole," she murmured, and strode for the door.

LYING ON HIS belly scoping out the warehouse in the pre-dawn dimness with Myers next to him, Callum had only a second to wonder what the hell Ivy meant before the office door visible through the open bay burst open.

Ivy appeared for an instant, her hand flashing out toward the tango guarding the door. His hand was still reaching for his weapon as the blade came up and drove into his kidney.

He jerked and dropped within a second. Before he'd even hit the floor Ivy pivoted and threw something toward the open side door on the far left.

The guards standing outside it scattered, but too late. An explosion tore through the air, lighting up the darkness in a brilliant burst of light, the concussion reverberating in his chest.

All three men fell and lay twitching and screaming on the ground.

Callum barely kept his jaw from falling open. Holy *shit*, Ivy.

"*Go*," he told Myers, and charged forward, heading straight for the open bay door.

The men inside never even saw them coming, too busy rushing toward their fallen comrades. Callum chose a target and fired, dropping the man in the lead. The others turned to confront him, blindly reaching for their weapons and returned fire. Bullets ripped through the air, the supersonic rounds whistling past him.

Ivy had moved out of the doorway to engage the men rushing for the side door on the left. She dropped one with a pistol shot as Callum fired again, hitting one running out of the shadows in the back. Next to him Myers took out two others.

The two of them moved together like they'd been doing it for years, bursting into the warehouse and methodically sweeping the space. Callum caught sight of someone hiding behind a stack of boxes near the far-left corner, fired two shots. The rounds ripped straight through and hit the man center mass. He dropped, his weapon clattering to the ground.

Callum stalked forward, scanning the shadows.

"Clear," Ivy called out from the other corner.

"Right side's clear," Myers said behind him. "Go get your girl."

Callum didn't have to be told twice. He ran for the closed office door.

TWENTY-TWO

Curled up on the filthy carpet, Nadia clenched her eyes shut, flinching at every shot, her ears still ringing from whatever had exploded moments ago. What was happening? Where was Ivy? Was she okay? Where was—

She went rigid when the office door ripped open, squinting against the light as a huge figure loomed in the opening. She bolted upright and shrank back against the wall, a scream rising in her throat.

"Nadia, it's me."

Everything stilled. "Callum?" Her voice was muffled behind the gag.

"Yeah, baby, I'm here." He knelt and quickly sliced the tape on her wrists with a knife, then cut the gag away.

Her throat was so tight all that came out was a choked sound. A heartbeat later his big, strong arms closed around her. She clung to him, reeling, praying this was real.

"I'm getting you out of here." He lifted her, held her to his chest as he shoved to his feet and ran outside with her.

Nadia glimpsed the bodies lying on the floor, closed her

eyes and buried her face in the side of his neck. "It's okay," he murmured as he ran. "You're okay now."

She nodded and forced her eyes open when they emerged through the open bay door. The guy who'd come to the orphanage that first time with Callum, Myers, was standing on one side of a truck, and Ivy on the other.

Myers climbed into the driver's seat while Callum put her in the back and climbed in next to her. He'd barely shut the door when Myers spun the truck around and sped away.

Still in shock, Nadia shuddered when Callum dragged her into his lap and wrapped his arms around her, holding her in a fierce grip. "You're okay," he whispered into her hair. "Everything's okay now."

She dimly realized she was shaking. A constant, uncontrollable tremor that was getting worse every moment. It took over her limbs, her lungs, even her jaw. Her teeth chattered, a bone-deep cold flooding her.

Callum's arms tightened. "It's all right." His voice was low and calm next to her ear.

She huddled against him, shoved her face harder into his neck and held on for dear life. "C-Callum," she choked out, and the dam finally burst.

All the fear she'd gone through. Everything she'd seen, everything that had happened. How close she'd come to being tortured and killed. It all poured out of her now, and there was no stopping it.

He held her tight through the torrent, murmuring low, reassuring things she didn't even hear, the truck bouncing slightly as it raced away from the warehouse. Finally, the storm blew itself out.

She slumped against his chest, shoulders hitching with residual sobs. Her eyes felt swollen and sore, too heavy to open. Every bruise on her face and body throbbed, and her chin…

She flinched when Callum set a hand on the side of her face and tilted it upward. She opened puffy eyes to stare up at him.

"Are you hurt anywhere besides here?" he asked, expression worried as his gaze dipped to her chin. There was blood on the front of his shirt right above where it disappeared under the top of his bulletproof vest.

She reached a hand up to touch her chin, but Callum caught it and angled her face toward him. In the faint morning light now seeping through the windows, he examined it. "Don't think it needs stitches, but it's bleeding pretty good. Hold still."

"Here." A hand thrust a first aid kit at him. Nadia focused on Ivy.

"H-hi again," she croaked.

Ivy gave her a warm smile. "Hi. Glad to have you back safe and sound."

"That was one hell of a diversion you pulled off," Callum said to her as he took out a bandage and antiseptic wipes. "Didn't see that coming."

"Neither did they," Ivy said.

"Getting captured was also one hell of a risky stunt to pull in the middle of our op," Myers told her, speeding along whatever road they were on.

"Calculated risk," she said with a shrug. "And there was no time to argue about it. I knew what I was doing."

Nadia's head was spinning. "Sorry, but...who are you?"

"Don't bother asking," Myers said. "She won't tell you."

Ivy raised an eyebrow at him. "Sure I will. Later." She tossed a wink at Nadia over her shoulder.

Callum tipped her face to the side. "This is gonna sting a bit."

Nadia braced herself, tried to hide a wince when the antiseptic wipe lit up the cut on her chin like fire.

Callum leaned in and blew on it, and the sting subsided.

"Just gonna put some pressure on it to slow the bleeding." He pressed a bandage to it, held it there with his big hand. "We're getting you out of the country."

She felt like crying again, but she was empty. Or maybe dehydrated, she wasn't sure. "Thank you," she whispered, gripping his thick wrist with her fingers. He was so warm, and she felt like she was encased in ice.

He kissed her forehead. "No. You know I would do anything to keep you safe. Anything."

She nodded. She'd thought it, but now she knew it on an intrinsic level. Big difference. "And both of you, too," she said to Myers and Ivy. "Thank you."

"It was our pleasure," Ivy said brightly, then clapped Myers on the shoulder, making him blink. "Right?"

"Yeah, well, don't drop your guards just yet, because we've still got a long way to go before we're in the clear. The Taliban are mobilizing all around the city, and they're using equipment and weapons our military dumped on the way out, so…"

Ivy rolled her eyes at Nadia and shook her head at him. "Such a pessimist."

Callum eased the bandage away, checked the wound, then put a strip of some sort of tape across it in two places. "There." He dropped a kiss on her upturned lips before cradling her face in his hands and studying her. "Are you hurt anywhere else?"

"No. Just banged up." And traumatized. Yeah, all of this was definitely going to leave a mark on her psyche.

He stroked her hair back from the side of her face, cupped her cheek. "I love you."

Her throat tightened and she curled her arms around his neck, burying her face against his neck again. "Love you too." This felt like a dream. One minute she'd been trapped and facing the reality of her torture and execution at the hands of a sadistic enemy. The next, she'd been freed and back in Callum's arms.

She laid her cheek on his shoulder and closed her eyes, a wave of utter exhaustion rolling over her. This wasn't over yet. Not even close, and it scared her to think of what other dangers they would face—but at least she had Callum and the others with her now.

"Let yourself go," Callum murmured, dropping a kiss on her forehead, his beard tickling her. "I've got you."

It felt like she'd barely dropped off when Myers's voice from up front brought her instantly awake. "Looks like we're gonna have to make a little detour. Taliban up ahead."

CALLUM TIGHTENED HIS hold on Nadia as Myers slowed, saw the truck barreling straight at them.

"Hang on," he warned Nadia, bracing his shoulder against the door and one foot against the opposite one. She tensed, then Myers swung them around in a tight one-eighty and sped back the way they'd come.

"Are they after us?" Nadia asked.

The fear in her voice ate at him. "It'll be all right," he said, stealing a glance behind them. An SUV had joined the chase as well. The patrol must have been alerted by someone at the warehouse before the firefight. "Get hold of Walker," he told Ivy.

"Already messaging him and Amber," she said, staring at her phone. "Walker's plotting out a route for us. Amber's diverting the helo."

"Helo?" Nadia said.

"Yep, we're blowing this joint in style," Ivy said, studying her phone. "Okay, follow my lead," she said to Myers, and began giving directions.

Callum braced Nadia against him as Myers took a hard right, the back end of the truck fishtailing around the corner. He glanced down at the open duffel next to his left foot.

They had all three M-4s and their side arms, but he wasn't sure how much ammo was left, or what kind of secret arsenal Ivy might have stashed away somewhere. Probably enough to hold off another Taliban patrol or two. He would do whatever it took to get Nadia out alive. Period.

She was stiff as a ramrod in his arms, her breathing shallow.

"It's gonna be okay," he soothed. "We're getting help from two of the best in the intel business. They'll get us out of here."

Nadia gave him an uncertain look, and after what she'd endured, he didn't blame her for being scared.

"Yeah, no problem," Myers muttered, navigating another sharp turn.

"Faster," Ivy urged a moment later, and cut a glance at him. "You want me to drive?"

"No," he growled, both hands gripping the wheel as he dodged slower moving traffic on the two-lane highway they were traveling on.

"Lemme know if you change your mind—turn right at the next intersection."

He did as he was told, jaw taut. Callum peered behind them. The pickup was nowhere in sight, but the SUV was still back there, and he could make out the silhouettes of at least four men in it. They would all be armed with AKs.

Come on, Walker. Help us lose these assholes.

A series of tight turns later, they shot out onto another stretch of highway and gained speed. The sun had just reached the top of the mountains, flooding the plain with golden rays of light.

"There we go," Ivy said. Then to Myers, "Not bad."

He shot her a dark look and didn't let up on the accelerator. "How about you just navigate and save the comments for after."

"Well, that's no fun."

"They remind me of my middle sisters," Nadia muttered, casting a furtive glance over his shoulder out the back window. "They bicker just like that constantly."

The SUV wasn't within firing range of them yet, but it was slowly gaining on them. Only a matter of time before he'd have to engage them. "Yeah? I'd like to meet the rest of your family sometime."

A faint smile twitched her lips. "You say that now." The smile vanished when Myers swerved around a semi, the big rig blasted its air horn.

"There's our pathway to freedom," Ivy said.

Callum looked past her, following her gaze off to the right where another stretch of road wound its way into the distance. Toward a desolate plain of parched, gray-brown earth. He could almost smell the scent of the dust in his nose.

"Hang on, this is gonna be tight," Myers said. He veered in front of a line of cars and cut across both lanes to the exit, the tires squealing in protest.

"Looks like we've got more company," Ivy said, and swung around in her seat.

Callum craned his neck to look back. Sure enough, the SUV made the exit with them, along with another pickup a little farther behind. "How far to the LZ?"

"Barring any slowdowns, maybe nine to eleven minutes," Ivy answered.

"Oh, God," Nadia groaned, putting her forehead against his vest.

He had work to do.

He hugged her close for a moment. "I'm gonna put you on the floor and I want you to lie flat on your stomach and not move until I tell you to," he told her, cutting off her protest with a finger over her lips.

"What are you going to do?" Her big brown eyes were wide, her features pinched with anxiety.

"I need to buy us some time for when we reach the LZ." And he needed her out of harm's way while he did it, or he'd never be able to concentrate.

"But—"

"Down now and cover your ears," he said, easing her from his lap and onto the floorboards. She shot him a worried look but did as he said, stretching out on her belly with her head down.

He grabbed an M-4, checked the partially used magazine. Eleven shots left, and more in the duffel if he needed to reload.

Shifting around, he set one knee on the back seat and slid open the center panel of the rear window. The SUV was still in the lead, the pickup not far behind it. "Slow down a bit," he told Myers.

While the truck slowed Callum took aim. As soon as the SUV was within range, he fired.

The round hit the windshield on the driver's side. The vehicle swerved but corrected its course and kept coming, telling him he'd narrowly missed the driver. A second later the passenger appeared through the open window and aimed a rifle at them.

"Slow down more," he commanded, staying where he was.

Myers eased his foot off the gas more. The passenger hanging out the window fired a burst but missed them by a mile.

Ignoring him, Callum fired again. This time he saw the blood spatter. The SUV careened off the road and out of view into a hollow.

He switched his attention to the pickup as it whipped past

the SUV. But unlike the SUV its driver slowed, hanging back out of range. "Again," Callum said to Myers.

Their truck slowed more, but so did the pursuing pickup, the driver smart enough to keep his distance. "Resume speed," he said to Myers. The pickup wasn't going to come within range here. But the real test would be once they reached the LZ and had to get out of the vehicle.

"Helo's eight minutes out," Ivy said.

Close to when they should be there. But it was going to be tight, and the race from the truck to the helo would leave them all exposed with the other pickup coming on fast.

He reached down for another rifle and handed it to Ivy. "Get ready. This is gonna be tight."

"How close are they?" Nadia asked.

He wouldn't lie to her. "Close." He ran his fingers through her hair briefly, his gaze still locked on the approaching enemy. They were so close to getting out of here. He wasn't going to let anything get in their way.

"When I tell you, you're going to get on your hands and knees and get ready. As soon as I get out, Myers is going to grab you and run for the helo. Don't stop, no matter what happens. Got it?" He made his voice hard, leaving no room for argument.

She nodded.

"Say the words, Nadia."

"I got it."

Satisfied, he gripped his rifle, mentally counting down the minutes.

"There's our ride," Ivy said.

He stole a glance out the passenger window and spotted the black dot approaching in the sky.

"Turn right in eight hundred meters," Ivy told Myers. "Last turn, everyone. Hang on."

The truck skidded as the tires slid off the asphalt and onto the softer terrain. Myers corrected it expertly and hit the accelerator, racing for the approaching helo. The Blackhawk banked away from them and began to descend.

Callum checked the pursuing pickup. It had maintained the same distance this whole time, and now all three passengers' heads and shoulders emerged out of the windows, along with the barrels of their weapons. Getting ready to open up the moment they came within range.

"Touchdown," Ivy said.

The helo was on the ground now, its rotors turning. Myers aimed right for it. Callum set a hand on Nadia's shoulder, squeezed. "Get ready."

She got to her hands and knees, face strained, eyes on the door, her shirt covered in blood and the bloodstained bandage on her chin. So brave in the face of everything she'd gone through. Christ, he loved her.

"Here we go," Myers said, and started a countdown from ten.

At one he hit the brakes. A cloud of dust rose up all around them.

Callum threw open the door and leaped out, Ivy right behind him. They stepped to the rear of the vehicle just as the other pickup appeared through the veil of dust.

He glanced over his shoulder, a measure of relief hitting him when he saw Myers charging Nadia toward the bird, his hand wrapped around her arm.

Turning to face the enemy, he and Ivy opened up at the same time as the tangos.

The staccato crack of automatic fire echoed above the noise of the helo's engines. He and Ivy peppered the windshield with rounds as they edged their way backward toward the bird. The pickup veered sharp left, heading away from them. The tangos bailed out, rolled in the dirt with their weapons.

"Go!" he shouted at Ivy, laying down more covering fire. The tangos returned fire. Rounds pinged off the bed of the truck in front of him.

He waited a few seconds before falling back toward the helo, firing continuously. Until the chamber clicked on empty. There was no time to reload.

He dropped the rifle and ran.

The right bay door of the helo was open. Myers was in the opening, reaching out a hand for him. Callum sprinted for him, flung out his hand as bullets raked across the fuselage, sending up sparks. He winced as something hit him in the chest, kept running.

Ivy popped out of nowhere, aimed over his head with her M4 and returned fire. He leapt aboard, shouting to the crew chief and pilots to take off. When he risked a glance behind him, three bodies lay on the ground near the other pickup.

Two tangos were still firing at them as the helo lifted and nosed forward. Poised in the open doorway, Ivy fired, picking them both off.

It was over.

Callum turned away to look for Nadia. She was near the tail with the crew chief, watching him with wide eyes. He got up and hurried toward her, the horror on her face making him stop where he was. "What?"

"There's a hole…" Her face was white with strain.

He looked down at himself. A ricochet had hit him in the center of his vest. "I'm okay." He undid the Velcro straps and pulled it off. "Just a ricochet."

She sagged, putting a hand to her heart, the anguish in her face all too real. "Oh my God…"

He hauled her to him. "It's okay now." Squeezed her hard,

one hand cradling the back of her head to his shoulder. "They're all down."

She threw her arms around him, fingers digging into his back. "So it's over?"

"Yes." He closed his eyes, savoring the moment, the feel of her finally safe in his arms.

The nightmare was over.

And now the rest of their life together was just beginning.

TWENTY-THREE

The next sixteen hours passed by in a blur for Nadia. The helo flew them into Pakistan, and then a military cargo plane took them from Karachi to a base in Germany. She slept most of the way, curled against Callum, and woke when they began their descent.

A team of American officials was waiting for them when they disembarked, along with Walker and a man named Alex Rycroft, who had apparently sent Ivy to help them.

They were taken to a building on base to be interviewed individually. Various people from different organizations asked her the same questions over and over until she could barely think straight, giving them all the information she could remember about her captors, their approximate locations.

By the time she was done, she was completely drained and wanted only to crawl into a bed to sleep.

Callum was waiting for her when she finally walked out of the room. The tired smile he gave her made her heart turn over. She'd fallen for him knowing what sort of man he was, and that he'd served in an elite military unit. But that was completely different from seeing him in action firsthand.

He'd put everything on the line for her. Risked his life to come back for her.

She'd never imagined a love this deep. Couldn't believe he was hers for the taking.

He wrapped her up in a hug, holding her to his chest. "Holding up okay?"

She nodded, drinking in the feel of him. The instant sense of security being close to him always gave her. "I kept asking about Ferhana, but no one seemed to know anything. It frustrates me. I wanted simple answers and to know she was okay. Better yet, I want to see her in person to make sure myself."

"We'll look into it together tomorrow. For now, let's get to our hotel."

Being alone in a western city hotel room with him sounded like heaven. Too good to be true.

They took a cab to the hotel. Walker had already arranged a room for them, and the keys were waiting at the front desk. A cart bearing food was waiting for them when they walked in.

She groaned and fell on the tray of finger sandwiches like a starving woman, caught the amusement on Callum's face as she wolfed down her fifth one with some fruit. "Don't judge," she mumbled through her mouthful. She'd been starving.

But rather than fortify her, once her stomach was full it was like her mind unplugged itself from her body. Fatigue crashed down on her like a heavy curtain. The king-size bed with its crisp white sheets and comforter looked so incredibly inviting she almost whimpered but felt too grimy and disgusting to slide into it yet.

"Let's get you cleaned up and into bed," Callum said, drawing her into the bathroom.

Under the hot spray of the shower, he held her to his naked body while his strong fingers worked the shampoo into her hair and scalp. She groaned and closed her eyes in bliss, feeling like she might float away. What he was doing felt incredible, and while normally she would be so turned on, she would be jumping him right now, the exhaustion was too strong.

"Rain check for as soon as I recharge, I promise," she murmured, nudging the solid length of his erection trapped against her abdomen.

"Shh," he said, and finished rinsing her off. Then he soaped up and quickly washed himself before shutting off the water and wrapping her up in a towel. She started for the bathroom door, but he swept her off her feet and carried her to the bed.

She smiled up at him adoringly. He'd done this at least a half-dozen times before, but it never got old. Every single time her belly flipped at the effortless show of strength, the romance of it. "I'm so tired," she mumbled. "You?"

"Yeah," he said, sliding between the crisp sheets with her. He tucked her against his chest and drew the covers over them.

Nadia sighed and let her heavy eyelids fall shut. Lying alone with him in the dark, quiet room was like being encased in a deliciously cozy cocoon.

She dropped off almost immediately into a deep, dreamless sleep. When she woke next it was still mostly dark in the room except for the faint gray light seeping in around the edges of the curtains over the window.

Her chest constricted as everything from yesterday came rushing back. *But you're safe now. Callum's here.*

Turning her head, she found him sprawled on his stomach facing away from her, fast asleep.

Tenderness and awe flooded her. He'd stuck by her through everything. Even in the face of what he'd viewed as her rejection. And now this strong, capable, incredibly courageous man was all hers.

Her muscles were stiff and achy, but she scooted over and

fitted herself to his broad back, rubbing her cheek against the smooth skin between his shoulder blades. A heady rush of arousal pulsed through her at being skin to skin with him, making the aches and pains fade more into the background.

He woke with a slow indrawn breath and gave a low, sleepy rumble of contentment that sent a rush of heat pooling between her legs. "Morning," he said quietly.

"Morning," she whispered, kissing her way down his spine, the heated arousal growing every second. There was no more danger. No one to interrupt them. There was only here and now, and this precious, newfound time for them to reconnect.

She wanted him desperately. Loved exploring the hollows and reacquainting herself with the contours of his body, all the ridges and dips of muscle, and now she finally had the chance again.

Her nipples tightened as they dragged along his warm skin, her clit already swelling and starting to throb. She slid a hand down his back, over the taut rise of his ass, then delved underneath and between his legs.

He let out a low growl when she cupped him, wrapped her fingers around the rigid length of his cock and squeezed. A heartbeat later he rolled over and pinned her flat beneath him.

The display of easy power and the shock of his warm weight shot a thrill through her. He turned her on so effortlessly.

His mouth brushed across her cheek. Her lips. Skimmed over the bandage on her chin before finding the edge of her jaw and placing open-mouthed kisses down her neck, his hands gripping her hips firmly.

She tipped her head back, surrendering to sensation. To him. Wanting all of him right *now*.

With one quick tug he ripped the covers off them and began

kissing her all over, seeking out every raw and bruised spot and giving it equal attention. She barely noticed the scrapes and cuts anymore, too preoccupied with the hum of arousal that had taken over her body.

Floating on a warm tide of bliss, she turned liquid in his arms. Her body became a wave rising to meet him, her gasps and sounds of pleasure filling the room.

He cradled her breasts as he sucked her tight, sensitive nipples, one big hand sliding between her legs to ease the unbearable ache. His long fingers slid through her wetness, making already tingling nerve endings burst into flame. They stroked around her swollen clit, zeroing in on the sweetest spot he'd memorized long ago.

"Callum," she whispered, winding her legs around his hips. Her lover. Her protector. Her partner and the man who held her whole heart in his hands.

His lips burned a path down her middle until it met his teasing fingers. She groaned and pushed up against his tongue as it slid over her clit, her fingers knotting in his hair. He didn't tease now, just gave her what she needed with slow, measured strokes and eased two fingers inside her, intensifying everything.

Within moments she was a trembling mass of need, her whole body alight with pleasure. She cried out in joy and relief when he pushed her over the edge, the orgasm rushing through her in a wild tide.

As she recovered, he kissed his way back up her body, his hands caressing her curves. She waited until his eyes met hers before running her fingers through his hair. "I love you so much," she whispered.

Something primal flared in his gaze. He rose up, looming above her with his weight braced on his forearms and took possession of her mouth. She wrapped an arm around his back and reached between them to close her fist around his cock.

He groaned, a deep sound of raw need that turned her inside out. He was so strong, so proud, his need for her made her feel like the luckiest, most desirable woman on the planet.

She stroked him, savoring the way he pushed into her hand, his muscles bunching, breathing turning shallow. "There's been no one else since you," he rasped against her lips.

His words sent a fresh wave of heat pumping through her. "Not for me either." Her body had known right from the start that he was it for her. Her mind had been too damn stubborn to admit it.

She kissed the corner of his mouth, pulled her head back to watch his face while she curled a leg around the back of his thigh and arched her hips. The head of his cock nestled directly against her slick folds. She rocked along his length, drew in a soft breath when it slid across her swelling clit.

All of a sudden, she was greedy all over again, another tide of arousal running through her. Callum gripped her hair in one fist, his other hand sliding down to play with a taut nipple.

"Slower," he murmured, drawing it out. "Slow down with me."

Slowing down was torture when she was revved up this much. But a delicious one, and she knew he would make the end result worth the wait.

She took a breath, a tiny shudder rippling through her, pleasure suffusing her body. When he'd pushed her close to the edge and she couldn't wait any more she whispered a plea and dug her nails into his ass, demanding he finish what he'd started.

They stared into each other's eyes as she guided him inside her. His grip on her hair tightened, his jaw going taut. He thrust forward, burying his length deep, his weight pinning her down.

She whimpered, slipped her fingers between them to play with her clit. "More," she said, her body catching fire at the dual sources of friction.

Callum drew his hips back and then thrust home again, establishing a firm, controlled rhythm while he angled to hit her just right with each stroke. Within moments her orgasm began to build.

She tightened around him, squeezing hard while she rocked into every thrust. Increasing the friction, reaching a whole new level of intimacy with him as she stared up into that molten hazel gaze. There was no stopping now. Only the inevitable rush toward the coming explosion.

"Oh, Christ, Nadia," he groaned, his face contorting, eyes closing as he neared the edge.

She shuddered, feeling it too. "Love you," she gasped out, her heart overflowing with everything she felt for him. There was no more hiding. No more holding back. He'd made that impossible. "Love you, love you…"

Callum drove deeper. Faster. She clung to him, choked back a sob as the friction pushed her over the edge once more. His tortured groan gusted against her ear, then he shuddered and went rigid with his own orgasm.

He lay on top of her for several long minutes until his fist finally relaxed in her hair. His fingers stroked through it as his warm weight blanketed her.

She was boneless beneath him, totally sated and content in a way she'd never been before. But now her mind was working overtime, reminding her of all the things she'd vowed to tell him.

"Pinch me," he said.

She angled her face toward him. "What?"

"Pinch me. Not too hard, because I'm sore. Just enough to prove this is really happening."

Her heart squeezed. She smoothed a hand down to his sculpted ass and gently pinched it. "There. Feel that?"

"Yeah." He nuzzled the spot where her neck curved into her shoulder, his beard raising goosebumps. "God, I've missed being with you like this."

She closed her eyes, hugging him close. Wishing she could undo all the hurt and doubt she'd caused for him before. "I've missed it too. And I'm sorry I kept pulling away for so long."

He pushed up slightly to look down at her, still lodged deep in her body. "Why did you?" The sight of him like that, his powerful frame braced over her, the devotion in his eyes, melted her and gave her the courage to finally come clean.

She focused on the smooth curve of his muscular shoulder as she ran her fingers over it, unable to look him in the eye as she said the rest. "I promised myself I'd tell you this if I made it out of Afghanistan, and… It's about my childhood—which sounds really cliché, but it really explains a lot. And it explains why I was…so afraid to let you in before." She felt dumb admitting it now, but he deserved to know why she'd run scared for the past year.

He propped himself up on one elbow, watching her with a level stare. "Tell me."

"I don't remember my birth parents. I have just a vague, fuzzy image of them in my head. I know they were young when they had me, and poor. They couldn't take care of me properly, so they gave me up. But I remember the day the Bishops came to the orphanage."

Everything about that time in her life was painfully vivid. "A lot of other kids had all been adopted soon after winding up there, but I'd been there for more than a year. I thought nobody wanted me because I was bad. Or unlovable."

He made a low sound and hugged her, but she kept going.

"Then the Bishops came, and they seemed to like me. I was on my best behavior."

She'd been too terrified not to be. "I was so afraid of messing up, scared that if I did or said one thing wrong, they would walk away. I barely said two words to them the entire time and used every manner I'd been taught. I thought it must have worked, because they adopted me and brought me to the States. They put me in school, and I worked with a tutor to accelerate my English.

"All of a sudden I had siblings and a new home," she continued. "It was noisy and hectic and crowded. Things were good, but... I felt like I never really bonded with my mom. Like I could never measure up to her expectations. And she would say things that reinforced my insecurities about her not considering me the same as her bio children."

"Like what?" he asked, frowning.

She lifted a shoulder. He came from a stable home with two loving parents and wouldn't be able to relate. But maybe this would help him understand more. "Like if I did something wrong, or something that disappointed her, she would tell me I should try harder to be better because they'd done me a favor by bringing me home. That maybe they'd made a mistake and should have picked a different kid to adopt instead."

"What the hell?" he growled.

It still hurt. A lot. "Or constantly reminding me of all the orphans they passed up by choosing me, and how I should be more grateful because I'd been given a chance the others back in Romania hadn't." Little cutting remarks like that, leaving no visible mark but doing plenty of damage inside.

His expression darkened. "Those are fucking cruel, toxic things to say to a child."

His reaction only made her love him more, his innate protectiveness of her ringing with each word. "I know that now, but I didn't then—I believed her and thought it was my fault. There were plenty of other incidents like that over the years. For years I thought it was just me she did it to but found out later it was all the adopted kids. She used guilt and shame with us like weapons, always holding up the example of her bio kids and making us all feel like we let her down."

"Why didn't your dad do anything about it?"

"Because he didn't know. He traveled a lot for work and was always out of town. I only told him when I was in my mid-teens while they were going through a divorce, because there was a custody situation unfolding. Anyway, I haven't really had much of a relationship with her since they split. She's my mom and I love her, but she's toxic and now I limit my contact. I stayed with my dad because I know he loved me unconditionally."

"Good," he said in a hard voice. "Sounds like a healthy decision."

"Yes." She skimmed her fingers across his chest, stroked the bruise where the ricochet had hit him. Seeing it sent a pang through her. Inches in any direction and she could have lost him. "Anyway, it sounds stupid now, but it was all that baggage that held me back with you."

"Why?"

She huffed out a breath. "I guess I just was afraid to put myself out there too much with anyone. Afraid to trust and make myself vulnerable in case you eventually decided I didn't measure up, or that I wasn't worth it in the end."

"Never." He captured the side of her face in his hand, tilted her head until she met his gaze. "I would never think that. But I get it now, especially why you feel so strongly about helping other kids, and I'm glad you told me."

A faint sting started behind her eyes, but the sense of relief at getting it off her chest was huge. "Me too. And by the way,

I'm done with my organization. I'm sending my resignation later today. I might make a public statement through the media about them too. Haven't made up my mind on that yet."

He nodded in approval, expression turning hard. "Good."

"I don't know what I want to do after this. I definitely want to keep helping orphans and vulnerable kids, but maybe not in combat zones for a while. Or ever, I haven't decided yet."

"You've got lots of time to think about all that. You don't need to make any decisions until you're ready," he murmured, brushing a tender kiss across her lips.

She loved that he didn't argue against her going back to that kind of work, that he understood how important it was to her and that she didn't want to give it up entirely. Not even for him. They would find a way forward together, however that panned out.

He stroked the hair back from her temple with his fingertips, his gaze thoughtful. "We didn't use a condom."

"No." She had zero regrets. She'd wanted him too badly to stop.

"You okay with it?"

"Yes." She kissed his shoulder. If she got pregnant from this one time, then it was meant to be. "I want to have a family with you eventually."

He pushed up on one arm to look down at her, his gaze soft in the light seeping in around the edges of the window next to the bed. "Yeah?" A smile curved his lips.

She traced a finger down the side of his beard, nodding. "Yeah. You?"

"Definitely. But I want to marry you first."

It made her smile. She'd suspected he felt that way, knew he was traditional when it came to that kind of thing, but hearing it out loud was amazing. Her life had been so unconventional, she wanted some traditional things for herself now. "Was that a proposal?"

His expression turned serious. "Yes." His stared directly into her eyes. "Say you'll marry me, Nadia."

Her smile widened even as her throat tightened. Against all odds, this incredible man was going to be hers forever. She wanted to pinch herself to make sure this was real. "Yes. I'll marry you."

TWENTY-FOUR

Walker glanced up from his laptop in the conference room on base early the next morning when the door opened and Ivy walked in, followed by Alex Rycroft. He jumped up, surprised to see them here. "Rycroft. Good to see you."

Rycroft stepped forward to shake his hand. Now in his fifties, his dark hair was liberally streaked with gray. But everything about him was still powerful and imposing, and his silver eyes were sharp as a blade. "You too."

"Thanks for the help."

"Happy to lend a hand." He glanced at Myers, Callum and Nadia, all seated around the table, nodded at them. "You all look pretty rested. Everyone get a good night's sleep last night?"

"Best I've had in weeks," Nadia said, looking much better than she had upon arrival yesterday. She'd removed the bandage on her chin, just the steri-strips showing now.

"I thought y'all flew out last night," Walker said, gesturing at him and Ivy, though most of his attention stayed on her.

Seeing her in person yesterday when the team stepped out of the aircraft had been one hell of a shock.

She was nothing like what he'd expected.

Mid-thirties, fit yet softly curved in all the best places. Her wavy, jaw-length brown hair framed a heart-shaped face and pointed chin, hazel eyes that were deceptively soft at first glance, because one look into them and he could tell she didn't miss a thing. Ever.

She met his eyes now, and the impact of that hazel gaze from twenty feet away hit him hard.

Rycroft shared a brief glance with her before addressing the group. "We're both flying out soon, but we wanted to show you all something before we go."

Walker didn't move as Ivy sauntered over to the table and paused next to him, close enough for him to catch her clean, citrusy scent, and gestured to his laptop. "Mind if I borrow this?" she asked, the slightly husky edge to her voice making every cell in his body sit up and pay attention.

"Be my guest." He started to rise from his chair, but she simply turned his laptop toward her and began typing fast commands into the keyboard.

He caught only a split-second glimpse at a military intelligence site, his eyebrows rising as she quickly hacked her way through a firewall that had probably cost millions to create. He stole another glance at her as she worked, burning with curiosity. His efforts to delve into her and her background had gone exactly nowhere. It was like she didn't exist.

"Here we go." She turned the laptop around so he and the others could see the screen, then hit play on a video feed.

It showed drone or aircraft footage of a target on the ground. A series of buildings in what appeared to be a remote area. "Where is this?" he asked.

"Twelve miles west of Jalalabad," Rycroft said. "Three hours ago."

Not yet understanding the significance of what he was looking at, Walker watched the aircraft circle and zoom in on one of the buildings in the center of the compound. There were vehicles scattered around it.

"Wait for it," Ivy murmured.

Seconds later something streaked toward the ground. The target building exploded in a brilliant flash of light.

"And there we have it. Bye bye Baasim," Ivy said, her voice laced with satisfaction.

Walker and the others stared at her in surprise. "Baasim's dead?" he asked.

She nodded and Rycroft spoke. "Already confirmed by the Taliban."

He couldn't believe it. "Who authorized it? Us?"

"I'm not at liberty to disclose that, but it was partly your intel that helped locate him. I just wanted you to see it for yourselves—" He looked across at Nadia. "And know he's never going to hurt or threaten anyone ever again."

"Thank you," Nadia said quietly, leaning into Callum's embrace. She looked tired but alert, and it was clear she drew comfort from Callum. "It's a big relief to know he's gone and won't pose a threat to the friends I left behind at the orphanage."

Rycroft nodded and flashed her a smile. "The latest intel I received said all the women and remaining children were accounted for and safe."

She expelled a relieved breath. "That's great news."

The others all started talking excitedly about what they'd seen, but Walker was too busy replaying the video. It was from a secure US intel site, the encrypted kind that was supposed to be unhackable, yet he'd just watched Ivy blow past every security measure protecting it in a matter of seconds.

And he was willing to bet his left nut that it wasn't her first or even fiftieth time doing something exactly like it. Was that who she was? A secret weapon hacker working for the US government?

Setting that aside for now, he enlarged the video, squinted to make out more detail on the ground showing in the frame. He'd seen a satellite picture of this same site a few days ago while gathering intel on Baasim and tapped it as being a possible base of operations for him. But Walker had never dreamed it would lead to anything like this. One of America's most wanted wiped off the face of the earth in a precision drone strike.

"I'll be damned," he murmured. It had been a while since he'd had a direct hand in something like this, and even though this time he'd been involved unknowingly, it still felt damn good.

He glanced up to ask Ivy about how she'd hacked through the security so fast, stopped short.

She was gone.

What? He glanced around. How had she left the room without him noticing?

He jumped up and went to the door, checked up and down the hallway. Empty.

Turning around, he scanned outside through the windows lining the back of the room. No sign of Ivy.

"She's gone."

He met Rycroft's gaze. The former NSA agent appeared to be trying not to smile, amusement twinkling in his silver eyes. "Gone where?" Walker asked.

Rycroft shrugged. "Your guess is as good as mine."

Walker highly doubted that.

Frowning, he shut the door and approached the former

agent. The others were still talking amongst themselves, gesturing to the video. Probably still oblivious that Ivy had just up and disappeared into thin air. "Who is she? And is Ivy her real name? Because I can't find *anything* about her, and no one else I've talked to can either."

"It's her real name. But you're not going to find anything about her online or through your sources."

"Then why is—"

Rycroft cut him off with a friendly clap on the shoulder. "See you around, Walker."

He stared after him as Rycroft walked out the door, left with twice as many questions as he'd entered the room with a few minutes ago.

As well as a handful of half-answers that didn't satisfy him in the least.

TWENTY-FIVE

Anticipation bubbled inside Nadia as the plane parked at the gate, along with a few nerves. After spending two days in Germany they'd flown out on a commercial flight rather than a military one, with comparatively cushy seats, TV screens in the headrests and inflight food service. The flight had felt downright luxurious after being in the back of a Blackhawk and a C-130.

"Feel good to be home?" Callum asked, nuzzling the top of her head.

"So good." Touching down on US soil had eased the residual tension she'd still been carrying. She looked up at him. "You sure you're ready for this? They're a lot all at once."

He raised a ginger eyebrow. "You worried I can't handle it?"

She grinned. "No." He'd risked his life to go back to Kabul for her and faced down armed Taliban patrols. Even her crazy family couldn't compare to that. "Just a little nervous."

"It's gonna be fine. And even if it doesn't go well, so what? You've got me."

His words suffused her with warmth. She was so damn

lucky. "I know." She squeezed his hand, leaned up to plant a kiss on his lips. He was the best.

"Hey, cut that PDA shit out," Myers teased as he rose from the seat behind them.

"Yeah, get a room," Walker added next to him.

"Plan to." Callum cupped her face in his hands and kissed her nice and slow.

Myers grunted and punched Callum's shoulder on the way by, making Nadia laugh. Callum lifted his head and grinned at her. "I love seeing you laugh."

"I love having something to laugh about again."

Callum laced his fingers through hers as they walked through the terminal to baggage claim and stood there visiting with Walker and Myers until their luggage arrived. They had meetings with the State Department the next morning, then would fly out to Oregon in the afternoon. She was going home with Callum to Crimson Point and planned to stay there indefinitely. All her stuff was in storage, so she could just move the most important things and sell the rest since Callum's place was already furnished.

As the crowd of passengers filed into the international arrivals terminal, Nadia craned her neck to see over the sea of heads in front of her. The moment they cleared the doors she spotted Anaya standing on her tiptoes near the back wall, waving an arm excitedly.

"There she is," Nadia said, and dumped her suitcase at Callum's feet to rush at her sister.

"Hey!" Anaya threw her arms around her and squeezed tight. "Oh my God, I'm so glad you're finally here." Her voice was rough, her embrace almost desperate.

Nadia hugged her hard. "Me too."

Their dad came up, smiling. "There's my girl. You're a sight for sore eyes, sweetheart."

She blinked against the unexpected sting of tears as his arms enveloped her. "Hi, Dad."

"Hey, peanut." He kissed the top of her head.

She pulled in a shaky breath and held on for a few moments until she'd steadied herself.

"Okay, you better introduce him to this hunk over here," Anaya said, her arm around Callum's waist.

With pleasure. Nadia shot him a smile. "Dad, this is Callum. Callum, my dad."

"Sir," Callum said with a polite nod.

Her dad stuck out his hand. "Call me Frank." He clasped Callum's hand, set his other one on top of it. "Thank you, son. Thank you for getting her out of there. I—" His voice cracked and he stopped, swallowing hard.

"It was my honor," Callum said.

Nadia almost swooned. Watching the three people she loved most together, she thought her heart might burst.

She wound both arms around Callum's waist and faced her dad and sister. "Guys, guess what?"

They looked at her expectantly. "What?" Anaya asked, excitement creeping over her pretty face.

Yeah, her sister had already figured it out. Nadia didn't want to hurt her by rubbing this in her face, but she was about to burst and knew Anaya would be happy for her. "We're getting married."

Her dad's eyes widened. Anaya squealed and launched herself at them, grabbing them both and hopping up and down. "Yes! Yes, I *knew* it! I'm soooo happy for you guys."

Laughing, Nadia glanced up at Callum. He was grinning, already charmed by her sister. Nadia didn't know why she'd been nervous. Stupid insecurities.

"Congratulations," her dad said with a proud smile. "I don't know him yet, but I can already tell you picked a good one."

The best. "Yeah, I did."

"She didn't make it easy," Callum said, looking down at her with a teasing gleam in his eyes.

"No, but the best things in life never come easy," her dad said.

"You're right about that," Callum murmured, staring deep into her eyes. She felt the pride in his gaze and tone all the way down to her toes.

Anaya let them go and stepped back to scan her face anxiously, her gaze pausing on the cut on Nadia's chin. "You really okay?"

"Yes, thanks to all these guys." She gestured to Callum, and Myers and Walker, who stood a polite distance away. "And Ivy. Oh, man, wait until I tell you about her. But in the meantime, this is—" She stopped, blinked at Walker. "I just realized I don't know your first name."

"It's just Walker," he said with a smile, coming forward to shake hands with Anaya and their dad.

"Then you must be Donovan," Anaya said to him, taking Nadia by surprise, then startled everyone—Myers especially—by walking up to him and flinging her arms around his shoulders.

THERE WAS NO time to dodge it. Donovan stood there like a damn statue while she hugged the crap out of him, unsure what was happening. Or why.

"Thank you," she gushed, squeezing him tighter. And oh, Christ, she smelled amazing and felt even better. The unexpected jolt of arousal that tore through him took him totally off guard.

This was Nadia's *sister*? "You're, uh, welcome," he muttered, patting her once awkwardly between the shoulder blades. Everyone was staring at them. Callum was grinning. Walker was smirking. Nadia looked like she was struggling not to laugh.

The sister released him but only took a half-step back and smiled up at him. "I'm Anaya. I called you the other—"

"I remember." Hard to forget something like that. And now that he'd seen her in person, he'd never forget her, period. Her voice definitely matched the rest of her. Sexy and soft, with a face he couldn't help but stare at.

She was stunning, with deep brown skin and eyes, and a mop of black curls pulled up into a tidy bun at the back of her head. And he could still feel the press of her body against the front of him. Firm but curvy, slapping his sleep-deprived senses to full alertness. All while simultaneously sending an unfortunate amount of blood rushing to his groin.

"I guess that was pretty weird for you, huh? Me calling you in the middle of a mission and all." She looked directly into his eyes as she spoke.

Her smile was so genuine, her manner so at ease he couldn't help but sort of smile back. It felt stiff, but that was probably because he was out of practice. Everything about this was awkward, but he didn't completely hate it. Except for the prickle of discomfort at the way she was looking at him, like she thought he was some sort of hero or something. When he wasn't. "A little bit, yeah."

"Sorry but not sorry. And we appreciate everything you did for Nadia more than you'll ever know. Normally I'm not that pushy. Right, Nadia?" She looked over at her sister.

Nadia faltered. "Well…"

"Okay, *most* of the time I'm not." Her head tipped to the side slightly as she studied him, her big brown eyes holding him captive. She had the longest, thickest eyelashes he'd ever seen. Her light, sweet scent swirled around him, her lush, full lips slicked with a shiny pink gloss he couldn't stop staring at. They were even softer than her smile.

"Right?" she asked.

He blinked, realized he'd been staring and not paying any attention to what she'd just said. "Sorry, what?" The tips of his ears started to get hot.

Her pretty eyes laughed up at him. "I said I'm planning to visit Nadia in Crimson Point next time I come out to the West Coast, so I hope I'll see you again then."

"Oh. Yeah, for sure." Wouldn't exactly be a hardship to see her again. Out of the corner of his eye he was aware of Walker standing ten feet away, still smirking at him. "Well." He cleared his throat, struggling to throw off the weird sort of fog she'd somehow thrown him into. "We'll leave you guys to it. Come on, Walker." He stepped past her and wheeled his suitcase for the automatic doors.

From start to finish, nothing about this trip had gone to plan. And for damn sure he'd never been hugged by a family member of someone he'd protected. He wouldn't mind getting another from her if their paths crossed again.

He shook the thought away. Right now, all he wanted was a double cheeseburger washed down with ice-cold American-brand beer, and the bed waiting for him at the hotel.

Walker pulled up beside him, wheeling his own suitcase. "Did I just see *the* Donovan Myers get tongue-tied by a pretty woman?" he drawled in a shocked tone as they strode for the exit.

"Shut up," he muttered, scowling. "She took me off guard."

"I'll say. You shoulda seen the look on your face." He laughed under his breath.

Whatever. "You call Shae yet to tell her we'll be home tomorrow?" They'd planned a dinner together for the three of them at Shae's favorite restaurant on the water about twenty minutes south down the coastal highway from Crimson Point. Donovan couldn't wait to see her. Wished he knew how to make up for all the time they'd lost together while she was growing up.

Walker gave him some serious side eye and stopped at the curb to wait for a cab. "Yeah. So, guess you'll be seeing more of Nadia's sister when she comes into town, huh?"

"Doubt it."

"That'll be interesting."

"No, it won't." He waved down a cab, anxious to be on their way.

The instant punch of attraction he'd felt a few minutes ago meant nothing. Anaya was the last woman he'd get involved with.

And he was the last guy she would be interested in if she knew the truth about him.

TWENTY-SIX

"Why are we here?" Nadia asked in confusion as their ride pulled up in front of the hotel.

"Last minute meeting," Callum told her, suppressing a smile. He'd been looking forward to springing this surprise for days, ever since Walker had helped him set it up before they'd flown from Germany. Seeing Anaya and their dad had helped Nadia a lot emotionally. But this would be even better.

"Ugh, okay, but after this we're done for the day and heading back to our hotel, right?"

He shrugged. "If that's what you want."

"It is."

"Okay." He had a feeling she was going to change her mind about that in short order though.

He opened the lobby door and led her to the waiting room of the office building they'd chosen. He'd wanted neutral ground with nothing to tip Nadia off about what was happening. "What time's dinner with your family tonight?" Four more of her siblings were driving into town for it.

"Seven. Why, you don't want to go anymore?" She looked concerned.

"No, I do." He settled back in his chair, rested his linked hands over his stomach, looking forward to her reaction when the person they were meeting arrived. "I was just checking."

"They're a lot to handle all at once, I know."

"I like your dad and Anaya. I'm sure I'll like the others too."

"Yeah, but all together they're pretty intense. You're tough, though," she said with an adoring grin. "I know you can take it."

He could. And he'd withstand anything to make her happy. Including sitting back and watching her go back overseas for another posting with a different organization if that's what she wanted.

She was fiercely committed to helping kids in tough situations. That determination and her big, caring heart were two of the things he loved most about her. So even if he hated the idea of her going somewhere dangerous again, he would deal with it and support her.

His phone chirped with a text message. He checked it. "They're here." *Show time.*

"Good, let's get this over with so we can get out of here."

The door opened. Callum sat back, unable to wipe the smile from his face as Ferhana toddled into the room, the aid worker standing back just outside the threshold.

Nadia shot out of her chair with a glad cry and rushed forward. "Ferhana!"

The baby froze for a split second, then recognized Nadia and her little face lit up. "Na!" she cried and launched herself at Nadia.

Nadia laughed and scooped her up, burying her face in the baby's neck to give smacking kisses there. Ferhana squealed and giggled in delight, then put her tiny hands on Nadia's cheeks.

The two of them stared at each other for a long moment, and a rush of warmth filled Callum's chest. He knew next to nothing about kids, but even he could see that Nadia and Ferhana's connection was obvious and palpable.

Nadia cooed to her in a mix of English and Dari. Ferhana patted Nadia's face, her four little front chipmunk teeth showing as she grinned. Nadia turned to face him, her smile lighting up the room and hitting him square in the heart. "You did this."

He shrugged. "Walker helped."

The love in her eyes made him feel like the luckiest man on earth. "Thank you." She kissed Ferhana's forehead, swayed back and forth in that innate way women had. "My brave little survivor. Do you remember Callum?"

Ferhana gazed at him with dark, solemn eyes, and he could see her mind working. Trying to place him and determine whether he was safe or not.

He smiled. "*Salaam alekum*, Ferhana."

He got a toothy grin for his efforts and she leaned toward him, stretching out a hand.

"Oh," Nadia said, bringing her closer. "I think she wants to pat your beard."

He angled his chin so she could touch it, watching the fascination in her little face as her palm patted him, a startled smile spreading across her lips.

"This is a big compliment," Nadia assured him. "It means she likes you."

"I like her too." Little sweetheart had been through so much and was still willing to trust people. It fucking humbled him.

Ferhana grew tired of his beard in under a minute and started to wriggle in Nadia's arms. Nadia sat on the floor with the baby in her lap. "How about the Itsy Bitsy Spider? Remember? I love that one. Watch." She began singing the song, using hand motions with every step, totally absorbed in connecting with the child, and Ferhana was captivated.

It was amazing to watch Nadia in her element, especially here back on US soil where she was safe and sound.

He thought of what she'd told him back in Germany. That she wanted to have a family with him one day.

She would be an absolutely incredible mother. He pictured them in his house in Crimson Point, two kids running around the big, fenced yard, them flying kites or building sandcastles at the beach together.

He hadn't considered himself ready for kids yet, but with Nadia in it, the picture felt right.

She sang a few more songs and then told Ferhana a story. Near the end of it, Ferhana let out a huge yawn and laid her head on Nadia's shoulder, doing a slow blink. Nadia kept going, and by the time she finished Ferhana was fast asleep, her lips parted and her long eyelashes casting shadows along the tops of her cheeks.

And the expression on Nadia's face as she looked down at Ferhana, the total adoration and pride…

A soft knock rapped on the door, and it cracked open. The female aid worker smiled when she saw Nadia and Ferhana. "I was going to warn you it's near her nap time. I need to get her back to the center for dinner."

"Oh. Sure." The woman approached and reached down for Ferhana, but Nadia shook her head. "I'll carry her out."

She didn't want to let Ferhana go.

Callum followed them out to the minivan parked near the entrance, stood back while Nadia buckled her little friend into the car seat and peppered the aid worker with questions. Was she eating and sleeping okay? Adjusting into her new environment?

"She loves seedless red grapes. And cheese, but you have to

cut the cheese into little cubes because she won't eat it in any other shape," Nadia told her.

The woman took it all in stride but shot Callum an amused look before responding. "I'll tell the kitchen staff at the center."

Then there was nothing more to say. Still Nadia hesitated, hovering over Ferhana protectively until the worker slid the door shut.

Callum walked up and wrapped an arm around her shoulders. Nadia leaned into him, rested her head on his chest as the van drove away. "Oh, God, I hate this. She's been through so much already. I know she's young, and I know from experience how resilient kids are, but what's going to happen to her? What if she's like me and doesn't get adopted until she's older? What if her adoptive parents are shit?"

"Maybe we should adopt her."

Her head jerked up, her eyes locking with his. "Are you joking?"

"No." He took a moment to collect his thoughts. "You're crazy about each other, I feel a strong connection to her, and you'll never stop worrying or wondering about her if we don't do this. Plus, we're getting married, so that should help our case with the adoption process."

She blinked fast. "Oh my God, you're serious," she whispered, her voice catching.

He took her by the waist and turned her to face him. "Dead serious. But only if this is what you want."

She nodded, giving a watery laugh as she wiped the heels of her hands under her eyes. "Yes. Yes, it's what I want. Oh my God, *thank* you." She flung her arms around his neck, almost choked him. "I love you so much, thank you."

Grinning, he held her close. Most newly engaged women would be all about picking out a ring. Nadia didn't care about that or making wedding plans. Ferhana meant more to her than any jewel he could ever buy her. "I love you too, but don't thank me yet."

She jerked back from him, face turning anxious. "Oh, there's so much we need to do, and we need to do it fast. Can we start now?"

He blinked at her, smile fading. "Now?" He hadn't considered that, but…

"Yeah, we can—" Her gaze strayed to the minivan as it turned out of the parking lot and started down the street. He wanted to stop it.

Nadia broke away from him and headed for the row of cabs parked along the curb past the entrance, waving her arms like a madwoman. "Taxi! Taxiiii!"

With one hand she absently waved Callum forward as a cab started toward them, but when he didn't move fast enough for her liking, lunged over to grab his hand and together they ran to the vehicle.

He chuckled and dutifully got in the back because she was already in the front passenger seat pointing through the windshield while she commanded the driver, "Follow that minivan! Hurry, don't lose it!"

Wide eyed, the driver took off like a shot, determination stamped on his face.

Callum smiled to himself and settled back to enjoy the ride.

∼

ANAYA BROKE into a smile the moment Nadia's face appeared on screen. "Hey, how's things?" It had only been two days since they'd seen each other, but now that they were on opposite sides of the country again, Anaya missed her like crazy.

"Things are unbelievable," Nadia said.

"Yeah?" Curiosity leapt inside her. She leaned closer to the screen, peering into the background. "Hey, Callum." He was over by the fridge in the kitchen of his house.

A dark-haired guy walked past him and out of the frame. For a second, she thought it might have been Donovan and her heart rate kicked up. He'd made one hell of an impression on her, first volunteering and risking his life to go back to Kabul for Nadia with Callum, and then seeing him in person at the airport.

She didn't know what she'd expected him to look like, but it hadn't been that. Tall, dark and drool-worthy with his powerful build and brooding good looks. The polar opposite of Bryan, and that was a good thing. It was also the first time she'd been attracted to anyone since him, which was as much of a surprise as it was a relief. For a long time, she'd worried that she would never recover from what happened.

"Hi," Callum called back, the dark-haired man no longer in sight.

"So?" she said, turning her attention back to Nadia. "I was calling to tell you some news, but you've obviously got something you're bursting to tell me, so go ahead."

"No, you first."

"Okay. I just got word from my boss. He wants me to represent the design team during the meetings with the French delegation at the Boeing factory in September."

"That's fantastic!"

"I know, and even better, it means I'll be able to spend a few days with you guys before or after. Or maybe both, if you can stand me for that long." Maybe she'd even cross paths with Donovan again while she was there, who knew.

"Girl, you know I'd move you in with me permanently if I could."

Her heart squeezed. Nadia was the dearest person to her in

the whole world, the one she trusted completely and without reservation. They weren't sisters by blood, but their bond was unbreakable. "I would so not enjoy feeling like a fifth wheel though," she teased. "You and Callum need time alone together after everything that's happened."

Her sister's expression changed, taking on an almost guilty look. "Yeah, about that…"

"What?" It wasn't like Nadia to hold back. "It's something good, right? You were smiling like a lunatic when you answered the call."

"No, it's amazing. It's…" She glanced back at Callum, now standing with his back to the counter, watching her as he drank something.

"Nadia, you're killing me," Anaya said. "What is it? You eloped so there's not going to be a wedding and I won't get to wear the bridesmaid gown I already picked out? Because I'll be happy for you, I really will, but damn, this dress was incredible."

"No," Nadia said with a chuckle, and Anaya sensed hesitation behind it. "Callum and I are adopting Ferhana. I'm going to be a mom," she finished in a rough voice.

Anaya's face froze for an instant before she could control it, and the swift, piercing pain in her chest shamed her. This wasn't about her. Not even a little bit. "Oh my God, that's amazing news!" she cried, putting on a wide smile. She meant it. She truly did. She was ecstatic for Nadia and Callum. "Oh, I'm going to be an auntie!"

Her sister's face lit up. "Yeah you are! And you're gonna be the best auntie *ever*." She blinked fast, wiped her fingers under her eyes even as she smiled again. "It was Callum's idea."

"How did it happen? Tell me everything." *Even if it hurts me.* She had to get past it.

She listened patiently while Nadia told her the story. It was beautiful, a perfect epilogue to her and Callum's love story. But it was also a painful reminder of everything Anaya had lost not that long ago.

If things had gone ahead as planned, she would have become a mother around this same time. Her child and Ferhana would have been cousins.

By the time Nadia finished, her eyes stung with the imminent threat of tears. Anaya put on another smile so her sister would think they were happy ones and tried her hardest to push her sadness aside. "I can't wait to meet her." She'd seen pictures of Ferhana, but getting to hug that sweet baby who had lived through so much trauma was going to be epic.

"Me too." Nadia sat back, an apology in her eyes. "Sweetie, I know that couldn't have been easy for you to hear. I—"

"No, stop it, are you kidding me right now? I'm about to burst over here, and if anyone was ever meant to be a mom, it's you. You deserve this. You deserve *everything*."

Her sister's smile was full of love, but touched with sympathy. "Thanks. You sure you're okay?"

She scoffed, touched but a little embarrassed that Nadia was so concerned about her. "Of course I'm okay, I'm already planning out Ferhana and auntie days at the mall, sleepovers, and getting her first mani and pedi together when she's a little older."

Relief bled into Nadia's expression. "She's going to adore you. Can't wait for you to get here in a few more weeks."

"Me neither." Shit, a lump was forming in her throat. She swallowed, the burning at the backs of her eyes getting worse, and grabbed her cell phone, pretending she'd just received a call. "Oh, it's my boss. I gotta take this."

"Sure. Send me the details when you know your travel dates."

"Will do, and congrats again. Love you."

"Love you too. Bye."

She hurriedly ended the call and closed the lid of her laptop, sucking in an unsteady breath as she blinked furiously and stared at the ceiling. Dammit. She refused to give into the urge to cry.

Grieving for something that might have been was no way to live the rest of her life.

EPILOGUE

Two months later

Nadia took Ferhana from Callum, sat her on her lap to stop her from fussing and popped a pacifier in their daughter's mouth. She wasn't a big fan of them in most instances, but sometimes a mom had to do what a mom had to do, and right now silence was more important. Callum's former roommate Asher and his fiancée Mia had offered to watch Ferhana at their new place near the beach, but Nadia had wanted to bring her here today.

Ferhana instantly relaxed, a contented look coming over her face as she leaned into Nadia's shoulder with a sigh. Crisis averted, Nadia shifted her attention back to the wedding ceremony taking place in front of her.

It was a gorgeous mid-September day in the Pacific Northwest. The sun was shining, its warm, golden rays filtering down through the towering evergreens that ringed most of Boyd and Ember's property. And she was mentally counting down the days until Anaya arrived next week.

The couple of honor stood in front of their guests under an

arbor draped in flowers at the edge of the back lawn, holding hands as they faced each other and smiled into each other's eyes. Boyd wore a tailored black suit and Ember was stunning in a simple ivory gown that flowed behind her into a short train spilling across the grass. Boyd's son Travis stood next to him as his best man, and Ryder's wife Danae stood beside Ember.

The minister waited until Boyd had slid the ring on Ember's finger and repeated the final vows before smiling at them. "By the power vested in me, I now pronounce you husband and wife."

A cheer went up from the twenty or so guests. Callum stuck his fingers in his mouth and let out a shrill whistle. "Go, Cap!"

Ferhana jolted, staring at him with wide eyes. Nadia laughed. "He's just happy for his buddy, sweetheart." She was too. Over the past few weeks they had spent a lot of time with Boyd and Ember.

It wasn't hard to see why Callum revered the man. Boyd was as solid and dependable as the mountain his home was built on, and he and Ember were perfect for each other.

Boyd didn't like being the center of attention, but he took it all in stride as he stopped to accept everyone's congratulations on the way back down the aisle.

Callum hugged him and clapped him on the back. "Captain Boyd Masterson, a married man." He grinned at him. "Looks good on you."

"Your turn's coming soon enough," Boyd said, shooting a wink at Nadia before moving to the next row.

Callum slid an arm around her and pulled her into his side. "What do you think? Should we do something like this?"

"That would be perfect." She didn't want a church or anything fancy. Just their families and the friends they'd made here in Crimson Point.

Everyone in their circle had accepted her into the fold

immediately, along with Ferhana. She loved it here and was excited about the life she and Callum were already building together. Right now she was on a break and living off savings she'd put away, but Callum made more than enough to pay their bills so there was no rush for her to find another job.

She glanced over as Noah, the local sheriff, helped his extremely pregnant wife out of her seat. Poppy winced and put a hand to her lower back.

Nadia winced in sympathy. "I have no idea what that feels like, but it looks uncomfortable." She squeezed Ferhana. "Luckily, I got you without having to go through any of that. But that won't be the case if we give you a brother or sister the old-fashioned way."

"I'm a big fan of making babies the old-fashioned way," Callum said, making her grin and elbow him gently in the ribs.

Ferhana's eyes crinkled at the corners in a smile as she contentedly sucked on her pacifier. She was learning more English every day, absorbing everything they taught her like a little sponge. It was amazing to watch.

They followed the other guests back across the lawn and into the house where the food was waiting. Apparently, Boyd had been baking bread for the past three days to make sure there was enough for everyone.

Partway to the house, her phone buzzed against her hip where it lay buried at the bottom of the diaper bag she now used as a purse and carryall. She moved to the side out of the way, shifting Ferhana to her other hip and fished the phone out.

It's Ivy, the message read. *Pick up.*

Whoa. None of them had heard from the mystery woman since they'd last seen each other in Germany. "Can you take her?" she said to Callum, passing Ferhana over. "It's Ivy."

"Ivy?" he said in surprise.

"Yeah. She wants to talk to me." She stepped away from the

group, Callum following her, and answered when the phone rang. "Hello?"

"Hey, sister. How are you?"

The *sister* part filled her with warmth. "I'm great, thanks. How are *you*? Any more thrilling missions you can or can't tell me about?"

She laughed softly. "Not recently. I hear congratulations are in order. You're officially parents now?"

"Yes. Technically we're her legal guardians for now, but the adoption process is rolling along really fast. After everything that happened, my former organization used all its muscle to help make this happen—probably to keep me from going public about what happened. But mostly we have Alex Rycroft to thank. He's been using his clout behind the scenes to expedite everything and cut through a lot of red tape on our behalf." He was an adoptive parent himself and had apparently used his influence to help another couple expedite the process last year. Nadia adored him and wanted to meet his wife and daughter someday soon.

"Yeah, Alex is pretty amazing that way."

"He is. I also talked to Homa the other day, still at the orphanage in Kabul. She was ecstatic when I told her the news." She and the other female workers were still safe, thankfully, and continuing to care for children who desperately needed their care.

"I'll bet she was. Ferhana couldn't have found a better family than you guys." She paused. "I hear a lot of activity in the background there. You at a party?"

"A wedding. Callum's former captain."

"Ah, nice. When are you guys tying the knot?"

"We haven't decided yet. No rush, and Ferhana's keeping us busy anyway."

"I'll bet. So, do you have a few minutes to talk right now?"

"Uh, sure." She glanced at Callum, gave him a reassuring nod and wandered away to the edge of the yard away from the chatter to hear Ivy better. "What's up?"

"I heard you're no longer with your organization."

"That's right." They were dead to her, and she would never forgive them for what had happened. For now, she wanted to have time with just Ferhana and Callum and get their daughter adjusted to her new life.

"Okay. I know your plate's pretty full right now as a new mom, but just in case you were thinking of looking for some work in the near future... One of my sisters does private work protecting orphans from exploitation and trafficking. I help her out when I can. Anyway, I told her all about you and your background, and she said she'd love to bring you on board. It's part time, highly private and sensitive work and wouldn't involve travel unless you wanted it to, and you could work from home while taking care of Ferhana. Is that something that would interest you? I can put you guys in touch if you want to talk to her about it."

Of course she was interested! "Yes, please, that sounds a*maz*ing."

"Great! Kiyomi will be in touch. I have a feeling you two will hit it off instantly. I won't keep you any longer, but say hi to Callum for me, and tell Ferhana that Auntie Ivy sends a kiss."

Auntie Ivy? It made her grin. "I will. Bye."

Callum and Ferhana were both watching her as she crossed back to them. "What was that all about?" Callum asked.

"Ivy's sister has a part time job offer for me. I wouldn't have to travel unless I wanted to, and I would be helping protect orphans."

"Her sister Amber?"

"No, she said her name's Kiyomi." Sounded Japanese.

He frowned. "How many sisters does she have?"

"No idea. Maybe they're all adopted too, I didn't get the chance to ask her." She closed the distance between them and put her arms around him and Ferhana, ready to burst with happiness. "I'm going to talk with her about it soon."

Ferhana leaned over to curl an arm around Nadia's neck and rest her cheek on her shoulder. Callum chuckled and kissed the top of their daughter's head. "Mama's girl."

"She's becoming more of a Daddy's girl every day." They stood together, linked as a circle of three. A family.

Nadia closed her eyes and smiled. Life didn't get any more perfect than this.

—The End—

*Read Anaya and Donovan's story next in **Protective Impulse**!*

Dear reader,

Thank you for reading ***Unsanctioned***. If you'd like to stay in touch with me and be the first to learn about new releases you can:

Join my newsletter at:
http://kayleacross.com/v2/newsletter/
Find me on Facebook:
https://www.facebook.com/KayleaCrossAuthor/
Follow me on Twitter:
https://twitter.com/kayleacross
Follow me on Instagram:
https://www.instagram.com/kaylea_cross_author/

Also, please consider leaving a review at your favorite online book retailer. It helps other readers discover new books.

Happy reading,
Kaylea

PROTECTIVE IMPULSE
CRIMSON POINT PROTECTORS SERIES

By Kaylea Cross
Copyright © 2022 Kaylea Cross

PROLOGUE

Port-au-Prince, Haiti
28 years ago

"Come on, hurry," her mother snapped, tugging impatiently on her hand.

Anaya lurched forward, her bare feet squishing in the sticky mud beneath the thigh-deep water they were slogging through down the ruined road they were traveling on. They had been walking for hours and she was so tired, didn't even know where they were going.

"I'm tired too, but we can't stop to rest yet."

She stayed quiet, watching around her and clutching her blanket tight with her free arm. Just like their village, everything around them here was destroyed too. Trucks and cars were swallowed up by water and mud, the tops just peeking through the surface. Some of the buildings and the people inside them had been swept away.

A terrible storm had been raging over the island. Hurricane Gordon, she'd heard *Maman* say. It had unleashed so much rain that the mountain above their village had melted like shaved ice in the sun, sending it tumbling down into the valley where they lived.

She shivered in the darkness even though it was humid and warm out. Last night had been terrifying. She'd woken when her mother dragged her out of bed in the middle of the night and run with her toward the forest.

The landslide had rumbled like thunder behind them. Anaya had heard people screaming and it had frightened her. She didn't know how long they had hidden in the trees, but when they had finally come out, their village was gone, along with many people Anaya had known.

Now they had no home, and no family to take them in. What would happen to them?

Her stomach rumbled angrily. It had been so long since she'd last eaten, a little plate of rice and beans one of the neighbors had shared with them yesterday afternoon because *Maman* couldn't get any fuel for their fire with the storm howling outside their little home.

It was starting to get lighter out now. They had been walking all night, the two of them part of a long line of people carrying their most prized possessions down from the mountains.

The winding, muddy road began to straighten out before them. Up ahead she could see signs of people moving around in the faint, gray light. A city loomed ahead, emerging out of the shadows. Some buildings and cars were ruined here too, but not as many as back home.

She wanted to go home. Wanted the doll her grandmother had made for her on her last birthday. Were they both buried in the mud too?

It seemed like they walked for another hour or more, now wading through water that came above her knees. Every step was a struggle, exhaustion pulling at her legs and feet. She wanted to stop. To curl up at the side of the road and sleep under her filthy, wet blanket.

Eventually the water and mud ran out, leaving puddles everywhere. Tall buildings rose like dark trees in the distance. When they got closer Anaya saw that these buildings were untouched. Cars were still driving on the roads, and people were busy carrying things to and from the market as if nothing had happened.

The hazy shapes up ahead became clearer. More buildings, far bigger than anything in their village. The spire of a church. And she couldn't stay quiet any longer. "Where are we going?"

Her mother's face was drawn and sad-looking, her lips tight. "Hush. We're almost there."

Where? she wanted to ask, but held her tongue. Her mother was upset, but at least seemed to know exactly where to go.

They passed the church, painted all white with blue lettering above the top of the front door, and started down a tiny, winding street nearby. A low building stood at the end of it.

Something about it made Anaya's stomach tighten. She stopped, but her mother muttered something under her breath and jerked her forward once more.

She couldn't shake away the thought that something bad was about to happen. Her heart thudded hard as they stood on the doorstep. Her mother pulled on a rope. A bell rang inside.

Moments later a woman opened the door. She was old, with pale skin, and only her face showed in the middle of a black and white flowing hat and robe that covered the rest of her. She looked at them both standing there in their wet, filthy clothes, and Anaya could see the woman felt sorry for them. "Come in, both of you."

Anaya was put in a chair near the window with a piece of bread and a glass of milk while her mother went into another room with the old woman and shut the door. She glanced down.

Her bare feet and legs were coated in orange mud. Her nightie was ruined, and her blanket might be too.

After finishing her bread her stomach rumbled for more but she was suddenly too tired to care. Her eyelids grew heavy, and then her head. It kept falling forward until she finally slid out of the chair and curled up on the hard stone floor, clutching her blanket to her.

Maybe this was all a bad dream. Maybe when she woke up everything would be all right again.

The next thing she knew, her mother was shaking her awake. Anaya blinked slowly, struggling to sit up. She was still so tired. Couldn't concentrate on what her mother was saying.

Then she saw the urgency on her mother's face and shot upright. She stared up into those wide brown eyes, the sheen of tears there frightening her. "I have to go."

Go?

"The sisters will take care of you." Her mother smiled but her lips trembled, and she looked so sad Anaya gripped her arm, her stomach pulled into a hard knot.

"I don't want to stay here. You already take care of me."

Tears spilled down her mother's cheeks. "I can't anymore. These people will give you what you need."

"No, *Maman*—"

"I want you to have this." Reaching up, she undid the thin gold chain from around her neck. The tiny cross pendant winked in the light coming through the window as she fastened it behind Anaya's neck.

She cupped Anaya's chin in her hand. "Be a good girl. Promise me you'll be good, and remember me." She dropped her hand and stood, turning away.

Anaya's heart lurched. She shot to her feet as her mother started for the door, panic roaring through her. "No," she cried, hurrying after her. She couldn't leave her here.

Her mother paused. Looked back at her. And the stricken look on her face made Anaya go cold all over. "I'm sorry, little one. I love you. I will always love you, but you deserve more than I can—" She choked out the last words and stopped, then spun away and rushed for the door.

Anaya raced after her, heart hammering. Terrified and not understanding what was happening. "*Maman!*"

This time her mother didn't stop. Didn't slow down. Just walked out the front door at a brisk pace.

A wave of terror crashed over her. Anaya bolted for the door, determined to go with her. "*Maman*, please!" she cried, her voice shaking as much as her limbs.

Adult arms caged her from behind. "Don't, my child."

She kicked. Struggled. Tried to wrestle out of that imprisoning grasp, her eyes glued to her mother's retreating form. *No! Don't leave me! Please don't leave me!*

Her mother kept going. Had reached the end of the narrow street they'd walked up earlier. "Come back!" she cried.

If Anaya didn't hurry she'd never catch her. She gulped in a breath, her chest hurting. Had she done something bad and made *Maman* angry with her? She must have, for her to leave her here. "I'll be good!" she screamed, sobbing. "*Maman*, please, I'll be good!"

Her mother stepped around the corner and vanished from sight.

Anaya stopped struggling and stood frozen inside the doorway, staring at that spot. The terrible realization hit her just like the wall of mud that had destroyed their home last night.

Her mother had left her. And Anaya already knew she wasn't coming back.

End Excerpt

ABOUT THE AUTHOR

NY Times and USA Today Bestselling author Kaylea Cross writes edge-of-your-seat military romantic suspense. Her work has won many awards, including the Daphne du Maurier Award of Excellence, and has been nominated multiple times for the National Readers' Choice Awards. A Registered Massage Therapist by trade, Kaylea is also an avid gardener, artist, Civil War buff, Special Ops aficionado, belly dance enthusiast and former nationally-carded softball pitcher. She lives in Vancouver, BC with her husband and family.

You can visit Kaylea at www.kayleacross.com. If you would like to be notified of future releases, please join her newsletter:

http://kayleacross.com/v2/newsletter/

COMPLETE BOOKLIST

ROMANTIC SUSPENSE

Crimson Point Protectors Series
Falling Hard
Cornered
Sudden Impact
Unsanctioned
Protective Impulse
Final Shot

Crimson Point Series
Fractured Honor
Buried Lies
Shattered Vows
Rocky Ground
Broken Bonds
Deadly Valor
Dangerous Survivor

Kill Devil Hills Series
Undercurrent
Submerged
Adrift

Rifle Creek Series
Lethal Edge
Lethal Temptation
Lethal Protector

Vengeance Series

COMPLETE BOOKLIST

Stealing Vengeance
Covert Vengeance
Explosive Vengeance
Toxic Vengeance
Beautiful Vengeance
Taking Vengeance

DEA FAST Series
Falling Fast
Fast Kill
Stand Fast
Strike Fast
Fast Fury
Fast Justice
Fast Vengeance

Colebrook Siblings Trilogy
Brody's Vow
Wyatt's Stand
Easton's Claim

Hostage Rescue Team Series
Marked
Targeted
Hunted
Disavowed
Avenged
Exposed
Seized
Wanted
Betrayed
Reclaimed
Shattered

COMPLETE BOOKLIST

Guarded

Titanium Security Series
Ignited
Singed
Burned
Extinguished
Rekindled
Blindsided: A Titanium Christmas novella

Bagram Special Ops Series
Deadly Descent
Tactical Strike
Lethal Pursuit
Danger Close
Collateral Damage
Never Surrender (a MacKenzie Family novella)

Suspense Series
Out of Her League
Cover of Darkness
No Turning Back
Relentless
Absolution
Silent Night, Deadly Night

PARANORMAL ROMANCE

Empowered Series
Darkest Caress

Historical Romance
The Vacant Chair

EROTIC ROMANCE (writing as *Callie Croix*)

Deacon's Touch
Dillon's Claim
No Holds Barred
Touch Me
Let Me In
Covert Seduction

Printed in Great Britain
by Amazon